Chapter 1

The one thing I was always afraid of, in the sack, was being a sack. I have no idea where this notion came from, but it was omnipresent. I was a good girl. I was more scared of teenage pregnancy, than the act involved. But, I'd heard only good things about doing the dirty.

So, I made it almost all the way to twenty before I took the plunge. (*I took the plunge? That sounds wrong.*) Lucky for me, I was a good girl. I had absolutely no intention of having shenanigans the night I did. I discovered a few months later from the girlfriend he had whilst simultaneously dating me - *(nice one, I sure can pick them)* – that **she** caught crabs and vaginal warts from him. *Strike one on the first go.*

Thank heavens I didn't keep dating him. Poor girl dated him for months and caught all of those nasties. Now I know where 'creep' comes from. They give you STDs that creep and crawl and freak you out. He was obviously cheating on her too. For months.

Right, so um, I thought this was a normal progression. I'd seen a few dirty movies and there was always lots of heavy breathing involved. Naive me, I had no idea this was caused by the sheer body weight of the male participant forcing the air out of you. Oof, breathe! Oof, breathe!

Yep, I had morphed into a hefty pair of bellows. I was young enough to care, so I insisted Mr Crabs 'teach me'. He had no intention at all of doing any such thing. Don't men get that we aren't programmed to be a femme fatale? It's not hardwired. It's something we hone, like a skill. Same with cooking. Don't assume we just know what the heck we're doing.

Oh, and just for the record, nothing I'd heard about doing the dirty was vaguely accurate. So I dumped the cheating, lying, conniving bastard and went on an 'I hate men' mission. They could buy me as many drinks as they liked, it wouldn't make a fudge of difference.

Then .... fate walked through my door. I was in my first employment. Footloose and fancy free. Loving life. It was a huge adventure. And I was a good girl desperate to break a few rules. My good friend Adelle phones and convinces me that we have to house-sit a home together, not too far from work.

"How did you arrange this? Whose house is it?"

"Oh come on! I can't do this alone. It was arranged for a model Alan works with, but he's got a photo-shoot."

My mind is already dancing the happy dance: FREEDOM.

"How long?"

"Two weeks."

"Okay, but you're buying the booze!"

Wait! Adelle: I must tell you about her. We've been friends since the sixth grade. She was my first friend to smoke. She started in the sixth grade, smoking her dad's cheroots. She and Alan were already having sex by grade nine, bumping uglies as often as possible. He would sleep over and sneak out of her bedroom window in the morning - (and they are still together), bumping uglies as often as possible. She was wild. No scratch that – insane! Good thing Adelle loves him; he works with models and she has moments of insecurity. Anyway, he hobnobs in the right crowd, so this house-sitting gig in Fresnaye should be fun.

* * *

Day two, called **Saturday!**

I waltz into the kitchen, my long blonde hair all over the place. This old house is colder than the morgue at the winter solstice, hence my nipples protrude without subtlety against the white T-shirt I slept in. But that's okay, because Adelle is twice my size and her boobs are the biggest I've ever seen. It's a tiny room for a kitchen. A miniature of the farm-style type. I guess that models don't have to cook. They live on carrot sticks and champagne don't they? Well, no one could serve a family from this little nook. *I know. I've helped Mom cook enough meals.* But the fridge, that's plenty big enough for carrot sticks and champagne.

Hey!

Gulp.

4

Clawback

by

Gemma Rice

.t Road
Kent TN23 2RJ
'3 655573
)kcollege.ac.uk

E-Hub
Resource

ISBN   1460935403

EAN   978-1460935408

'Clawback' was first published by Night Publishing, a trading name of Valley Strategies Ltd., a UK-registered private limited-liability company, registration number 5796186. Night Publishing can be contacted at: http://www.nightpublishing.com.

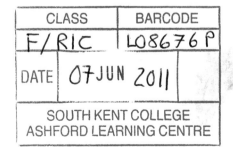

There's a really, *really*, dishy guy smiling at me; he's sitting in the kitchen at the pathetic square called an island. Down girl. Shit. I still have a nipple stand.

Adelle doesn't seem the least bit fazed as her udders jiggle around, unrestrained, in her loose T-shirt. She grins at me, blue eyes twinkling in a brunette bob frame, and points at the dude, "Stef, this is Gary."

I smile. What the hell am I supposed to say? This is **girls only!**

She hands me steaming coffee in an amber-hued mug. "He's an old friend of Al's."

Riiigggght! I vaguely recall meeting him once when we went to play pool. So basically this is the first time he's making an impact.

Hey dude: keep your eyes on my face! Look out the window. Not fair. You're unannounced.

I decide I should say something. I look at blondie, with the death-by-grin, grin. "So what are you doing here?" Wait, that sounds rude. "So early?" I add. Gulp.

I'm folding my arms trying to hide these erect nipples that have nothing to do with his blue hypnotist's eyes. It's called 'Cold as the Mausoleum Syndrome', okay?

Darn, that smile is naughty. He's aiming it at me and he's shooting to thrill.

"I'm looking after you."

Oh I bet you are. I smile, kinda. "Oh … *Reaaally*?" (Dripping sarcasm.)

I give him the, 'I can look after myself just fine thank-you-very-much,' stare. It's a challenge. I dare you to say I need a man! To quote Adelle. A woman needs a man, like a tree needs roller-skates.

Oh, be still my rioting heart: he's just pushed his sleeves up. That darn white knitted shirt of his is just clinging to defined arms and ripply shoulders. Those forearms. Phew, hang on, I just need to breathe for a moment; coming over all weird.

Okay, you can stay as *loooong* as you like, handsome.

Wait. If my mother finds out a guy is staying here I am dead. DEAD! Hung and flogged in public until death do I depart.

He shoots those steaming eyes, brimming with 'I want to do bad things to you' at Adelle, "So baby, what are we doing today? It's Saturday!"

Swoon. He makes it sound like it's our last day on earth to do anything: the whole 'now or never' vibe. I am losing my will here. If he told me to crawl around and snort like a pig, I'd probably do it.

Adelle is the most conniving, manipulating, best friend, ever!

"Let's have the guys over. Play some coinage or something?"

It's seven-thirty in the morning and these people are already planning our let's get shit-faced day? I need to brush my teeth. And put a bra on, dammit. *Guys? What guys?*

They both look at me expectantly. I shrug. Miss Cool.

"Sure." Making out like I don't give a damn either way. When all I want to do is watch this boy for the rest of my horny days. Hang on. I'm horny! How the hell did that happen? And how come I've known Adelle for eight years, and I am only meeting this boy properly, **now**? She and I are going to have to talk.

Aaaah, she's a genius.

"Gary you go out and get what we need for lunch, I'll cook. And get shooters while you're at it."

He stands. Whoa! This is a sin. **No one** is allowed to look that scrummy in plain blue jeans. He's lean *and* muscly in all the right places, with a real gladiator ass. He gives me a cocked eyebrow as he picks up his keys, "Be good while I'm gone."

Gulp. *Ha ha.* I smile. How do I answer that?

I can't breathe. My insides are trying to climb out of my throat. My heart's pounding. (Is it obvious?)

I had no idea, right there and then, I submitted. This boy was going to do very bad things to me. He would turn the sack into his own version of the Pussycat Dolls. And I would wear stilettos and corsets, doing the Kama Sutra, willingly.

Chapter 2

It's March. Summer in Cape Town is just magical. Although I went to a snob school and hung out in the snob crowd, I personally prefer the surfer type. Adelle has always been my most relaxed and rebellious friend. It's normal for her to hang out with older guys; she's used to drinking, smoking, and chilling. Me, however, I'm realising that I've lived a fairly sheltered good-girl existence, up until now.

Oh dear. Being a closet nerd leaves you unprepared for hardened drinkers. Who, by the way, are expert at bouncing a coin into a shot glass, even when slurring words. They are all gunning for me.

Every coin ends up with me downing the creamy Amarula alcoholic beverage, which I am washing down with apple cider. I've got that warm *buzzzzzzzzz* just humming through my veins. I'm kind of on diet, so I haven't eaten very much today. Anyway, I can't eat when I'm feeling self-conscious, and Gary has been here **all** day. So this stuff is just smacking me around like Mike Tyson with a midget.

Magically, Alan's photo shoot ended early, and he's pitched up in time for dinner. (What happened to two weeks?) Gary's friend Charl, who reminds me of Al Bundy from 'Married with Children', is also staying the night. So now we're short on beds, there are only two double beds. Talking of double, darn now I have to down three? *Hey! This isn't fair.*

Woooooooo! I am going to bed. I can barely focus. What was that? Gary will sleep with me, Charl in the lounge, Alan with Adelle. Fine.

Hang on a sec! *Gary is sleeping with **me**?! In my bed? Um ... shit!* Now I'm sober as a druggie on the twenty-eighth day of rehab.

It's somewhere around 3:30 a.m. and I'm still wide awake. I'm pretending to sleep, but I can't. He is a foot away from me and it's all I can think about. He's been making moves on me all day. I know he manipulated his way into my bed. And now we're 'sleeping'?

Not to mention this old creaky house is just creepy. Absently I examine the pressed ceiling above the bed, reflecting moonlight off the perfect white paint. All of the old houses are overly decorative. It's taken for granted in this moist climate that everyone has wooden floors and window frames. All of these old houses have gigantic rooms that a normal double bed looks pathetic in. I don't like the old houses. They just seem sad and lonely to me.

Flippenheck, scare me why don't you!

Eyes are watching me. "Can't sleep either, huh?"

I shake my head. I really wish I could sleep. I'm just way too nervous to sleep.

"It's because you're cold."

Aaaah, cunning viper.

This place is like a mortuary. It's not a lie. Carpets might help. Curtains too, for that matter.

"You can lay next to me if you want."

Sure thing. Would you like a blow job with that? A foot rub? A cigar and a martini?

He smiles that snake charmer grin at me, "Come on."

How come he's so friggin' sober anyway? Oh what the hell. I guess this is called the first move. So I shimmy closer. Why did I bring only thongs with me? My T-shirt isn't long enough.

Ooooh looooordy. My skin is on fire. Naked legs on naked legs ... *Go-To-Sleep-You-Slut.*

I close my eyes and pretend that this is much better. Truth is, now I'm definitely not going to get any sleep. Mmmm, but he is really warm. Cosy.

* * *

I wake up with the blinding sun streaming in through the unsheathed window. It's impaling my eyeballs to my eye sockets. **Fuckenhell.** My heartbeat accelerates to 170 mph. There is a hand over my right one. Yes sir! And fuck me, it feels really good. I inch my arm up and peek at the time on my watch. I have had three hours sleep, and I know I'm not going to get any more. And the fucker is awake. Mister, 'I'm pretending to feel you up in my sleep'. *Pleeeeease* stop moving your fingers like that. I am not trained to make nipple erections disappear.

I swivel my tousled head and stare at him pointedly with slate blue eyes. Should I break his arrogant nose, or encourage this? I only met him yesterday. Good girls don't do this. Oh come on, who am I kidding? I'm on the pill; I can do whatever the hell I want. And right now sinning seems like a p-r-e-t-t-y fine idea.

He smiles. The wicked charm is already switched on. He's waiting to see how I'm going to react.

Okay. Game on.

"Is that all you can do?"

Aaaaah ... oof. Oh no, I'd forgotten about the bellows. No, actually all he's doing is kissing me ... hang on, sorry ... my mind goes completely blank the minute someone sucks on my earlobe.

... Pause ...

... Play ...

Sorry, where were we? Oh right. Yes! Can you believe it? Nothing happened. Just some fondling and kissing. He turned me on like a sauna, and then buggered off to have a smoke with his scary friend Charl. (I am not joking about scary. This guy exudes genetic throwback.)

I use the opportunity to dive into clothes. Brush my teeth and hair, and get a smoke of my own. Okay, so we can all do dragon impersonations, we can blow smoke. What was the point of getting me shit-faced, getting into my bed, for that?

Stuff that. I'm not playing games. I go walking back to the bedroom across creaky yellow-wood floorboards. HEY! He's in my Hermès bag. And he's holding my packet of contraception!

He drops them on the bed, gives me his, 'I am going to make you scream' seduction stare, and says, "Just checking."

Right. What is this? Do I get strip searched now too? Fucker!

So that's why he didn't do anything last night.

Mmmm, he's way too close. Okay why don't you just kiss me. *Oooh* and slide your hand under my shirt. Haha, what a pro. Unclipping it with one hand.

Adelle! Knock, girl!

Chapter 3

There was something about Gary I can't put my finger on. He had a quality of reckless abandon. He was also the most persuasive male I have ever met.

So he stayed for the whole two weeks, and this 'good girl' managed to keep that a secret from her prying mother. But how could I hide the glow that sex gave me? Which had nothing to do with bellows that went oof. Instead, it became a journey of discovery. At the first available opportunity, I went before the jury to plead my case. Ignorance! I was ignorant. And I required a tutor. (*You've heard the expression 'famous last words'– right?*)

It started with a simple game of pool. He is after all a master, with his own cue - *wiggles eyebrows*. It seemed of paramount importance that I should learn that a girl must **never** jerk a cue. But should build up momentum slowly before releasing the tip into the ball – *(or is that the ball into the tip?)* After hours of patience, I got it right. And so I graduated to pupil of grand master.

No matter where we were, the minute we hit that Audi of his, things got steamy. I had started 'forgetting' to wear underwear. Fold down seats are such a great invention. And thank the goddess Venus that mankind - (or horny young men) – invented the drive-in. I became a regular. I was a religious zealot about Friday and Saturday night movies under the African stars. And I'm talking *double feature*.

He could play me like a cello, move to harp, back to synthesiser, over the piano keyboards and down the flute. Move aside Beethoven, here comes Gary! (Did I just say that? Oops, no he never jumped the gun like that. He had the control of a Zen master.)

My life became tactile. I spent every penny I earned on risqué underwear (hidden from mother of course) and exotic perfume. I also intended to woo him with my delectable cooking. So I invented the midnight picnic. Everything a girl needs. In my arsenal I had lots of long lasting candles. Ridiculously expensive KWV cabernet sauvignon, (matured for at least five years), my new favourite Nachtmusik, and plenty of finger food in the picnic basket. I became the proud owner of suspenders, hold-up black Dior stockings, transparent bras and now only wore clothing that could be unbuttoned, never wore earrings (they snag), grew my nails, and painted them as religiously as I went to the drive-in with my new beau.

Sucking on his fingers started the game. He became the Lion King, sprawled supine on his back on a picnic blanket next to a midnight black Atlantic ocean. Candles surrounded us between the boulders of Llandudno, seclusion and fire, making this look like a blue moon voodoo seduction. Wearing shiny black Errol Arendz heels – (so practical for the beach) – the shortest schoolgirl skirt I could legally get away with - oh, and did I mention I somehow lost my top between dessert and my next smoke?

I sat on Gary, (he was still dressed), trailing my tongue down his neck. Nibbling, biting softly. I always knew what he liked because his hands would tighten on my hips and he'd hold onto me like an anchor looking for safe harbour.

Why do men wear belts? Would someone please explain this to me? I'd get his faded blue jeans off, just enough. And that's where he'd stop me and give me that salacious smile, which dissolved me into mush. He melted me from the inside. (His eyes had the effect of a blow torch.) All it took was that naughty grin and a softly pleading, 'Oh, come on.'

Right. How could I forget? The girl doesn't get to play unless there is Chanel lipstick on the dipstick. Chalking the cue is apparently the only way to sink anything.

* * *

I know my descent into debauchery is all rather graphic. But this is how it was.

Gary had an appetite like a wendigo. I have only ever met one other man that can go and go and go, making that fluffy pink bunny in the advert more like a playmate than I could ever have realised. Not to mention that it's incredibly romantic: learning the art of lovemaking with a sea breeze tousling your mermaid's locks. Tasting fine wine off his full lips; pure white talc-soft sand surrounding a mohair blanket, casting ghostly light; the waves serenading our rhythm. It was perfect. My blond hunk sculpted in caressing moonlight, his strong hands feeling my breeze-teased nipples, you can't buy memories like that. It was at once new and primal. It was exciting, clandestine and wicked.

You see, Gary was my first long-term boyfriend. What we did, I just thought, was how it was done. Mr Crabs didn't have time to teach the potato sack how to dance, so when I did learn, I had no idea that I was shacking up with the demon-lord of sexual depravity.

There were rules. And if I wanted to keep him, I had to abide. If I was disobedient, he managed to make me feel as though I had betrayed him in an all night orgy with every person I could find at a moments notice. I was his puppet. He made me into who I became. I was addicted and lived, breathed, for him. (And my next fix of him.)

When the rules began trickling between us, I accepted them. I had no reason to question them, or him. No, not for years.

Rule Number 1:
The woman serves. That means she gets what she wants. First you give the man what he wants, for as long as he wants it. Then you get to have your say.

Rule Number 2:
If the pants are off, fellatio is the introduction. Without it, nothing is going to happen.

Rule Number 3:
Always do what he says and we'll get along just fine. Otherwise there's the door. It's over.

Rule number 4:
Sex is as vital as water. Without it, a man and his 'loving' demeanour are doomed. Put out, or piss off.

Rule Number 5:
Be available when I want you. No matter who died, or is getting married. Your previous life is over. If you want me, then you have to be mine.

I would do ANYTHING to avoid breaking rule three. This guy was hotter than chip oil and the other girls were going to have me on my feet and ready to please him no matter what. They had balls those girls. Cheeky wenches would phone him, hit on him, all in front of me. I had to get a ring on my finger. And the only way to do that was to give him one made of lipstick, every time I saw him.

Hence, I discovered a way to make sure he was always happy to see me. He'd pick me up, off we'd whisk into the day. I never knew where we were going, or what we were going to get up to, or with whom. Life was one endless surprise. (Now I hate surprises.) But it always took us at least fifteen minutes to get there. At the first traffic light, that guy looked like he was driving the car, and was alone.

I'm telling you, how I lived to tell this tale is a miracle. A BJ at top speed in the fast lane on the highway, um, how many laws did I break? But this became my signature move. And he became an expert driver. He was behind the wheel and I was going to ride that highway all the way to the end.

Which reminds me of that song by Tom Cochrane which sings about life being a highway. It's so apt.

But instead what I have ringing in my ears is AC/DC - 'Highway to hell'.

Chapter 4

Within the first three months of my seduction, I had gone from 'hardly ever been kissed' to 'let's get it on'. We were inseparable. (What can I say? He was obviously enjoying tutoring me.) I drank far too much alcohol, (he liked me drunk, said it lowered my inhibitions and made me more fun); smoked too many slimline cigarettes, and learned to dance like I was permanently attached to a stripper's pole.

I learned to head bang to his heavy metal as if I was seducing the gods of rock; I call it the snake dance. Snaking from side to side, but the long blonde hair went too. I learned to pout, was finally given my bedroom eyes, and the master key.

I also beat all of the other girls to the finish line. I met the parents. He was so strung out I was beginning to fear he would violate me unconscionably if I 'fucked up'. I had to be the Virgin Madonna for his parents. And I was to be raunchy Madonna Ciccone for him. (Big secret – he was like a double agent. His parents had no clue that he drank, smoked, listened to heavy metal ... oh , and was the spawn of the devil.)

My demure prissy-missy upbringing had me in good stead. I wooed his refined and sweet parents living in their sprawling and expensive home in Groot Constantia, and we were given the thumbs up. Finally, I was moving in with the hottest man this side of the universe.

His laugh, smile and eyes were seductive. And I have witnessed this charmer seduce friends and work foe alike. He can talk the talk and twist the most resistant mind around his little finger, (or his pen ...oopsy ... or his pool cue.)

* * *

I'm ready for this. My things are unpacked in this refurbished home in Rondebosch.   Finally we have our first night alone, legitimately. The candles are lit, dinner is made, the music is on, and I am wearing suspenders, hold up stockings, a camisole, g-string and stilettos. Oh and Van Cleef and Arples.

Game on!

So **that's** why men wear ties. (Blasphemes like a sailor under breath). Blondie walks through the carved door and doesn't give a damn about the perfect roast waiting for his arrival. He pulls off his silk tie, kicks off his shoes, and targets me like a homing missile. I'm thinking, 'Oh yay!' expecting the usual. This was the day my life changed: he had plenty of ties – oh and handcuffs. WITHOUT A FLIPPING KEY.

Picture this if you will. I am blindfolded with the tie he took off when he got home, his evil grin charming me into compliance. His whims are, after all, my commands. Whatever he wants, he gets. And if he wants me to suck on his toes, I'll do it. He was pretty darned adamant that I could not see anything before leading me off into the spacious boudoir. I am placed on the bed, listening to his chuckling.

Christmas came early for Gary! I am scolded for wearing so many clothes. *Oookay.* I went to all this effort, why? No, he must not be displeased. He's torrid when displeased. And he can be pretty ruthless too when he gets that way. In hindsight, he is worse than a woman.

You know how we get accused of 'sulking' for days? Well Gary had it down to a fine art. He knew there was nothing I wouldn't do to make him a happy man again. So he used this technique to break my mind and every boundary I ever owned.

I'm stripped in under fifty-five seconds. Then I am tied with more ties to the bed. He thinks this is great fun. I'm not minding it myself. He is a master, and seriously knows how to work it.

Hang on! "What are you doing?"

"Having some fun." More baritone chuckling. "How does that feel?"

"Cold."

I'm hearing noises. "What are you doing?"

"Taking my clothes off." The clincher. "Don't you trust me?"

"Of course I do."

"Then trust me and stop asking questions."

"Gary, this is hurting."

He whispers into my ear, "I thought you'd like my present. You look so good in handcuffs."

Naturally I think this is amusing. So I laugh and relax. But those buggers bite into soft skin worse than piranha.

He was tireless. I mean it when I say he was like a demon. But, he wanted me on top now, so off came the blindfold. He untied my ankles, and then leaned his toned torso over me to take off the handcuffs – and those bastards weren't going anywhere. Every time he tried to 'unhinge' them, they became tighter. I'm not that into S&M yet, and I'm not enjoying this at all.

He finds it hilariously funny and pisses off to get himself a beer and a Marlboro. He waltzes back in, sits himself down like the don of the Mafia – (he was such a confident, arrogant prick) – and laughs through the smoky candlelight, "Looks like I'll be eating alone."

"You're joking, right? Come on Gary. Where's the key?"

"There isn't one."

"Haven't you done this before?"

"Plenty."

"So? How did you get them off then?"

"Like I just tried. It usually works."

I'm beginning to get cold and I'm not having fun anymore.

He puts his smoke down, rifles through my bag, finds a hair-clip and comes back again. This time I hear a satisfactory click. I hadn't realised my hands had gone numb, until I can move them. My arm muscles are aching.

(**Hello!** What is wrong with me? Why do I not stop and think, um, how come this dude can pick handcuffs anyway? Don't fall for refined. Where a man lives, the school he went to, the money he has, none of it gives you any warning about his character.)

This dear man doesn't offer me a drink, a smoke or a hug. He doesn't care that the roast is drying out. All he does is grab my hair and haul me in for chalking the cue. I have my pride. And there is no way I'm giving my mother the satisfaction of knowing I've just moved in with a sadist.

So, I'm not leaving. But regret: now that's a word to use. (Okay, I admit it. She doesn't like him. I am stubborn and determined to prove her wrong.)

Yep, we did every position I know inside that carpeted monochrome bedroom, until 2 a.m. I had my tush thrashed a few times, it seems he likes the satisfying slap of his hand on my skin.

16

Then he decides he wants a massage. Head to toe baby. (And you have to use the talc, not the greasy oil.) Finally at 3 a.m.-ish, we get to eat roast chicken, roast potatoes, baby carrots, gravy, onion, all the trimmings. I am no longer hungry.

Grrr! He makes all the right noises. Says all the right things. That fishing line has me hooked and the heart angler is reeling me back in. That cocky smile that melts my heart. The possessive way he runs his hand up my chaffed thigh. The way he whispers softly to me as though I'm the only person he could ever care for. I've finished the wine, and I'm doing fine! I am the best cook in the world. The hottest lover. To prove it I get more AC/DC therapy: 'Got you by the balls.' Alluding to the fact that I'm IT. THE ONE.

I'm relaxed. I light his smoke. I light mine. I at least have my satin g-string back on. The scented candles are burning low. When THWAP! That flippin hand connects with my rump again and he says, "Woman, go get me a drink."

I looked at the burning ember at the end of my cigarette and considered putting it into his eye. But he'd kill me if he lived to find me. (I loved him. I cannot explain to you how much I was willing to live through, because he was hot, delicious, and knew how to mess with my mind.)

My face is burning with degradation and I'm fighting my reflex to punch him. I am so angry I can hardly breathe.

He grabs my hand and I lose my balance, ending up in his lap, "I mean that in a loving way. From now on I'm calling you 'woman'."

I look at what I consider to be a moment of insanity flirting in his eyes. It's so dim they look charcoal. His hand assertively rubs my thigh, "Oh come on. Don't be so old fashioned. I love you."

The kiss sealed the deal. Right. From now on, I was nothing more than 'woman'.

Chapter 5

So it's another cold, gusty, depressingly grey and wet winter. And I live to please Gary. In a spurt of what later would be deemed momentary madness, I go out during my lunch hour to my usual snob shop. (Stuttafords in Cavendish Square, if you must know.) I forgot to mention that I like designer clothing. And in winter, I like real wool. (This too will change.)

Perhaps I have seen too many movies, but I thought it would be a great idea to get one of those long black woollen coats that I can wear when it's freezing. And then I can wear nothing but my sexy underwear and those arousing stilettos underneath it. That should surprise him nicely.

Finally, I find one that is just **perfect**. I don't think twice at the money I'm spending. I earned it. It's mine. And anyway, this is completely justified. It's for Gary. (What most men don't know is that flimsy underwear is crazily expensive. I would spend this much on underwear in a month. And he just snaps it off me. So I have to keep on replacing it.)

I get home after him. And I'm happy as a hornet on a stinging mission, when the scowl from those beautiful blue eyes stops me dead. My stomach starts to tremble. I know it's bad.

What have I done?

I can't get that image out of my head. He is beautiful. He has eyes that stop meteors, hair blonder than pollen, and is sculpted to athletic perfection. The owner of the haughtiest dark eyebrows and the most sensuous smile ever owned, by any man, woman or child. But the image of that beauty livid with rage, his tie half undone, a Castle Lager in one hand (bottle), I stopped dead. I didn't even close the front door. I began shivering just from the impact of that angry scowl.

"Take it back."

Huh?

He's advancing, across the plush carpet and onto the white tiles, closer to the front door, and my instinct is yelling at me to RUN. Oh that would work on anyone else *but* me. I don't run from a confrontation. I run toward it.

He has the black woollen lapel and is yanking it, "Get it off and get it OUT OF MY HOUSE."

What the fuck?

"No."

"Woman, I won't tell you twice. Don't come back until it's gone."

This is insane. I thought it would be so sexy, and make him happy. And he's behaving as though I just brought a boyfriend home.

* * *

I never got the chance to explain why I bought it. But, I wasn't going anywhere, and it was too late to take my sexy, long black coat, back today. It was the first real fight, and **I did not** like being dictated to about what I could or could not wear, **or** how I spent **my** money.

What a bad night. One I will never forget. I cooked dinner in silence. I ate in silence. I cleaned up in silence. I was torn. I wanted to fight him, but I didn't. I just kept quiet. Biting my tongue with tears duelling for supremacy. I didn't want to cry from hurt, or fear. I was so bitterly livid, I wanted to cry tears of frustration.

We drank together in the spacious lounge, reclining in deep chairs and staring at a wide screen LED TV – (he always has to have the latest.) We smoked together. And we went to bed together. When that commanding hand reached for me, for the first time I pulled away. For once, his outer beauty could not hide the beast that lived inside. But no one denied Gary, especially not his woman.

I didn't know this ... yet.

I was property. And I had allowed myself to become property, willingly. I woke up sometime between midnight and sunrise. He was taking me from behind as I lay asleep on my stomach. He knew I'd wake up. He did not care. He had a point to make. And he was nailing it home. Now the black sheets seemed fitting. His darkness closed in on me, suffocating the life out of my independent spirit. Holding me down, deriving dominant pleasure by teaching me a lesson I will never forget, all I could feel was the freshly ironed obsidian sheet I was clutching. Silent tears baptising the linen, choking my pride silent.

19

(Blame the heating in his home. That's what you get if you go to bed naked. Because he scolds you for having any degree of modesty.)

* * *

I took the coat back.

It was the first time I ever returned a purchase. That was the night I should have taken a stand. That was the night, he knew he had the power to dictate and I would blindly, compliantly and without resistance, follow.

It was a power play. And I chose to lose.

Chapter 6

Something that happens to all couples, is routine. Saturday was King Day. And my king liked his routine. (I can see I have to explain that. Hello? Every man likes to be the 'king of his own castle' ... get it?)

I am not a morning person. Gary is. As usual my day starts with blaring Metallica. He likes to kick start his day. With metal and beer. The 'Master of Puppets' – (no pun intended) – album is drilling a hole through my hangover, as I make my way to the rambling white kitchen for the drugs to kill the disease. The tiles are icy under my soles as the shining perfection of our state of the art, heart of the home, threatens to blind me with sterile reflection.

He walks in behind me, beaming with cheer. I am naked. He grabs a fondle and whispers, "What a good woman. Getting up to cook me breakfast."

Oh! *(So, he thinks I got up to serve him?) OOOOOH! (Realisation dawns.)*

THWACK.

One day I am going to thwack him back with a cast-iron frying pan.

"I saw a movie once with a broad cooking breakfast in nothing but an apron." The *hmmmmm* in my ear gets the hint across. I make myself coffee and don the apron. Bacon and eggs coming up, master.

He yells from the lounge, "Where's my tea, Woman?"

I make his breakfast with precision, and feel good about his pleasure at being served by a not yet fully compos mentis me. When he is happy, he's so loving. That's when he smiles, cuddles and gives me a warm happy feeling. He's showered and dressed after eating. He's ready!

"Hurry up, woman! We're going to be late!"

"Where are we going?"

"Out."

Great. Thanks for clearing that up. So I dig, "What must I wear?"

"Jeans!"

I pull on my jeans, my Doc Marten's, over a skin-tight body suit and give my nipples a modicum of decency by covering them with a waistcoat. (Gone are the designer classy days.) I flip my wavy tresses and fluff them out. Grab my smokes, stuff them into my pocket. Put on my sunglasses, and walk to my master.

... Pause ...

(Catch a wake up! You know you're in a screwball, highball, tea-ball relationship when you have to ask **him** what to wear!)

It was a slow poisoning of my taste. Endless criticism, to downright, "I'm not being seen with you dressed like that." And each time, I bought the clothes he wanted me to be in, I wore the clothes he preferred for each occasion. It was often subtle, but it undermined my self-confidence perfectly.

... Play ...

The cocky smile says he approves.

THWACK.

That manages to successfully catapult me out the door. Two helmets. *Right, we're taking the bike then.*

"Why are we taking the bike?"

"Because you get a nipple stand from the wind and I like to feel you press them into my back."

Is everything in life about sex?

No. I should have known. Where there is sex; there's drugs and rock 'n roll.

It's an amazing sunny day. The perfect kind, where you ache to go to the beach. The sky is perfectly sun-bleached cobalt, not a cloud to be witnessed, the warmth of the sun feeling like a soothing caress. I understand why he decided to take the blood red Suzuki. I discover where we are going when we get there. Alan broke it off with tall and voluptuous Adelle some time back, and is now dating a seriously cute brunette with a mane of wild hair, a-la Tawny Kitane. She looks like a model, about five-foot-five, with a heart-shaped face and vivid green eyes, and is sunnier than margarine. We climb off the bike at Alan's new digs. A rambling house in Durbanville.

I'm hauled straight to the homely kitchen to help Kristy with culinary preparations for the gang. Gary pisses off outside to smoke a joint with Alan. (Male bonding.) I hear a voice yell from beyond the open kitchen door, "Woman, be a doll and bring us a few cold ones!"

Kristy looks at me, "Woman?"

I laugh, "Yeah. It's my pet name." *All that's missing is my leash.*

I do as I'm ordered. The men are watching the new puppies playing in the immaculate yard. Lording it up, doing nothing. As I walk back into the terra-cotta tiled kitchen, a full glass of chardonnay is pushed into my hand by a knowing Kristy. She makes me feel at home. She brings sanity back into my life. She giggles and gossips. Oh, and she's allowed to spend her own money. *Lucky bitch.* She breaks every rule, and puts on 'Don't want no short-dicked man.' Her favourite song, (Alan's age must have rubbed off on her.) She never stops telling me how *amaaaazing* Alan is in bed. The downfall of many a good woman is how good her man is in bed. Call us shallow. Or **stupid**.

Gary walks in with towering Alan, and glowers at Kristy, "Who put this crap on?"

Alan walks up behind her, giggling like a teenager. Dope can do that to you I hear. He starts fondling her cleavage and I watch her cheeks turn puce. "Alaaaan..." she objects shyly.

Then we get **blasted** with more AC/DC. I can see why Kristy thinks Alan is hot. He is reminiscent of a younger Val Kilmer, but at least six-foot-five, with a very sexy mouth. (Have you ever seen a Michelle Pfeifer mouth on a man?)

A happy Gary strolls back through the kitchen with the other sidekick. Charl has arrived: Creepy Charl, with his imaginary chin. His mouth just slopes off into his neck, it freaks me out. His cheekbones are non-existent which makes his face look like a fish, streamlined for swimming, it makes his eyes look freaky, and his nose too large for his face.

And off they go for joint number two. I'm happy and while the day away with a vivacious Kristy. We end up sitting in the lounge on their burgundy leather couches, surrounding a very costly oriental carpet. They're into this stuff and can tell you about pile, the oils in the wool maintaining lustre and strength ... I zone out and suck on my smoke and drink my wine.

I watch the three men walk past the lounge to the bedrooms, and wonder what the heck is going on. I stand up and walk, a tad unsteadily, over wooden floors to Alan's bedroom. Gary blocks the door, "Woman! Hey baby! You shouldn't be here. We're doing guy stuff."

I like him in this mood. I wrap my arms around his waist and whisper, "I'm horny." It's true. Red wine turns me into a whore.

This is one thing I don't like about Gary. He never believes a word you say. He has to check. He moves my waistcoat, and sure as atoms, they're standing to attention. He smiles and gives me a wink, "We'll go in a bit." He turns me and THWACK. "Off you go."

Humiliated, I walk to the bathroom. I smell all of Kristy's perfumes and envy her budget. Then I sneak back out and peek through the tiny gap made by the bedroom door hinges. Alan is snorting cocaine. I fear that I'll get caught, so tiptoe back to the lounge, sit down with a very intoxicated Kristy, and light a smoke before downing my 2006 Simonsig Cabernet. I feel like crying.

A very cheerful Gary swaggers into the room. I watch him advance, seductive to my hormones, in his black leather waistcoat and porcelain white shirt, exposing his strong, tanned, kissable neck. He flops down next to me, shamelessly ensconcing his hand between my legs. Kristy is way past the point of caring about decorum. (Why do parents pay for private schools anyway? If this bunch is any indication of money well invested.) Alan walks in with Charl, a bottle of shooters in each hand, "Let's drink."

Coinage it is. Some games never get old. I never get any better at them either.

Somewhere around three, we get back on that bike and go home. No one can handle liquor and drugs like Gary. He seems as sober as a Monday morning, he's lucid. I'm not.

My head spins and lurches with every corner we lower into. I don't care that my long blonde hair is wrapping a noose around my neck. I just want to get home alive.

As we get inside the front door, I help to close it as Gary pins me against it. Tearing off my clothes. *Oh right. Shit! It's Saturday night.* I'm glad I'm so drunk. Within minutes my naked master sprawls atop the evilly black duvet, while I dine on his toes. Massaging the arch of his foot, applying delicate pressure to muscles, kissing calves, running my tongue up the inside of his thigh. I start proceedings the way I've been taught. With my submissive lips coating the maypole, preceded with a caressing and moistly executed tea-bag. Usually I have to be on top first, but he disarms me by flipping me onto my knees. I'm hardly resistant with all the alcohol in my veins.

That was the night I learned what the wheelbarrow is. Maybe that's why I remember it.

Chapter 7

Sunday is coitus day. And friends' day. Friends come over to watch movies, get drunk, smoke up a storm, leave me and my resplendent home, wasted. But we indulge in copulation all day, until they arrive. My underwear has gone through a few transformations over the past year. And the Sunday practising of spawning starts off with handcuffs and blindfolds. (He's so classy. A real class act.)

Let's rename Sunday to 'Indulge Your Master Day'. Today, he knows exactly what he wants, he's going to try out the Kama Sutra. And I'm the idiot with the engagement ring on my finger. So guess who he's testing the theory on?

Please, I'm begging you: don't do it. I did ballet and gymnastics, could still do the splits, and I found the Sutra too much like contortionist masochism. But Gary was having a ball. And I was getting two. (Yes. To answer your question, every single one of those positions was recreated.)

I have never been happier to have his friends arrive to disrupt my life. In nanoseconds the chains, cuffs and ties were hidden. I launched into the bedroom and shut the door to get clothes on. Gary just pulled on his jeans, lit a smoke to disguise remnants of activity, and opened the hefty door to his alcohol-wielding friends. The goofy musketeers were reunited. Two more friends followed. A decent couple: Cindy and Graham.

I walk out and smile, lighting a smoke with a trembling hand, cheeks flushed.

Charl is probably the most depraved man I have known. And he hones into that picture book like an addict needing a fix, "What's this?"

(Which is **creepy** to observe: picture someone with bulbous fish eyes offset with a caricature potato nose, alighting with demented anticipation, almost drooling ... yeah you get the picture ...)

Gary does his deliciously wicked chuckle that still makes my knees turn to goo, "The Sutra."

Charl's steel-hued eyes light up, (glistening like the old black and white version of the Hunchback of Notre Dame), "Does it work?"

Gary flops into a recliner, his diabolical smirk illuminating his face, "I'll let you know."

(How come, when he does that, he looks handsome - not demented?)

Alan drops the afternoon's entertainment on the table in front of Gary. Porno movies just brought in by his boss. Kristy picks up the Sutra and leafs through it. She passes the book to Alan. He opens it and informs Gary, "I'm borrowing this."

Gary picks up the movie on the top, "Then I'm keeping this."

Alan smiles and throws an unlit joint to Gary, "Deal."

* * *

The drink flows like the fountain of youth. (It works that way, have you noticed? Everyone looks better – even Charl – once you're sozzled.) My home is a smoky haze and I'm giggly on fumes. We drink, we eat, and we watch porno stars show us their stars. It's disgusting I know. But inevitably a long afternoon and evening morphs into sex talk, Irish coffees, and the last joint of the weekend.

I don't care who's done what with whom. I'm learning secrets from Cindy. She has a friend who's a nurse, and she's telling me how to prevent ejaculation so that it lasts longer. Kristy is flipping through Cosmo and reading to us how to successfully perform a blow job.

"It says to hold it and lick it like an ice-cream cone."

Cindy laughs sarcastically, "We know how to do it, Kristy."

Kristy drops the glossy mag as though it's anthrax, "I can't believe they have to explain that! How can you **not** know?"

I keep quiet. I didn't know. Gary's sadistic lifestyle taught me that and *waaaay* more. (*In fact I naively thought it WAS a BLOW job. I had heard the expression and had a vague idea of what went on during the act, but I had no idea back then that he did the blowing (up) not me.*) Two accusing and perceptive pairs of eyes pin me to my cigarette.

"What?"

Kristy starts jiggling with raucous giggling, "Stef! *OH MYYYY GOOOOD!*"

The room stops, and all men present are staring to see what the commotion is about. I feel my cheeks getting hotter. Gary is smiling at me. Instigating, he eggs, "Show her how it's done, Cindy."

There is still a lady inside me somewhere, and she wants to crawl under the sleeper-wood table as Cindy grabs her empty beer bottle and starts performing her version of oral sex on it. I notice that Charl's perverted hands have just snaked into his loose dirty red baggies. *He is so gross. (*Did he honestly think that none of us would notice?)

I can't watch and avert my eyes to stare morbidly at the taupe carpet, listening to the mocking laughter as Cindy performs her expert craft on a piece of cold moulded glass. Music blares, breaking the tension, when a hand grips me and hauls me into the arms of my lover. He smiles with understanding and squeezes me tight. Whispering confidentially into my ear, hotly, "It's okay woman. I won't tell them." I love him. I really do.

Eeuw, Charl's just made his way into the marine blue bathroom. To jack off no doubt. I hold on and kiss my man. He's my haven in this never-ending flurry. He's in a romantic mood for a change and holds my hand. Expelling his friends from our abode at last. We all have work tomorrow. A part of me is dreading having to do more Kama Sutra, or gymnastics like the flippin' wheelbarrow. If he was any taller that wouldn't work.

I look at the mess and sigh. I clean up ashtrays, bottles and greasy glasses, while he watches Miss Magic Boobs in her porno movie. I walk in just after midnight and have an education on the flat screen burned into my retina, the multiple facets of using an ice cube. A long ice cube. A long, rounded, ice cube. I shudder.

He flips it off, we're cloaked in blinding darkness. Strong arms surround me. He kidnaps me to the bedroom. Wow, kisses and cuddles. For a change he's making love to me as he strips my body naked. Caressing me. Sucking my youthful skin with his magnificent mouth. Turning my relaxation into exquisite anticipation. I am so relieved to just lie back and be indulged. Tonight he's being slow, gentle, no violence or hard, punishing, invasive manoeuvres. Letting him rock my body with the motion of the ocean, I succumb to a heightening. Each time he eases himself into me, I become more aroused. I'm twenty-two, and something happens. It's divine. It's

28

unlike anything I've ever experienced. I have never felt this good in my life.

A hand clamps over my mouth, "Shut up, the neighbours will hear you."

I don't care, just keep moving. I DON'T CARE. (Houston, we have lift off!) I wasn't even conscious of my voice moaning out of me. Now I'm done. It's official. This is the man for me. He looks like a god, and finally he's giving me what girls have been talking about since high school. I'm not going anywhere. Just keep doing that and I'll stay with you.

Chapter 8

One thing I loved about being with Gary, was the lifestyle. It was chaotic and wild. Perfect Cape ocean-view bike runs at least twice a month along the coast.

Sometimes doing the wine route, other times following the scenic coastline to the Cape of Good Hope Nature Reserve, where we'd end up swimming naked together on secluded beaches we had to illegally hike to; endless pubbing and clubbing, from Mercury Live to Stones in Tableview; socialising eight days a week. It kept me motivated.

I can't say when the switch happened. It was that insidious. He often kept me waiting at work, insisting on fetching me. So my best friend was the security guard. He was a very nice guy, with fair hair and big blue eyes. A tall and lanky dude who came from the same town as Gary. I worked in a particularly seedy and crime-ridden area at the wrong end of Adderley Street; so waiting outside after dark was not even a consideration.

When Gary came to the door, looking through the glass to see me laughing and joking with Mr Security Guard, I was completely unprepared for the jealous repercussions. He could have any girl he wanted. I knew my place. I would **never** cheat on him. A: I didn't have the energy – (you've heard the expression, 'I'm fucked', right?) – and B: I loved him so much, I would have laid down my life for him.

I was the recipient of the sulky-silent treatment all the way home. Not knowing what I'd done, I can take it no longer and as we walk inside I broach the subject.

"What is your problem?"

"Why were you talking to him?"

"Gary, he is the security guard. No one else is there at that time! What must I do, sit and stare at the wall? He's just a friend."

I get The Look. Wow, he must be angry. He fetched his own beer.

"What were you talking about?"

I look at his face and know he's a cobweb away from violently angry. I know that look and I never want to see it again.

"Music. We like the same music."

I get the '**yeah right!**' look.

Half an hour later I sit down with him in the lounge, waiting for dinner to finish cooking. He looks across at me with those smouldering blue eyes and states, "You don't love me."

WHAT!

He's breaking up with me because I spoke to the security guard about the kick ass rock band, Feedback? *Are you kidding me?* He's ripping my heart out of my ribcage with his wounded stare. I can't lose him. **I can't**.

I can barely breathe, "That's not true. I do love you."

"Prove it."

I'm shaking. Why am I so afraid?

"How?"

"Never talk to him again."

Okay, that's impossible. I work there. How can I never talk to the man who opens and closes the door for me? It's irrational. I know I can't keep my word if that's what he wants.

"I can't *not* talk to him. That's unreasonable."

Silence.

I know Gary. I've been with him for a long time. So I get on my knees and crawl over to him. This always works.

He pushes me away, "I don't want you anymore."

Cue: Sledgehammer. Pounding me into emotional smithereens.

Tears. I can't help it.

"Why not?"

"I don't want what another man has had."

I'm shocked breathless. "Gary, nothing happened! I **promise**."

"You were alone. You just said so."

God give me strength. "That doesn't mean a thing. I can't wait in the dark for you. Gary, I would never ..."

Saved by the dinner buzzer. I get off my knees and walk in these ridiculous heels to the kitchen. Gary has rearranged my wardrobe. Tight, tight or tight. Jeans even tighter. He criticised me endlessly, until I became his image of arm candy. I serve dinner. I'm not hungry and go to the coldly spacious bathroom.

That night was the first time Gary and I did not engage in any form of physical activity, other than our very first night in a frigid bed. The situation was bad. Cataclysmically bad.

* * *

Days followed days. I tried to maintain my distance from Mr Security Guard. I had to explain why though. And I felt really stupid telling him about the fight. We had an arrangement. We would sit across the office from each other. Chat from afar. As soon as we heard a car door or any activity, I would pretend to work, he would pretend to be listening to his earphones. I guess it was obvious. The silent confrontations each day, between my friend and my lover, at a door I walked through each and every day at work.

But, tonight is pool night. Finally I can have a sense of normal. I rush dinner, get ready, when the bullet impales me.

"It's just the lads tonight. Sorry woman. I need time alone with them. We're all sick of women interfering."

I'm deflated. I try to justify it. I can see that he needs time alone with his friends. That's not unreasonable.

"Okay."

How stupid of me to think that this issue would be just tonight. This was the beginning of the end. I watched him pick up the case with his pool cue in it. He looked dashing, he smelled fuckable. I loved his smell. (He was the pheromone lord!)

Chapter 9

By now, I know most of you think I'm exaggerating and writing a load of rubbish. If you do think this, then you are so very lucky. This is my life. It is my normal everyday reality. And if you've never been someone's walking blow up doll, then consider yourself blessed. (I was in a dysfunctional relationship and I didn't even know it.)

The first step to becoming someone's slave, is the severing of all previous ties. You deliberately cut off your network. And it's easy to do. It started for me with my friends of colour. Lovely, kind people. Gary was the worst racist I have ever known. Blondie hated dark skins. He had a derogatory statement for anyone who wasn't vampire white.

Because I loved and respected my friends, I 'phased' them out of my life (because I didn't want Gary to hurt them). I knew they wouldn't understand. Then came my family and old friends. In his opinion my mother hated him, my brother was gay – (he was homophobic too) – he had an issue with every single friend, (even Adelle), until all I had were his friends girlfriends. I did everything he told me to do.

I did anything and everything I had to, to keep him happy. So, when Gary pushed me away and kept me at a distance, I was miserable.

I still could not take my eyes off him. He was stunning. No man, (other than Calvin Klein models), looked that jaw-dropping in nothing but plain old blue jeans. And he chose to walk around in just the blues so often that I was in a permanent state of arousal.

Gary kept me at arm's distance for two weeks. He rejected every advance I made, but had to feed the beast. I cannot convey how it shattered my heart (and self-esteem – the little I had left) – that he refused to speak to me, to engage with me in any way, until I was fast asleep. For two weeks I was woken with him skewering me in the middle of the night. When he was done, he'd just roll over and go to sleep. Two hours later he'd wake me up again. Just a shake.

"What?" I'd mumble sleepily.

He would smile. I would fall for it, thinking that redemption was going to be mine. When he pulls my head into the top of his thighs, I give him what he likes.

My hopeful eyes would meet his, just to be met with that triumphant gloat.

He was killing me with degradation and humiliation. (I fell for this multiple times. Ha ha. You can tell I'm a natural blonde.) And I had no one I could share my pain with. My only real friend now, was Gary.

Once he'd decided that I'd suffered enough for being attractive to other men, he took me back. Gary style. The dynamics were changing faster than I could comprehend. But I was just so grateful he wanted me. He picked me up from work, drowning out any conversation with blaring Metallica. I stared sullenly out of my window at the back end of Table Mountain. The beauty lost on me in my haze of misery. Craving him with every breath and hating him for my sufferance.

When I got home, I walked in through the door expecting to simply make dinner. The kitchen was the first room as you walked in through the door. I dropped my Gucci bag on the table and put the kettle on. I opened the fridge and took out the cold brew to slake his hard day's thirst. He's wearing his wicked grin.

My heartbeat accelerates. Oh, how I've missed that look. His eyes sparkle deceptively as he puts his noosed tie around my neck. He takes the beer and places it onto the table next to us. His grin is a smile now. He's touching me. YAY, thank God he still wants to touch me. My dress falls to the floor. My bra follows. I step out of my shoes and become diminutive, looking up at him, wondering what he's going to do. He pulls off his button-down work shirt and drops it to caress my dress. With my leash he leads me to the bedroom. I'm melting. The thought of him has my body in biological response-ready mode.

He pushes me rather forcefully onto the edge of the king sized bed. Face down. I hear the zipper and my body explodes when he unlocks me. Tears of gratitude and relief well up. I'm into it. The rhythm. I feel the hardening before he ices my cake and instantly feel robbed as he pulls out of me and sprays hot ectoplasm all over my naked back. I swallow hard, fighting back bitter tears. I'm given hope again as the noose tightens and he pulls my head back by the hair. He re-enters the chamber of secrets and starts doing his thing again.

Hope restored! I'm used to his games. If Gary is anything, he's unpredictable. And he gets bored easily. The bedroom dynamic was constantly morphing, an endless kaleidoscope of sadistic creativity.

I am shamed when he pulls out and repeats the process. When he does it a third time, I am broken. He pulls me up off the bed backwards, with the noose tight around my throat, and turns me to face him. I cannot meet his eyes. My emotional pain is too excruciating. I don't want him to know what he's just done to me. I stare fixedly at his amazing pecs, my eyes caressing the shape that is perfection.

A commanding hand lifts my chin until I finally look into his eyes with my own. I hate Gary. He knows me better than anyone ever will. He loves to make me angry and hurt, because my eyes turn a deep sapphire. He deliberately shames and humiliates me, because he relishes my eyes when they're that shade of blue. I know that my eyes are betraying me, because his smile communicates that he has achieved what he set out to.

He hasn't spoken a word. Neither have I. I wait for the next instruction. He sits down on the kohl black sheet and pulls my body by the tie to stand between his legs. He looks at my erect nipples and a gloating smirk morphs his handsome face. He waits expectantly. I remember belatedly that this is my cue. (Hah! No pun intended).

I kneel and watch his eyes close, as a low moan escapes his throat when my warm mouth cossets one of the twins. He flops back and the noose gets tighter. I can hardly breathe and with the erection in my mouth, the lack of oxygen is making my vision blur. I've read about people dying like this. Squashing my fear, I choose to trust him. It's odd, but it's an adrenalin rush. Erotic extreme sports has entered our dynamic. He finally relinquishes the leash.

I'm in!

I loosen the tie slightly as I become the dominant partner. Looking down at my victim who is enjoying lying back with expectant anticipation. I've learned the art of masochism from Gary. And it's pay-back time. I'm hornier than a blowfish, but I've waited this long, a little while longer won't be any harder to take. Those hands grip my hips, and I take the noose off and restrain his hands to the bed with it. No way is he interfering in this.

Ha!

His eyes opened and I saw startled surprise. I smile back at my master. He's forgotten that he's trained me well. Sub or dom, top or bottom, I can do both.

I learned the Asian art of making love using all of the pelvic floor muscles. My body can do better than my lips can. I ride him until I anticipate the precipice, and using the nurse's technique of stalling a detonation, I make him wait. It's a brilliant technique.

I start the slow build up again. He's my victim now, and I'm relishing torturing him. I fondle my own pink skin and watch his eyes cloud with anger. The motion doesn't stop. My body is working its erotic pleasure on him, he moans loudly ... I cut it off again.

Three times he humiliated me.

Three times is payback.

So I initiate joyride number three. I'm getting my own fix. Two weeks without the explosion of a new galaxy is a lifetime when you've been having two or three a day for years. I'm now as sick as Gary. He has made his needs my needs. I cannot change who he's conditioned me to be.

I've never heard Gary yell like that ever. When I let him have the release, it looked like it could almost have been painful. I stay on him, smiling.

Game, set and match.

Respect won, he smiles back. The smile that conveys openly,' I love you, bitch'.

Feeling secure, I undo his hands and free him. My head lurches as he grabs me and pins me underneath him. He's angry and has to work off that energy. He's nailing me hard. (And I'm loving it.) Since that first time I have never had a vocal climax again. The only way to shut up, is to hold my breath. He knows I'm cumming when I stop breathing. A long groan breaks the never-ending slapping of skin on skin. Not from me. He drops heavily against me. A tear of relief and satisfaction escapes out of the corner of my eye. He leans away and grips my face. His explorative kiss feels like rape. I savagely kiss him back, returning the mingling of lips and tongues. I'm hungry. I've been craving this sustenance. His hand tightens around my neck and squeezes. Kissing and asphyxiating me.

My vision starts blurring again. Fear hammers my heart. Would he really kill me? Is this a power trip? I'm too breathless to scream. You never beg with Gary. You never ask. If you do, he'll show you the door. So I watch through tearing eyes as his head pulls away from mine.

(Thanks to Gary I can hold my breath for an indeterminate amount of time.)

He lets my throat go and laughs happily. A gentle kiss is placed on my swollen lips. Swollen from kissing. The soul-soothing voice speaks in my ear as he pinches my nipple, "Fuck, I love you." The first words of the night.

I can't tell you a time when I have felt this happy. My heart is blowing evanescent bubbles of joy as I walk naked to make us dinner. That night he engaged with my body repeatedly. And I felt loved. This was love. (Or so I thought.) I lost count of the orgasms we had between us. After dinner he put in Miss Magic Boobs and doggie'd me in the dark, watching her writhing. I'm addicted to his smell, it turns me inside out. I never object to his overwhelming appetite for my lips on his cue. I crave his hands all over my body. I adore him inside me. In short, I worship him.

(In retrospect I think he had turned me into a sex addict who missed her calling as a porn star.)

I knew I'd won him back when we went out together for drinks with the goofy gang on Friday night to the V&A Waterfront. Cindy is short, really short: four-foot-two or something ridiculous like that. And she can drink an alcoholic into surrender. Her joy at our being reunited is palpable, and she intends to rejoice with shooters. Shoving money into my hand she grabs the other and pulls me off my bar stool, "Come!"

She pushes me through throngs of men to the bar. I know the routine. She can't see over the bar so someone else has to get the drinks for her.

"What are we having?"

She grins and flicks back wildly curly, long blonde hair, "Two Slippery Nipples."

I laugh, and feel my cheeks heat up as every man around us is suddenly giving our nipples their undivided attention. *Shit. They are reacting to the attention! Great. Thanks nipples!*

The tall, dark-haired beefcake behind the bar smiles and asks, "What can I give you?"

I order, "Two Slippery Nipples, please." His eyes move to my nipples, he grins, "Sure thing." The suggestion is obvious.

As he walks away Cindy pulls on my arm and yells, "And a Blow Job!"

I raise my eyebrows because now we're becoming the object of commentary and scrutiny. She laughs and, too loud, says, "I'm craving one."

I'm not. I had a lifetime's supply just yesterday. Sleep is becoming an indulgence of luxurious proportions.

The bar-tender returns with the shooters and quirks an eyebrow, "Anything else?"

I blush for real, "A Blow Job too, please."

His smile causes sunlight to break through the night and he unzips his jeans, "With pleasure."

I clarify, "The shooter."

He gives me a wink, his mischievous glance said very clearly, 'It is the shooter, angel,' but he pulls it back up. His throaty laugh causes my cheeks to burn with fervour. (This is my give-away. It reveals that no matter what happens between Gary and me behind closed doors, I'm still naive and easily embarrassed around strangers. Especially men.)

Laughs erupt from the baritones and muscles surrounding us. A huge scary looking guy leers at me, "I'll give you one."

This isn't going well. If Gary sees other men talking to me, I'm in endless shit. And I've only just been allowed out to play again. My flushed cheeks drain as his wide shoulders push through them and he stands towering behind Cindy. His look of displeasure sends fluttering panic through my loins. Cindy fears no repercussion and is encouraging the lewd behaviour. Gary scowls at the men, puts his arm around my waist and slides his hand into the back of my jeans.

"Woman, is there a problem?"

I shake my head as the bartender returns to me with a Blow Job. I pay him, my eyes pleading silently for him not to joke any further.

As he hands me the change, Gary knifes him with two cold, hard, blue eyes and orders, "Two Castle's!"

Gary is used to ordering people around. You can tell. He never says please. Gary moves his arm to around my shoulders and blatantly cups my right breast. Angry eyes seem insulted as they watch him. I feel shamed and carefully pick up the drinks, handing Cindy her Blow Job, avoiding all eye contact with the audience around us, at any cost. She downs it and I put the empty glass back on the bar. I hand her the Slippery Nipple and get ready to walk back to our table with mine.

As I move through our audience, one man says to me, "What are you doing with a loser like that, sister?"

I freeze, dizzy with fear. I keep my eyes riveted to the floor and force myself to start moving as Gary's voice confronts him, "Fuck you!"

I glance back at the Good Samaritan. Gary is facing him, ready for a confrontation. I mouth "Sorry!" His eyes communicate so much. I felt genuine caring for my well-being in them. Cindy grabs Gary and pushes him, "Stop being a wanker, Gary!"

Gary knows he's outnumbered. He can withdraw with his pride intact. Glaring daggers, he allows Cindy to drag him away. When she reaches me she gives me the 'What the hell is wrong with your man?' look.

Charl and Alan immediately start teasing him for being highly strung, pushing smokes and alcohol at him. The instant solution to every problem.

My eyes meet his and I want to die, and cry. I'm going to pay for this.

I stare out at the luxury boats docked in the harbour. It's too late to hear the seals barking now. The lights dance ecstatically across the inky ocean, the smell strongly greasy from the tankers out of sight. I feel my exuberance drowning, like the moon sinking below the horizon. My emotional death is not that beautiful. Eventually, I drag my eyes back to watch him with ill-disguised trepidation. I smile half-heartedly at Cindy head-banging to one of our fine local bands. Cutting Jade are grinding out 'I will fight you, every step of the way ...'

I haven't. I don't have the guts to fight him.

Later, a voice whispers at me as I enter the ladies, "You can do better."

My eyes stare nervously up into gentle brown ones. For the first time, I'm sensing that I'm a catch, and Gary's possessive behaviour not only shamed me, but made me wish I didn't have an audience to witness it. I smile, averting my gaze in case my tormentor is watching, and whisper, "Thanks."

Chapter 10

Okay, I'll admit that it took endless reassurances and every persuasive technique in my repertoire to convince him that I was not at fault for Friday's issue. I also had to finally submit to some bedroom antics I am still staunchly opposed to. (Keep reading, I'll dish them out later.) By Monday morning, the game was back on.

Gary played games. Constantly. Underlying every one of them was a seriousness that kept me captive. One thing I would never attempt, was the undermining of his authority. He named the game. I had to play.

Nothing prepared me for him dropping me off for work. He grabs my wrist and stalls me from exiting the leather seat. His smile disarms me.

What's going on?

"Wait."

It's a command.

I wait.

*What are you **doing**?*

His hand slips into my knickers and his fingers bury in like a tortoise getting shy.

My cheeks instantly heat up as my body reacts to the stimulation. I watch the bodies thronging past the car. I'm grateful that Monday morning is a sedative. People stroll past in their own private trance. No one notices. He pulls open my blouse and pops out my nipple, his mouth covers it. I am molten. Instinct just takes over and obliterates any thought processes I was entertaining.

He pulls his hand away along with his head, laughs demonically, and smiles at me. "Get out."

"What?"

"Get out. I'm going to be late."

Hastily I try to straighten my clothing and step out of his impatient transportation capsule. He pulls off and does not look back. I draw deep breaths to try and still my arousal. My body is on fire and my legs have lost the blood flow that mobilises muscles. I stagger to the door and walk past it to the steps beyond. I flop down heavily, waiting for my cheeks to calm down. I light a smoke with shaking fingers and sit and stare blankly at traffic and strangers trickling past my view to the street.

A blond head appears at the window. Arched eyebrows convey a silent query. I smile and mouth, "I'm fine."

I finish my smoke, spritz on more perfume and force my legs to walk to the door.

The blond head opens the door for me, one hand for some reason on the gun at his hip, "Are you okay?"

I am so horny I am sure if I meet his eyes he'll see it, and know it. Embarrassed I mumble, "I'm fine."

I half meet his eyes, before nervously looking away and walking to my desk. I sit too close to him the entire day, every day. He knows my routine. This is how we became friends. Through close proximity, daily. If anyone can tell there's something different about me, it's the guy that doesn't have to answer phones and push paper. He sits down, a frown marring his peaches and cream face.

I don't get coffee, I just immerse myself in work.

* * *

I have a problem. I have one of 'those' voices. Once, a few weeks ago, I phoned the radio station to enter a competition on 5fm and landed up having a debate with the DJ about me doing radio. He insisted I had just the right voice for radio. He told me it was so sexy the listeners would lap it up. Thanks, but no thanks: (like Gary would ever let that happen.)

(Okay, fine. I admit it. I asked him if I could and he said NO.)

I also have clients who are pretty blatant about it. They phone me for no other reason than to say hi and hear my voice. A few of them have told me I should be doing phone sex, and they'd be my number one caller. **Great**. I know it's meant to be a compliment, but I'm pretty uncomfortable with strangers saying things like this to me. And no, I have never told Gary.

So the **last** thing I want to do today is answer that flippin' telephone. If they think that about me when I'm not feeling frisky, then those men will just *know* and start saying naughty things to me, and I just can't handle that today.

When Monica walks in, I tell her, "I'm not feeling well today. Can I ask you to take the calls?"

She nods, and drops her bag as she places her cute derriere into the chair at the desk pushed up against mine, "No problem. Just take it easy."

Mr Security Guard overhears and now he's staring through me as if he's trying to read my mind.

One of 'those' clients is actually on a mission to get my attention. He has come into the bank to meet me numerous times and doesn't know how to take 'no' for an answer. He is a tall Indian man with contrasting azure eyes. If Gary knew, he'd throw a FIT. Not just about me talking to other men – full stop – but to one who isn't snow white, I shudder to think of the repercussions.

Of all the days to pull a stunt on me, today is my cursed day.

Flowers arrive for me. From blue eyes: my Indian suitor who is, by the way, married and has a new-born.

I cannot function today. I don't react like someone should at receiving flowers. I do pluck up the courage to phone him and say thank you. He is adamant about taking me to lunch. Oh yes, he can sense the disease eating me from the inside out. My answer is **no**. My excuse, "I'm not feeling well today."

How do you answer, 'What is wrong my darling?'– 'Oh I'm just so horny that if Gary doesn't shag me soon, I may end up in an institution.'?

By evening, when everyone has left, I get up from my desk. I have sat there all day without moving. I have made as little eye contact with everyone as possible. And I need air! I grab my bag and my flowers and make my way to the staff door. I'm breaking the rule. I'm waiting outside.

This sets off alarm bells in Mr Security Guard, and he refuses to open the door. He grabs my elbow, "Are you okay?"

"I'm fine."

"No, you're not. You haven't been yourself today."

Finally, I look up at his eyes and feel deeply touched by his concern. It draws moisture into my eyes.

"I'm fine. Promise."

"Did he ...? You know you can talk to me if you're having problems right?"

Worry seeps through my weak legs. *Great, now he thinks Gary is beating me or something. I have to stop this.*

"I'm just not feeling well today. I swear, otherwise I'm fine."

He pauses, waiting for me to say more, giving me the opportunity to look for support. I don't need support. I need Gary.

He releases my elbow and opens the door. I smile, "Thanks."

I walk back to the steps, sit down and light a smoke. He's worried as all hell and opens the door and walks to me. He hands me a slip of paper. I glance at it as I take it. It's a phone number.

"If you need help, phone me."

Okay, now I'm all mushy and feel like I'm seriously going to cry. My lips tremor and my voice sounds shaky, "Thanks."

Please go inside, if Gary sees you I'm going to be in it DEEP.

I put the number into my bag and watch him walk away back behind the door. He doesn't take his eyes off me until I leave with Gary. I consider how impractical his dialling code has made him. I live in Rondebosch, he lives in Milnerton. He is nowhere near my side of the world.

I couldn't wait to see Gary. My anticipation had morphed my body back into an amoeba. I step into his capsule and the scowl paralyses me.

"Who the fuck gave you those?"

Gulp. "A client."

"Why? Does he want to fuck you?"

"No. It's just to say thank you for helping him with an issue." (What a lie.)

"Throw them away." He stops the car next to a trash bin.

"No!"

I never get flowers and don't particularly feel like giving these carnations up right now.

He gets out of the car, stalks around to my side and yanks open the S3's door. I struggle with him as he attempts to yank the flowers out of my hands. I'm **not** giving them up.

Big mistake. Now it's war.

He gets back in behind the wheel and glares at me, "Who is he?"

"A customer."

His expression conveys I'm retarded.

"WHAT. IS. HIS. NAME?"

44

I start quivering. I can't let Gary make shit with the clients. I'll get fired.

Whisper, "Mr Pillay."

"A FUCKING SAMOOSA GAVE THAT TO YOU?"

I nod.

"THROW THEM AWAY."

I shake my head. I'm too afraid to speak.

"Get out."

I stare at him, incredulous.

"I said GET OUT."

Wiping away tears, I get out of the vehicle with my bag and my flowers. I watch as Gary speeds away into a blinding sunset. I breathe with difficulty and become aware of the danger I am in. Moving briskly, I begin the long walk to the bus depot.

I got home sometime after eight o'clock. The night cloaked me with depressing black ink, saturating into me with its darkness, so very dark, and I wasn't completely convinced the locks wouldn't be changed by the time I get home.

What was I thinking? Armageddon exploded when I walked in with those flowers. I was a lying, cheating whore, who was secretly dating other men behind his back.

Cue: Atomic bomb. He blew up for hours.

Cue: Nuclear demolition. The tears a torrent of seeping misery.

Cue: monsoon flood. Is it so hard to believe that someone would give me flowers without fucking me first?

My eyelids are swollen from crying, and I stare at the object of my pain. I now hate those flowers. Giving it more thought, who in their right mind sends flowers as a romantic gesture? (*Here, have something pretty and watch it die. Not exactly a good omen for a relationship* ... oh ... and Gary doesn't do romantic.)

Then he goes through my bag looking for evidence of my soliciting. I want to vanish as he gloats, wielding a phone number.

Oh shit.

"Whose number is this?"

"A friend."

He's way too close, pushing the paper up to my nose to emphasise that I can't deny its existence.

"A male?"

I shake my head.

He glares further, I shrink away from the baleful glare. Convulsions begin when he picks up the phone and dials the number. I am so afraid I feel like I'm going to vomit. Gary's outrage is transparent when a male baritone answers the call. I can hear it from here.

Gary disconnects, turning his body to face me, quivering in a foetal position in a chair a few feet away from him. He's radiating waves of aggression. I can taste it.

He picked up his keys and left. I cried all night. I didn't sleep. He came home at around 4 a.m. and didn't even acknowledge me. I stayed in the lounge all night. Smoking, crying, blowing my nose. It was over. And I had done nothing wrong.

Chapter 11

I'm dressed for work and about to leave to catch the bus, when he approached me. He still seemed stern, but now exuded mild anxiety.

"Where are you going?"

Duh. Isn't it obvious? "To work."

My voice is husky, my throat is raw. I have an evil fairy with an ice-pick doing incessant damage to my brain. Light hurts my eyes. I've tried my best to hide my despair behind make-up.

"Aren't I taking you?"

I stare at him. He's offering me the floatation ring after the flooding and capsizing of my precarious ship. The dam bursts, and I blurt, "I love you."

He doesn't miss a beat this guy. One moment of weakness, "One condition."

I nod. Name your price, I'm going cheap.

"You destroy those fucking flowers."

I nod and agree. He smiles the evil 'I'm going to do bad things to you' smile. His demeanour instantly morphs, and he's happy as a junkie on a high.

How do men manage to plot a flower execution between 4.00 a.m. and 6:30 a.m.? He took me straight to Chapman's Peak drive and pushed me to the edge of the rock overhang, overlooking the ocean with a sheer drop. Waiting for me to throw them. I stare at the pretty flowers in my hands and hesitate. It seems such a waste to destroy the ceramic bowl too. *Can't I keep the bowl?*

He rips them from my hands and hurls them like an expert baseball pitcher, "For fuck's sake woman!"

I feel pretty sad about their extreme death. I don't feel right. Something inside is missing. I'm feeling oddly emotionally numb, and return to the transportation capsule to go to work. Sullenly, I observe the early morning divers pulling on wet-suits as he noisily throttles past them, drawing attention to us. I sink down in my seat, embarrassed.

With less than two minutes before reaching the destination he wiggles his eyebrows at me and gives me that instigating grin, "Aren't you forgetting something?"

I look back at him, blankly.

He looks meaningfully down at his crotch. I stare at it and debate with myself internally. This means the game's still on. I sigh and adjust my safety belt to lean over.

I left him high and dry in that vehicle as I walked to the door to enter the building through the staff side entrance. He would be so pissed, and today, I just don't care.

Mr Security Guard takes one look at me and bolts out of the door. *Great! I guess the make-up doesn't successfully hide my puffy eyes.*

"Jesus, what happened?"

Ha! Um ... you are sweet, but somehow I don't think you'd understand.

"He didn't like me getting flowers. We had a fight."

This guy is sharp, I'll give him that. Oh, and for the record ladies, don't tell another man you've had a fight, when what you've really had is an argument.

"He phoned me didn't he?"

Unwilling to confess to that, I simply look at him, pondering how to answer.

"I stayed up all night worrying about you after that."

Fuck. He knows.

"I'm sorry. I was too scared to phone you and explain. He found the number in my bag and thought the worst."

Ooookay, that didn't sound too good either. Shit this slope is slippery.

"You look like shit."

Thanks a lot.

My mouth morphs into a generic smile, "I didn't get much sleep."

He examines my arms and stares hard at me, "Are you okay?"

*Well now, where do I start? **No. I'm not okay**. But I know what you mean, so that makes the answer yes.*

"Of course I am."

You can look at me as doubtfully as you want. My heart is torn to shreds over unfair accusations. I don't know where the hell he was for at least eight hours, and I'll never find out.

I didn't sleep, I didn't eat, but **hey***, I'm* **fine***. My body is unharmed so you can just STOP thinking that. He's a lot of things, but he's not that.*

We have an eye clash. He's challenging me with his expression. I'm defiantly staring back. Finally he moves out of my way and opens the door for me.

I walk to my desk and pretty much behave the same way I did yesterday. As I am now well aware 'I look like shit', I don't particularly feel like having other people noticing that too.

I'm engrossed in the adding of numbers and balancing of investments when I become aware of the blue uniform standing at my desk. Startled, I look up into Mr Security Guard's worried face.

"Do you still have my number?"

I shake my head. He smiles and hands me a new one.

"Hide it properly."

Okay, I'm going to cry. This is so touching. He hardly knows me and he wants to save me.

I take the secret code to his phone from him, bury it under some paper, and scoot as fast as humanly possible with my head down for the ladies. He saw the tears. I hide inside a stall and cry as quietly as I can.

(In hindsight I have to thank him. His sympathy, gave me strength he will never know.)

* * *

Night falls, and I wonder if I'm supposed to catch the bus and just don't know this yet. I've been having a silent stand-off of ocular clashes with 'my hero' all day and now he's got his arms crossed glaring at me. He wants me to 'fess up. I have nothing to 'fess up about. It's my life. It's my pain. I don't want to share it. I finally run out of paperwork and fold my hands on my desk and stare back.

"Stefanie, I don't like him."

Well now, that's your problem not mine. I remain silent.

"No one should make you this unhappy."

Thanks, I appreciate that. How do I change that though? My eyes stare into his and I feel tears threatening, again. Damn it!

He can see it, and gets up off his chair and starts walking toward me, when Gary's blond head appears at the door. He immediately gets the wrong idea which is plain to see from his expression.

Oh God. These two are about to have a confrontation over me, and it's all one big misunderstanding.

(I will never understand men.)

Mr Security Guard squares his shoulders and unclips the clip that keeps his gun in the holster. He walks to the door with unveiled aggression. Whoa! Shit! Gary squares up too. He's ready for a stand-off.

I grab my bag, panicked.

The door opens marginally behind the security chains and I almost want to laugh when my hero talks through the gap, as if to a stranger, "Can I help you?"

"I'm here for my woman!"

"Sorry, who are you looking for?"

Oh, this is delicious.

"STEFANIE!"

Waaahahaha, this is classic.

"I'll see if she's ready to leave."

Hahahaha, and he closes the door on Gary and bolts it! I am the only person here, in full view.

My problem? I see the humour in this and want to laugh. But they're both deadly serious.

He looks at me, his hand still on his gun, "You don't have to go with him."

I smile, I can't disguise it. (Oopsy, that's seriously pissed off Gary. He's looking like he's having cardiac arrest out there. I've never seen his face turn that scarlet.) Truth? I have to go.

I pat his arm as I walk past him, "Thanks. I'll be fine." (Looking at Gary's expression, I'm not so sure.)

He blocks the door, "Stefanie, don't. You don't have to."

Yes. I do!

Taking a deep breath, I tell him sincerely, "It will be fine, really. I appreciate what you're doing, but I love him. We're just having some issues. Don't worry about me so much." I smile and whisper, "I have your number and I will call you if I need you, okay?"

This seems to appease him, "Promise?"

"I promise."

He opens the door and glowers at Gary. Both of them taller than me, Mr Security, taller than Gary. I halt, standing between them. I take hold of Gary's arm and tug, "Let's go."

Gary hesitates. This stand off of glares over my head is unnerving me. I look at my hero and **fuckenhell** – no wonder he's a security guard. He obviously has what it takes.

I'm adrenalised. I don't want any blood spilled on my behalf. I order forcefully, "Gary, we're leaving!"

He looks down at me livid with hatred. Oh Fuck. Why is it always my flipping fault? He doesn't break eye contact with the man with the gun, as I drag him away from the door. As I get to his white S3, he corners me against it, "What were you talking about?"

"Nothing."

"Then why wouldn't he open the fucking door?"

Yeah, blame me. Go on.

Boldly meeting his eyes, I drop sarcasm, "I. Don't. Know."

"WHAT DID YOU TELL HIM?"

Deep sigh. Count to five. Actually, you know what, I'm just too tired and emotional for this. I look away and see the 'I'm about to run out there and save you from yourself' expression from blondie, behind the office window, watching us. Shit. Why is life so complicated? Man! I'm feeling like everything is horribly unfair and I'm hot-listed for the persecution queue.

I stare at Gary, and for the first time, do not care. "Gary, nothing I say or do makes any difference. Believe whatever the hell you want."

I stalk off toward the bus stop. I'm running out of patience for this melodramatic existence. I don't have the energy any more.

A car idles next to me, "Get in!"

Fuck off, asshole.

He pulls it to a stop in front of me and gets out, "Woman, would you please get in the car?"

I stop dead in shock. He said 'please'. Wow. Oh wow! Who knew he actually loves me. He's upset and it's showing.

I glare – (keeping it cool) – and get in. We drive home in silence. No music blaring, just a long uncomfortable silence.

When I get home I kick into autopilot and make dinner. I do everything that I do everyday. Yes, you heard me. Everything.

I was under house arrest for three months for that day. I am now twenty-three and being treated like a naughty toddler. I may not have phone calls, or go out.

Why did I just compliantly do this? Where was my spine? Where was my head? *Ooooh yeah, right.* So far up Gary's ass I couldn't see Nirvana any longer.

He became irrational. He would go out – (a man has to do what a man has to do) – and come home over the weekends, sporadically. He would walk in, leaving the door open, and run his hand over the curtain rail, "There's dust on here! It'd better be clean when I get home!"

What do you mean when you get home? You just got home!

And he would leave as dramatically as he arrived. I cooked everyday, I cleaned everything. (I even washed the fucking walls.) The house and routine were so amazing that I would have eaten confidently off my own floors: the Queens of Clean, Aggie and Kim, would have been so proud. He made life as awkward as he could, putting pressure on me daily to "change jobs".

Reason set in. I'd had to catch the bus for months. He no longer cared if I got mugged on my way home. So, using the few brain cells I still engaged, I found employment doing exactly the same thing for a branch much closer to home. Close enough to walk.

This made Gary happier. He was reborn as Mr Charming, 'I'm going to fuck you until you walk like a cowgirl', Gary. Gary: the one and only master of the deranged.

In truth, I'm happier too. The crowd at this place are my age, and out together every weekend. I feel like one of the crowd, and welcome.

Three months, and I take a stand one Sunday afternoon. Gary didn't have to answer to me. He never did. He came and went as though I was his house slave. (Which I am: let's face facts here.) But I am no longer content with it. He walked to the door primped and ready, when I demanded, "Where are you going?"

"Out."

Oh, I can see that, asshole!

"**Where** are you going?"

Hey, where did that authority in my voice come from?

He throws me a stunned expression, "To play pool."

"I'm coming with you."

I wasn't asking. I was telling. If he'd said no, I would not have been there when he got home. And I think he sensed this.

"Okay. Sure. Why not."

I grab my smokes, giving him no reason to stall, or find an excuse. The house is bloody perfect in every aspect, so that one's off the board. I stalk past through the open door and to his vehicle.

In silence we drive to the pool place down the road from UCT . He seems strangely nervous. I don't know if it's because of the stunt I just pulled, or some other reason.

(You are about to find out why blondes are considered **stupid**.)

Gary and I never hold hands, or make a display of being a couple in public, (unless another man is looking at me.) So, I trail him into the room filled with pool tables, and stop dead as this pretty, young, willowy wisp of a girl comes running across the expanse and throws her arms around his neck, "GAREEEEE."

He looks embarrassed, "Oh, hi."

I see this for what it is and calmly walk past to the gang, who are all waiting at a table already playing. (I need a fucking cigarette. *Now*. Hands, if you shake, I will **chop you off**.)

I light a smoke and watch the spectacle.

The old me resurfaced. The girl who would break a nose because she knew she could – and **you are out of line.**

It was almost funny watching his friends scatter. The men all dived for excuses to leave their game unfinished. I stood with Cindy to my left, and a very nervous Kristy on the other side of the table, gulping at me with gigantic green eyes. Everyone was waiting for my reaction. Gary drops 'cookie' like a hot coal, and dives for the bar. (What a man!)

Sweet little Miss Sunflower flounces around the table, and smiles her big brown eyes at me, "Hi!"

I smile, "Hi." Calmly smoking.

I watch her ogling Gary with obvious adoration. I don't blame her. This isn't her fault. I ask her über casually, "So how long have you being seeing Gary?"

She's beaming, she's so proud to be his girl, "Three months."

53

I see myself in her. I stood in those dancer's shoes. I know how she feels.

She suddenly assumes the cat-fight stance, sensing that I have a 'claim' on her man. My rage is giving me lucidity I haven't had in years. *Want to fight, baby girl? You are how old? Eighteen?*

I face her, and put my smoke down in an ashtray right next to us. "Oh, that's interesting." I hold up my hand and shove the emerald engagement ring in her face, "I've been engaged and living with him for three years."

(She can thank me now for saving her from him. I hope you get to read this book, baby girl.)

Her face becomes instantly ashen. Her eyes are swallowing her nose and her mouth is gasping for air. She goes into shock, "I am so sorry ... I didn't know ... If I ... I would never ..."

I know she didn't know. My smile, although warning, also contains masses of sympathetic understanding. "I know."

She runs like a banshee apparition from the pool tables. Long, straight brown hair flowing out behind her. She is so upset, she doesn't say a word to Gary.

Now get this!

Gary comes bolting over with brews in his hand, a cue case in the other, and yells at me, "What the fuck did you just say to her?"

Excuse me?

My mouth sets into a rigid line, I'm trying to stop myself from **killing him**. I repeat the exchange, word for word. He drops everything onto the green felt of the table and goes running out **after her**.

I pick up my smoke and stare at the silent and guilty faces watching me. Alan, Graham, Cindy, Kristy and Charl. I think, 'And fuck **ALL** of you'.

Cindy blabbers as she grapples with my arm, "I wanted to tell you!"

I'm still smoking and know that all human emotion has left my eyes. I'm not intimidating – (come on, I'm five-foot-two) – and they all look as scared as boiling lobster.

Kristy beseeches, "I wanted to, but didn't know how."

I say nothing. I put out my smoke and stuff the box back into my pocket. I stare at each one of them in turn. Then so calmly – (man, I wish someone had recorded that. I'd get such a kick out of seeing pride gel my bone marrow again, resurrecting dignity) – I take my engagement ring off and place it onto the green felt next to the case and condensing beer cans.

With pride that had been missing for years, I walked out of the room and out of the glass doors.

Gary was pleading with the pretty baby girl as she drove her car away from him.

I walk past, and keep walking.

"Woman. **Woman**! Where are you going?"

I don't look back as I lift my hand and raise my middle finger.

I'm in shock. I am not feeling anything at all. No tears, no pain ... nothing.

Chapter 12

A huge part of me naively hoped that he would come rushing after me to beg for forgiveness and to salvage my loyalty. Yes, I'm a dreamer. No, actually scratch that. **I am delusional.**

(*How could I think he loved me? He obviously didn't! How much proof did I need?*)

Anyway, so I'm walking. My hopes are dashed and I'm panicking about how much shit I'm going to be in for ruining his rendezvous. Okay, Sunday afternoon seems like the perfect time to go for a run. Run? Hahaha. I'm sprinting as if I'd just stolen the Queen's tiara. I have to get home before him. I have to get out before he pitches up to twist my mind to his will again.

(I'm a dedicated member of the Gary cult. He could talk me into doing *anything*. I'm aware enough to recognise this, so am fleeing as if my life depends on it.)

Due to past occurrences, I don't go anywhere without my own key. I never know when he's going to pull his superiority shit on me and turn me into the peasant who has to make her own way home. Breathless, I open the front door. My heart is pounding from the exercise, making hearing difficult. I am faint with relief that he's not there. In nanoseconds I pack work clothes, some weekend gear and other essentials.

Then I have a stand-off with the telephone mounted on the wall. Who am I going to call? My pride won't let me call Mom. So I swallow hard and phone the only 'outside of Gary' friend I have, a new friend from work, Selene. (I was so scared that Gary would find My Hero's number, I chucked it. He's now left that division and I can't locate him. I regret this!)

Thank the angels that she lives in the same area. And he will never know where to look for me.

Shaking, with violently trembling hands, I call her.

"Selene. Hi, it's Stefanie ... No, I'm not okay. I hate to do this, but can I ask you if I can stay at your place tonight?"

(I'm scrambling. If I can't stay there indefinitely, I'll have to make another plan tomorrow. Right now I just have to get out before he gets home.)

Selene is a very special person. She never asks questions. She's just *there*. No matter what. She doesn't need to know why, or how, or what, the fact that I need to get out is reason enough for her.

"I'm on my way!"

"I'll meet you halfway. I'm leaving now."

I take my keys, slam the door and run.

(Cue: *Chariots of Fire* theme music.)

She finds me not four minutes later. I get into her red pick-up with a huge stuffed tote bag on my lap. She takes one look at me and says, "You need a drink."

I am so embarrassed I start rambling, "I'm so sorry. I had no one else I could call."

She gives me one stare of her chocolate mousse eyes, "It's okay. Don't explain. You can stay as long as you want."

Her dependability just makes emotional perception flood into me. And I stare persistently out of the window choking back tears. (I'm big into 'I can do this! I can handle it! I'm brave! I can be strong!')

Somewhat uncomfortably, I follow her into her home, where she shows me the spare room. I leave my bag on the bed and unearth my smokes. She smokes too, thank heavens.

She pours me a huge glass of wine and puts music on. She likes alternative, and we get along really well for a host of reasons. I love the band playing, Surrounded By Idiots. I light a smoke just as she lights her own. She raises her glass.

"To dumping losers!"

I smile. "Cheers."

Her eyes are examining me with undisguised concern.

I swallow my embarrassment and pride and tell her what transpired earlier, although I never ever tell her about the rest of that story. It's my shame, and I try very hard to hide the truth from everyone.

She nods, "You're better off without him."

* * *

I am a looney. I should have taken the day off work, but I don't. Monday morning we arrive at work together. I'm still shaken and can't eat. Hence, I'm not myself and very pale.

I've made a few friends at this place, and most of them sense that I'm not okay. I can tell, because they keep on asking me if I'm okay.

"I'll be fine."

I must say that work is a total blessing. It keeps me distracted and busy. By midday I'm feeling almost normal.

The phone on my desk rings. I deal with investment clients from 8 a.m. daily. So, this isn't a cause for me to panic. If he cared, he would have phoned by now anyway.

"Stefanie speaking, how may I help you?"

"Woman ..."

I hang up, instantly adrenalised and **angry**. I will *not* speak to anyone who starts a sentence calling me, 'woman'. My hands start shaking, and I push myself forcefully away from the desk. I stalk to the switchboard and tell the adorable lady, (who becomes another friend), "If that guy calls again, please just take a message. It's a personal call and I only have time today for business calls."

"What's his name?" she asks me, as if I'd just reprimanded her.

"Gary Fuchs."

"Okay," she nods. She takes her duties seriously and keeps me safe from him. None of his calls are put through to me for the rest of the day.

* * *

That evening, I need time alone. Selene lives on a high hill with a stunning view. At night it looks like a wonderland, and you can stare down at traffic, lights and traffic lights from afar. The colours of all the lights in the dark, remind me of alluring sprinkles dusting a cupcake. Just too enticing to resist.

It's time for me to face my feelings. I take a walk out there and get comfortable on a rock. I have a new box of smokes with me and light one, then stare miserably at the twinkling wonderland.

The puzzle pieces start falling into place. Since my house arrest, Gary had begun badgering me to stop being 'such a prude and so old fashioned'.

He wanted a threesome. I am a one man woman. I don't share my man.

CLICK. He was priming baby girl to be his third party victim in his *ménage à trois*. (So call me old fashioned. I justified everything because I was in a 'monogamous' relationship. Oy vey, what a hopeless, clueless, blow up doll I am.)

CLICK: "I need time alone with the lads. We're sick of women interfering."

Oh yeah, I bet. Having your partner there when you're trying to pick up new blood would never work.

CLICK: "I'm not going to make it. I have to work late. Maybe you should catch the bus."

So you can pick up your girlfriend and shag her before coming home!

I'm a daft twit. AC/DC has been warning me for weeks. We're nowhere near Christmas, yet, 'Mistress for Christmas' was played every morning as the wake-up song.

Okay, this isn't good. The anger is surfacing and it's **crushing** me. I think back to how many times over the last few months that he has only reached home after 10 p.m. at night. How strangely he's more tired than he's ever been. And this **stupid idiot** made dinner and waited for him before eating it. Waited for hours!

Oh, and suddenly he has a pager. Funny how convenient it is that Charl works with him at the I.T. company and can page him at any hour, and it looks like a call out. All times, even over weekends, 8 p.m., 10 p.m., 2 a.m.

I feel so stupid and ANGRRRREEYYY.

What's worse is I'm not angry with him. I'm angry with *myself.*

Bitter hot tears start dropping onto my cigarette, it fizzles out with a hiss. The past four years just went phissss, along with that ember.

I met Gary just before I turned twenty. I've been with him for four years, and he's had me jumping like a fire-walker since six months in. I am twenty-three and I feel old and used. I feel ugly and worthless. I hate myself.

I have done things that have made me lose my self-respect. I loathe who I am. I am ashamed to walk amongst women. I shame us all.

Gary didn't buy me soft toys or cute gifts; he didn't want anything girly cluttering up his home with 'crap'. He was my toy. If I wanted something to hold onto, he was the one to be my teddy. (Except teddies don't have conditions and rules and 'needs'.)

He didn't buy me jewellery, (except twice, my twenty-first and our engagement). Instead, he gave me what he considered to be fitting jewellery. A pearl necklace, at least four times a week. He had this fantasy that he enjoyed acting out. It's called, by him, the Bombay roll. Lucky me. I get the kind of jewellery that you have to wash out of your hair and off your flaming face. Now, if they had been pearls of wisdom, I might not have minded so much. (I guess he did have to do some diving to give me pearls ... but let's face facts, I'm the one that can hold my breath like a natural pearl diver, not him. When he goes diving, he doesn't even wear a wet-suit.)

For the record: handcuffs with keys do **not** count as jewellery, even if they look like bangles.

CLICK: I have nothing personal up in that home. There's no sign that a woman lives there. After all this time, I'm a ghost. A convenient ghost. The shoemaker's elf, that not only cooks and cleans but also the genie in the bottle, making all wishes come true.

(So what does that make Gary? The Magi, or Aladdin?)

CLICK: He has been missing all weekend for the past three months. Popping in at random, to find a reason to keep me home and busy, ensuring my endless servitude to his unreasonable demands – **because** he was out wooing his new lady.

CLICK: I haven't been able to save a cent. Not for years. He allocates my salary every month. He takes me grocery shopping to police what I buy, and to make sure that I am never alone. **So that I can never leave.**

CLICK: He's sick. And I'm not **ever** going to let a man degrade and treat me like that ever again.

Click click click click click click click click click click – like someone driving me insane with a pen and they have a nervous condition or twitch.

I stare at the smudging night. I have no idea where all of these tears are coming from, but they're breaking me in half. I bow my head and bury my nose between my knees; wracked and broken, I weep.

The worst. The absolute worst, is what he's done recently. He wouldn't leave it.

He kept on insisting that we have anal intercourse. **Why? What for?** I even researched it, to understand where the pleasure could lie in such an act. I discovered that the prostate gland is there in men, and if 'agitated' induces an orgasm. But women have no such thing. I **refused** to do it. And I told him why!

Sigh. He had recently being playing that song a lot ... and singing with it ... something about a back door male.

Cue song: SBI, 'Violently Opposed'.

Did I need a bigger sign board?

(Actually, I'm so ridiculously trusting, that what I needed was the front page of the newspaper announcing it to me, whilst a plane writes it in smoke in the sky, and every radio station broadcasts, 'WAKE UP ZOMBIE!')

But when you're handcuffed on your knees, he can pretty much do whatever he wants. And he did. (Am I a dumb blonde or am I just dumb?) You've heard the saying, right? Never be too open minded, your brains may fall out.

No offence, if you enjoy buggery. I personally find being buggered unappealing.

Cue: Feedback: Friends ... 'I try to see into your eyes, There is no one inside, and through the pain I hear your cries, But all I'm feeling is numb, numb ... Hold on ... Hold on to this ... Fake me, show me all those lies ...'

Okay. Now I **hate** him. I have been a Stepford Wife who blows him away whenever he needs a shuttle launch, for years. He has held the remote control that makes sure his woman does **everything** he desires. (The mute button even worked – for Pete's sake, he probably wrote that script.) Talk about his fantasy come true.

I have never loved anyone the way I love Gary. And no one has hurt me the way he just has. This is the problem with love. You can't just switch the flipping thing off. And it feels as though someone is cutting my flesh into strips with a rusty razor blade. I'm bleeding. But only I can feel it. Only I can see it. I feel spiked by the butcher's hook, and any moment Gary will morph into Hannibal Lector.

Selene has become worried and I jump, startled, as her hand rubs my back. She has no idea why I'm crying. She lights a smoke and hands it to me.

"It's gonna be okay. Cry. Let it all out."

Cue: Feedback: Hollow ... 'On this road running, and starting to slow, The size of life daunting, it makes me grow old, I give in, there's no real end ...'

Chapter 13

Tuesday Morning, Michelle comes to me with a hand full of message slips. She gives me a seriously worried expression. "These messages are all for you." She lowers her voice, "From that guy."

I take them with a heavy heart, and wonder why she's brought them to me. It was obviously weighing on her, because she's cornered me early.

She pushes up her spectacles and almost pleads, "I have to put him through. I'm not allowed to screen calls like this. I could lose my job, because every caller is a potential client."

I nod. I do get it. "I understand." I give her a warm smile, "Thanks."

She jerks her head in an awkward nod and storms back to her post, already fretting that she's left it for too long.

I sink into my chair and dread the telephone ringing. It's only seven-thirty – (I like to be early and catch up before the day starts) – and my stomach plummets as my phone starts ringing. That can either be Gary, Gary or Gary.

Selene sits opposite me and stops her filing, and gives me an expression full of girl power support.

"Stefanie speaking, how may I help you?"

"I am *so* sorry. Please forgive me! I feel just *awful.*"

I smile and nod at Selene. Indicating that all is cool.

"Hi Kristy."

Wailing comes pouring into my ear. "*Pleeeease* don't hate me."

I examine my desk and feel sorry for her, "It's not your fault, Kristy. How can I hate you? We all just do as we're told. He made you do it. I don't blame you."

Man, she's seriously crying over this. She sounds more torn up than I feel.

Sniiiiiffffff. "Promise?"

I nod, even though she can't see me. "Kristy, we're cool. Honest."

"Will I ever see you again?"

How the hell should I know? Not if it means seeing Aladdin. "I don't know, right now."

She bursts into tears and manages to get out, "I have to go."

I have a huge lump in my throat, "Okay. Thanks for calling."

"Stef, I love you! I'll miss you."

My eyes are prickly and my nose is hot, "Me too!"

Click.

I look up and meet Selene's eyes, "I'm going for a smoke."

She nods supportively, "I'll take your calls."

"Thanks."

* * *

Oh yeah, it's going to be just a peachy, all round happy day. The moment I return to my desk, my phone rings again. We only open at eight-thirty, and it's not even eight yet.

Taking a deep breath, I say, "Stefanie speaking, how may I help you?"

"Wait!"

Fuck.

"Don't hang up!"

I'm flooding with tension at Gary's voice.

"Did you get my messages?"

"Yes."

"Why didn't you phone me back?"

"Because, **I have nothing to say to you.**"

And I hang up.

Oh *sheeees*. My boss, her boss, and everyone else in the open plan office stares at me with horrified shock.

My cheeks throb with instantaneous embarrassment, "My ex-boyfriend." I announce in explanation.

No one looks convinced. I open my drawer, grab my smokes again and tell Selene, "I'm going outside. I'll be back before we open."

* * *

Selene decides the only thing that can save me is party therapy. So, we get dressed after dinner, to go out. My eyes nearly explode out of their sockets at my friend's dress. It's short. It's skin-tight. And it has a huge hole cut on either side that gives the perfect view

64

of skin and the wrong side of cleavage. She gives a whole new meaning to the word cleavage. (I wonder how many boys will have their eyes cleaved straight out of their skulls when they see that!) Selene is buxom; she has boobs that rival Adelle's and is obviously proud of them. We've never done this before, I've only ever seen her dressed for work.

She looks at my jeans and hauls me to her room, rifles through her closet for a dress, and throws it at me, "Put this on."

I take the skimpy thing that doesn't even look big enough to be a negligée and grin with shyness. I go back to my room and change. Then I return to stare into her body-length mirror.

Fuck me blind.

She smiles, "That should do it."

It's exactly the same as hers, except the sides aren't missing. My back is completely open and it leaves *nothing* to the imagination.

I'm suddenly delirious with rebellion. I'm **free**.

It hits me: I can do whatever I want and I won't get into shit. Yipeekayaymotherfuckers, let's start this party!

Selene has thick, almost black, straight hair. She has that whole Egyptian princess look about her. What's really funny is she's as 'good' and as 'shy' as I am, (during the day at work, anyway). But this is an education. She wears court shoes; I wear high heels. (I only own high heels to go with a dress.)

Smokes. Money. Eyeliner. Let's go!

(I urge you to picture Robert Palmer's video here *Addicted to Love* – which I see on MTV and VH1 regularly – well, Selene and I, looked like that, with hair down and loads of cleavage popping out.)

We hit the smoky dance floor and dance, laugh, drink and smoke. It's been a long time since I've had to listen to music like this and it's like forgetting how to drive. I'm awkward, all hands and feet.

She can read minds this girl, "It gets better. They have to play this crap for the trendies."

I nod.

Poof! Magic spell, a guy manifests next to Selene. My insides contract as the creepy sidekick hones in on me.

I can't do this and escape to get drinks. I watch Selene's professional flirting skills and am thoroughly impressed. I pay for the drinks and sag with relief as I spy Michelle. I wave her over and yell over the loud music, "**Hi! What are you doing here?**"

I buy her a drink too and nod as she points at Selene instead of shouting back. I take the drinks and hand them out, relieved to be dancing with Michelle. I keep turning my back on the creep. Seriously, I cannot handle this shit.

After a while Mishi and myself go off to a table and vegetate. We have one objective: let's get drunk.

Mishi is adorable, very sweet and a complete geek. Together we drink cocktails as though we're dying today and voyeur in on Selene's man snatching techniques. She is shameless. (And ruthless. Yep, she lost her ruth long ago.)

Erm......okaaaay, the 'single' young men at the bar where we order have noticed the pattern. So now drinks just magically arrive the minute ours are close to empty.

(You saw this happening didn't you? I'm out of practice myself.)

A fairly yummy dude strolls over, takes a seat and extends a hand that matches his predator smile, "Hi, I'm Stewart."

I laugh. (I'm toasted already.)

"Hi! Thanks for all the drinks!"

Whoa! Fuckenhell. **Never** lean in to speak into a man's ear to be heard.

He thinks this is my pick-up technique and, **gaboing**, he plants his lips on mine. I'm shocked and horrified. This guy is pulling in fast and I'm way too drunk. I feel like I'm cheating. I have this sick knot contorting my stomach and I feel ill, instantly, with self-disgust. I put my hand against his chest and SHOVE.

"Sorry Stewart, I can't do this."

Mishi is looking embarrassed and like she wants to leave. (Nooo. Stay. Don't you **dare** leave me alone.)

Na uh. 'No' wasn't uttered: (we have to say it right?)

Stewy just kisses me again. Like this is somehow going to convert me and change my mind. (Nope, I'm not a believer. Conversion unsuccessful.) Mildly panicked I pull away to shoot my about-to-be-roadkill eyes to Mishi in a silent plea for *heeellp*. She stands, (sober as a judge my little nerd is. Wow, how come I'm drunk when no one else is?)

"We're going!" she announces, and grabs my arm and hauls me to my feet, away from him and out the door, before I can say 'Boo'. In the passage she examines my face with worry, "Are you okay?"

(Okay wait. I have to give you the vibe. Michelle manages to make you feel like she's your mother and you're about to get a scolding. She's very good at giving disapproving glares. So I'm feeling like I'm about to get a lecture here.)

I nod. "Just scared the crap out of me."

She scowls and states, as if it explains everything, "Men!"

"I must tell Selene ..."

"Selene, is too busy to notice. I'll keep you company until she gets home."

Phew. Okay then.

So, off we whisk up to our hill and sit together smoking, enjoying fresh air and night silence.

Finally she hears who Gary is and I tell her why I don't particularly wish to speak to him right now.

She stares out at the night, exhaling her cigarette smoke, "Men!"

(Did I mention I adore this pumpkin?)

Chapter 14

For two blissful weeks I was rebellious. The crowd at work ranged from eighteen to twenty-three and they were all thankfully normal and in normal relationships.

Between Dianne, Julie, Selene and James, we had every ladies night plotted and planned. We knew up to what hour ladies could get in free, with a free drink to boot. We were booked every night of the week. I laughed, I flirted, I **thrived** like algae in sludge. My self-confidence just flourished, and I now knew without a doubt that I am not the ugliest girl in the room.

Unfortunately, the side effect of bonding with colleagues, is they find out why you're suddenly single. Even some of the guys at work seemed ambitious about getting to know me. I was one of the crowd, these were my people. We worked together; we played together; on Friday nights after work, we drank together at the work bar.

But – I can't stress this enough – one thing I knew I would never do again, is dress the way Selene dresses. We looked like wannabe prostitutes that night, and I did not like the way men just assumed that they could examine the merchandise. You know what I'm saying?

So, I'm happy. I honestly am. I still love Gary but we're over. He phones me every day at work and every day I hang up on him. He crossed a line and I wasn't that hard up that I needed to stay with a guy who not only made me feel like a cheap harlot, then stuffs around with other women behind my back. I could not have tried any harder to please him. And my best obviously wasn't enough. I wasn't going to waste another day of my glorious life following the leader of the pack down the dry dusty road to hell.

Right, so I've been flirting up a storm the last two weeks. I'm hurt. I'm seriously not ready for a new Mr Right, **but**, flirting makes you feel so delicious. It validates that you're not half bad. So on Thursday morning, when flowers arrive at work for me without a card, **I have no idea** who they're from. Seriously.

All of the girls at work, 'Ooh' and 'Aaah'. "Who are those from?"

I stare at the two dozen red roses making my desk look like a telephone table and shrug. "I have no idea!"

This day goes down in office history. I pick them up, move my trash can, and dump the whole lot into the bin underneath my desk.

In unison the ladies all exhale, "Gaaaaasp"

"You can't do that!"

I smile at Frank, "Oh, yes I can!"

His girlfriend also works with me, and from across the office I hear Julie, "If you don't want them, I'll take them."

I look at Frank for confirmation that this is in order. He nods and smiles, retorting back across the office, "Don't say I never buy you flowers. I just organised for you!"

Julie literally skips to my desk, as I remove the flowers from my trash can and hand them to her. She even kisses me, "Thanks."

She flounces to Frank and kisses him, "Hmmm, you are the best. I expect this every week from now on."

The office is smiling when my phone rings. It's the internal ring.

"Hello?"

"Stefanie, please come to reception."

I'm suspicious, "Why?"

"You have more flowers."

I roll my eyes, "Coming."

I stalk off to reception and pick up pink Amaranths. No card. Just flippin great. Now I'm psychic too, have you noticed? I doubt the same guy sent both bouquets. Men! (To quote Mishi.)

I walk back to our open plan office and announce from the doorway, "Who would like these?"

Five chorus 'Me!' I place them down on the sign in table, "First one here gets them then."

The entire office is laughing as the girls bolt for the flowers like a bunch of singles catching the bridal bouquet. Selene gets there first. I giggle as I walk back to my desk. She follows me and asks the question on everyone's mind, "Who are they from?"

"God only knows! There's no card!"

(I wonder if tarot cards work? A tall dark stranger will send you flowers ...)

My boss raises her eyebrows. I suppose it doesn't look that good to get flowers and not know who they're from. Whatever.

My phone rings and I lunge, "Stefanie speaking, how may I help you?"

"Hello, gorgeous."

Um ... "Hello."

I have no idea who I'm speaking to.

"Did you get my flowers?"

Um ... crikey. I have **no** idea what to say here. I wing it. "Yes, they just arrived." So I dig, "Why didn't you send a card with it?"

"I did."

Oh crap.

"Oh!" (Trying to sound surprised and flirty.) "I guess it fell off somewhere."

He laughs. Oooh he does sound nice. I wonder who he is?

"So when do I get to see you again?"

Fucked if I know sunshine, I have no idea who you are. "I'll be at the Stagger Inn tonight."

Another deep, throaty laugh. Lordy, he sounds delicious. How drunk was I that I don't remember this guy?

"See you there."

I giggle *waaay* nervously . "Can't wait!"

I feel shaky as I hang up. I think I'm in over my head here.

Riiiing...

"Hello?"

"Aren't you the popular one? More flowers!"

I feel stunned and almost panicked by this freaky turn of events, "Be right there.

Two minutes later I walk back in with a yellow and white bouquet of flowers. The card is from some guy named Jason. I guess he was the one that phoned. At least tonight I'll know his name. I get clever and give them to my boss, "For you."

She smiles, "Why don't you want them?"

The whole office is in pause mode, especially the men. Yes, everyone wants to know what my problem is.

"I can't stand watching something die."

Suddenly the girls who have flowers seem disturbed by the thought.

Shayne comments quietly from his desk next to mine, "I'll never understand women."

I smile at him, "Me neither." I giggle and feel elated. I haven't felt this good in forever. The ego is pumped up now.

* * *

That night I make sure the cleavage is blossoming with my new secrets. (You get that, right? I got my secrets from Victoria. Please tell me you get this?)

My long hair is down, I'm wearing tight black jeans and reinforced toe boots, (the only shoes for the sane to wear on a dance floor!)

I smell good and feel as though I look good. The girls and guys from work surround me as we dance and joke up a party together, when this tall, geeky looking guy, comes up to me, with a huge smile. He leans down and kisses my neck, "Hi gorgeous."

My mind is racing. Shit shit shit. I don't recognise this man at all, but I'm gathering he is Jason, because he's the only person I told where I'd be found tonight.

I smile and laugh, "Hi!" (Way too enthusiastic. I'm not one hundred percent sure that this is Jason, to be honest.)

Thank the lord men are forward. Frank gets all protective and holds out his hand, "Hi, I'm Frank. AND YOU ARE?"

The music is loud, but the way he did that made me want to laugh.

"Jason."

Oookay, this is Jason. So I play all coy, "Thanks for the flowers."

Frank interjects, "Which ones did you send?"

Oooooh nooooo. Now I could just **kick** Frank. Just pop his ego, why don't you?

Jason arches one eyebrow at me, "Yellow and white thing."

I smile, feeling like a slug caught under this poor man's shoe.

Jason grabs my elbow and glides me away from the pack to a dark corner. I'm expecting to be in shit now. Isn't that what happens?

My heart is racing with nervousness as I look up into his face. He's not bad, he's just not Gary. He's got short, dark blond hair. Greenish eyes: (hard to tell, it's a bit dark here). He seems nice. He's nice and tall. (I still have no recollection of him. Period.)

He leans over me, resting his arm on the wall, speaking intimately, "So who else are you dating?"

71

Fuck.

"No one." (And that's the God honest truth. I'm not dating anyone. It's not my fault complete strangers are sending me flowers.)

He laughs that delicious laugh, okay this is the same guy that was on the phone. "Chill out. It's just good to tell a guy he has some competition."

I'm so relieved, I could kiss him. I reach out a hand and place it against ... oooh, a wash board stomach ... HELLO.

"Thank you for the flowers. Really. But please don't do that again." I step onto my toes and kiss his neck. (He's much too tall.) It's a thank you kiss.

He covers my hand with his own and holds onto it, "Why?"

Here goes nothing. "I don't like flowers." I do, just not ones that will die in front of me. Cut flowers die, it's inevitable.

He smiles. He has a gentle smile. He's so different from what I'm used to.

"Well, am I allowed to get you a drink?"

Giggle. (A relieved giggle.) "Yes!"

He entwines his fingers through mine and takes me with him to the bar and orders for both of us. I spent a lot of my time with him that evening. By the end of it I knew we had nothing in common. Which is a pity.

Friday morning Frank corners me as I get into work, "He's awful! A girl like you can do better."

I'm going to change his name to Counsellor Frank. "There's nothing wrong with him."

He grabs my elbow and spins me around and points at James, "Look at him."

I look, "Yeah, so?"

"That's a man."

Ha ha ha. I know that. He's certainly not a woman

Frank eyeballs me again, "Listen to me girly. Jason isn't secure in himself. You are. You need a man that knows who he is and what he wants."

I arch eyebrows. I'm feeling mildly insulted. "Frank, it's none of your business."

He walks back to his desk, "You'll be sorry."

Somehow my happy bubble is burst. I feel chastised and full of doubt. I knew for myself that Jason and I wouldn't last longer than a week. But James? Come on! He's definitely not my type.

Oh *all right.* James is huge. He's about six-foot-four and built like a wrestler. I find that excessively intimidating. I really like him as a person, but gigantic men make me feel paranoid and intimidated. I can't help this.

* * *

Wednesday morning I'm mildly hung over, (the routine is established). I'm at work, life is good, coffee is maintaining my equilibrium for me, I'm competent, I'm fairly dishy myself and I have a phone-sex voice. I am ready to conquer!

Riiiing ...

"Stefanie speaking, how may I help you?"

"I need you."

The voice is so croaky, I can barely hear it properly.

"Hello?"

"Stefanie, I need you."

Oh My God. It's Gary. He sounds terrible!

"Gary?"

"NOW!"

My heart starts racing. I'm panicked. He sounds like he's dying. "Gary, what's wrong? Is everything all right?"

Long pause, before he croaks, "Can you get home? Now?"

Oh God. He's cut his wrists or something. Had too much alcohol and something else? Pills? I don't know. Don't tell me he's tried to end it because I refused to speak to him.

Full-blown guilt overload. Short circuiting brain, logic and everything else. I fear this is his last phone call. He's reaching out. Urgency pumps through me.

"I'll try."

"Hurry."

Click.

FREAK OUT!

"What? Stefanie, what's the matter?"

I look at Selene, "It's Gary. Something's horribly wrong. If Mrs Sinclaire lets me off, can you take me there now?"

Her eyes look alarmed, "Sure!"

She phones switchboard to inform Michelle that we won't be at our desks. Giving her the first inside scoop. I tell Sinclaire I have a family emergency. No problem she'll let Selene take me, I can take the rest of the day off. I am shrinking inwardly with panic and fear. It's as if someone just diminished my nervous system with a Tazer. Selene can't wait for me when she drops me off, she has to cover for me at work.

"Call me if you need me."

"Thanks."

I watch her drive away, and turn and run for Gary's front door. My insides nearly bottom out when I see a note attached to the front door with my name on it.

With violently shaking hands I unpin the white envelope and open it.

First reading the bold 'Stefanie' on the front. My fear that this is a suicide note is making me dizzy and on the verge of hyperventilating.

I try the front door. It's unlocked. I push it open and call, "Gary?"

Nothing.

Oh God.

Chapter 15

I ran through the house looking for him. Not caring at all about the note. Eventually I ran outside. Gary was nowhere to be found.

A cold chill tap-dances up my vertebrae as a sinister thought floods my consciousness. Kristy's ex had tried to shoot her, saying she could never leave *him*. My eyes grow larger as my breathing gets shallower; it occurs to me this might be a set-up.

Damn it. Why do I always react without thinking things through? I try to suppress the gonging of my beating heart, so I can listen, my eyes scanning every tree, bush, car in the street. Nothing. Shit man! This is unhinging me.

My stomach is now firmly lodged in the base of my throat. I'm so scared, I feel ill. Finally, I take the note out of the envelope.

Follow the arrows

Frowning, I look for arrows. I'm so distraught that I didn't even notice them. Taped to the floor are arrows. Gulp. Am I following arrows to my untimely death? I want to cry. This isn't fair! Why me?

I follow the path slowly. Carefully. With fear induced palpitations. I'm jumpier than popcorn. Through the dining room into the sitting room, I follow them to behind the couch. (My fear, honestly, is that he's lying bleeding to death behind that three-seater.) What waits for me shocks me rigid. I stop walking and stare in disbelief. What? What is this?

I look up, panicked. Everything feels **wrong**. You know when your instincts are **yelling** at you? You feel like you're being watched, and you have no idea how far someone else could go. It could be innocent. But, it might not be. Doubt is clawing at me.

I'm staring at the row of arrows leading to the cutest, puppy dog plush toy, I've ever seen. I'm afraid to touch it. It could be a bomb. It could be laced with poison. I leave it right there and keep following the arrows.

They take me into the bathroom. I'm faint with fear. They lead to the closed shower. My dread resurfaces: that I'm going to move that curtain away and he'll be slumped there, staring up at me with accusing glassy eyes. My hands are trembling so severely that I almost rip the curtain out of those ridiculously pathetic rings. I become dizzy with relief. A box lies next to the outlet cover. I stare at it. It could be another trap. Breathe. Keep breathing.

Agitated, I keep on looking behind me. Images of Psycho and the dude with the huge knife (but it was his mom right?) stabbing her to death in the shower, keep on fading in and out of my mind's eye. I keep following arrows into the bedroom. I'm like a cop from TV as I quickly glance in and withdraw, looking behind the door and beyond the closet which obscures the entrance. In – out. Dash – dash. (It looks empty – at least he's not lying unconscious on the bed next to an empty bottle of vodka and pills.)

Heebie-jeebies hug me, I shift a glance behind myself again. Nothing. Fuckenhell. I am freaking out so badly I am three steps behind my shadow with fear.

Taking a deep breath I tiptoe quietly into the bedroom. Now all but unhinged, I fling open every closet door defensively. Just clothes. I close them again, then stare at the arrows. Walking to my side of the bed I see another envelope. I pick it up off my pillow and open it. Looking at the doorway and the window behind me again in reflexive paranoia.

I sag onto the edge of the bed with weakening knees. It's a pink card. Relief and tears flood my veins. I am so relieved I'm not here to die. That he's not here to die. I open the card.

Stefanie, I love you!
I'm sorry!

Silent sobbing begins welling up. Gary **never** apologises, even when he's wrong. And I haven't heard him use my name for years. Except in the past two weeks of him phoning me. I gulp. I have to stay strong. It's not over yet. I'm not in the clear yet. He could be saying, 'Sorry I have to kill you'. Sorry? **Sorry**! Yeah, maybe I should wait to make a judgement call to find out just why he's sorry. (Oh, I'm sorry, but I have to hang you up like a deer I just shot.)

Images of Gary turning into Hannibal Lector resurface. **I am creeping myself out.**

Then I notice another envelope. I pick it up and open it.

76

Keep following the arrows.

Cold whispers over my skin. My hairs stand on end. Right here, this is what I've been trying to tell you. Gary knows me better than anyone ever will. How did he know? How could he? That I would stop here and think it's the end of the arrow hunt.

Ready to make a break for it, I look up and scan the area again. I am so stressed out. Gary is like a psychic. He knows what I'm going to do before I do. (Oh wait, actually, the day I took my ring off and left, he never saw that coming. Yay! Thank you for that thought. Anger is a whole lot better than this soppy fear.)

I nearly shed my fingernails in fright as the phone starts ringing, jarring the oppressive silence. My heart is pounding. That's him! I bet it is.

I run for the phone next to the front door.

Oookay. Right. So I usually lose bets too!

"Hello?"

"Are you okay? What's happening?"

I swallow hard as I watch around me, skittishly, with large fearful eyes. "Selene, I can't find him. I'm flipping out. It's all weird. I'll call you as soon as I have news."

"Please. Dammit Stef: I can't handle this!"

"*You* can't? I'm freaking!"

"Just call me! I have to go, your phone is ringing."

"I'll wait. Maybe it's him."

"Okay, hang on."

I wait, twisting anxiously, keeping my eyes on everything. The front door is still open: (why did I leave it open? Now it makes me feel vulnerable.) From here I can see into the kitchen, dining room and lounge. I need a drink. And a cigarette, dammit!

"Stef?"

Relief at her voice. "Yes?"

"I have to go, this call is going to take a while. It's not him. *Phone me.*"

"Okay. Bye."

Crud. Now I still don't know what's going on. I stare at the arrows leading into the kitchen and finally summon the courage to follow them. Next to the kettle are flowers waiting for me.

Okay? Now you see: a normal male would not begin to comprehend why I have a problem with any of this. I am totally losing my sanity, because this scares me witless. When you have known someone for four years and they have never bought you a soft toy or flowers, it sets off alarm bells in your head. Why now? What's different about today? When someone says sorry and they have never cared enough to say that to you before, it's Freddie Kruger scary. Premonition, suspicion, paranoia kick in.

"Stefanie."

I whip around. My legs have turned to jelly. They can't hold me up. **God Gary, scare the shit out of me, why don't you!**

I'm gripping the counter with all of my might and mentally counting the steps to the knife drawer. I stare, afraid to say anything. I'm sure that right now I am paler than the white tiles under my feet.

He looks normal. He doesn't look like he's about to shoot me. What does someone look like when they're about to commit cold-blooded murder?

I watch him. My silence triggers something. His face is changing colour. He's wearing the same shirt he wore the day I met him. It still makes him look like a god. I watch his brilliant blue eyes flood and can't believe that I am witnessing Gary with tears coming out of his eyes. He's like a robot. I forget he has emotions because he so seldom reveals them to anyone.

Did someone die? Crap. Maybe something happened to his parents?

I take an unsure step toward him, "Are your parents okay?"

He nods. (Okay, can I just say that it's totally NOT fair that men have such long legs?) He takes one stride and is standing right in front of me. I stare into his chest, unsure. Afraid. Shit, he's too close. I'm reacting. My body is tuned like a pitch fork to his tone. To his vibration. It's like my heart wants to fuse with his. It feels as though it's straining against my ribcage.

Gary grabs me and wraps his arms tightly around my shoulders, his face burying into my hair. He holds me tight like that for what feels like ages. I have no idea what's going on. Why's he so upset? But I can feel his pain. I'm flattered that when he needed someone, he called me. But this is bizarre and I'm afraid and my body just wants to jump him, and I'm fighting my libido about that too.

Tentatively, I put my arms around his waist. Soothingly, "Gary? Gary you're scaring me."

He lifts his head and looks down at me. Tears free-flowing out of eyes, some drip off his nose. I love him. I know I do. My instinct is to soothe his pain. To take it away. To distract him from whatever it is that has him this upset. Worry causes my own eyes to prickle, "Gary? Talk to me. What happened?"

He tightens his hold and I'm afraid he's going to crush me. He's much taller than me, and I only have a view of a white knit shirt and a few buttons. My heart breaks as his shoulders start shaking so much, that it dawns on me that he's stricken with tears. Gary does not feel like the rest of us. Life is one long game. We're all just pawns. He doesn't emotionally engage with the characters on the board. He just urges them to move, then laughs inwardly when they obediently follow his command or manipulation.

I know it's seriously, cataclysmically bad, for Gary to be crying. I cuddle him back, waiting for him to regain enough self-control to tell me what's bothering him.

I also hate myself for this. I am so weak. I'm thrilled he reached out for me. Of all the people in his life, he's here with me.

He pulls away and turns his back on me. (I am so confused.)

After a few moments, he faces me again, and seems ashamed of his own weakness, "Can I get you some coffee or something?"

What?

Wow, just hang on a second here. I am feeling emotional myself now. This entire experience has been surreal and outlandish and totally scary, he's in tears and now, he's offering me *coffee*?

And since when does Gary make coffee?

I nod. I have no idea how to respond. I'm surprised he even knows how to make coffee the way I drink it.

He walks to the kettle and stares at the flowers next to it. His voice is cracked and hoarse, "Did you get my flowers?"

My mind starts racing. Shit. Flowers! Three bouquets the same day. Two didn't have cards. Crap. I don't know which ones he sent!

79

I nod nervously, beginning to nibble my lip. I'm ready to flee.

He leans his narrow hips against the counter, folding his arms as he studies me. "Why didn't you phone me then?"

Because I didn't know you'd sent any! You never send flowers, **ever**. *And after the way you reacted to those other flowers I never thought you would ever send me flowers.*

I'm watching him and the hurt is obvious. He's made a real effort and expected recognition for it, at least acknowledgement, My eyes start flooding. "I'm sorry."

I wipe my eyes, bitter with myself for crying. I have to keep the upper hand here or I'll be handcuffed to that bed before the kettle has even started boiling. I manage with a shaking voice, "Thank you, they were lovely." (Did you send the pink amaranths or the roses?)

A vague smile flirts with his lips. I watch in silence as he makes coffee. This is the first 'normal', Gary and I have ever had. It leaves me feeling unstable.

He offers my mug to me, I take it.

"Will you stay long enough for a chat? I want to talk to you."

(I could argue and ask what was the bloody emergency?)

Instead, I nod. I'm in emotional carnage right now. I'm not sure I'm strong enough to do this. God help me but this boy is so sexy. My eyes watch him walk out of the kitchen. He's wearing grey track pants and white socks. He's still got the hottest derriere ever owned by anyone. Every man I've met in the past two and a half weeks pales in comparison with this one. He charges the room like a Van der Graaf generator. Every hair follicle I have stands to attention when he's present.

We sit down on chairs facing each other. My coffee is too hot so I place it onto the table next to my chair. His father made this table.

"Smoke?"

I nod.

He lights my cigarette for me after I take one from his packet. (Gary does not light my cigarettes. What is going on?)

This day goes down in Stefanie and Gary history. He's charming. He's a gentleman. And he cries.

Chapter 16

He smiles across to me. It's disconcerting.

"I missed you."

Like hell you did.

I arch an eyebrow and watch him. Choosing silence until I know what I'm doing here. I have a certain amount of satisfaction at his obvious nervousness. I've never seen him nervous before.

"Did you like the hound?"

What?

I gather my expression conveys the dumb blonde moment, because he reaches behind his chair and picks up the fluffy dog and presents it with obvious glee, "I thought you'd like him. Don't you think it's cute?"

So it's not a set-up. *Get to the point, Gary.*

"Yes, he's cute." I stare at the dog that reminds me of a Basset. Forgive me for my reservations but I don't trust Gary.

I watch him falter and place it awkwardly next to his leg. Track pants, eh? Clinging to toned thigh muscles from playing squash. I sigh slowly, exhaling smoke, as I appreciate the view.

My eyes travel back up him to meet his. He's watching me, waiting.

"What am I doing here, Gary? I'm supposed to be at work."

I enjoy satisfaction at the twitch at the corner of his mouth.

"I'm sorry, Woman."

My free hand tightens, "I beg your pardon?"

"Stefanie. Shit man! I'm no good at this. No matter what I do I'm going to fuck it up."

I stare coldly at him, anger simmering at being reduced to a gender again.

I watch his own hand curl into a fist, glistening with golden hairs. Midas hands.

He pleads, "I need you. Please ..."

State your case: this is your only chance. I arch an eyebrow. Tears escape his eyes again. I swallow the lump in my throat.

"I fucked up. I can't ... please come back."

He unfurls the clenched hand that was assisting him in containing his self control and it reaches across and glides over my knee to my thigh.

Breathe. Just breathe, dammit. Aladdin is unleashing the genie I had tightly corked in her bottle. My veins become sluggish as they pump the rising mercury. I pick up my coffee and sip it, watching him over the rim of the black edged mug. Slowly exhale.

"What happened to your girlfriend?"

He reacts as though I slapped him. He pulls away sharply and folds his arms. Outlining biceps and triceps. Gulp.

"She's not interested."

"Uh huh."

"Stef ..."

His voice chokes and I watch him fighting himself. He looks away, out of the window, as tears escape his simmering eyes. I'm already back, but I'm not going to make this easy. I can feel his magnetism from here. It's calling me. I can't resist the pull. I'm fighting myself as much as he's fighting his own weakness.

He looks back, his shoulders moving with silent sobbing. "I'm sorry. I don't know how else to say it."

I nod, and exchange my coffee for the fading cigarette in the ashtray on the table next to me. Nonchalantly, I demand, "Gary, we can't go back to the way we were. Things are going to have to change."

I flick the ash and look up at his desperate expression. He nods enthusiastically.

Waaaaayhaaaay! Finally, my opportunity for a few rules.

I smile, I can't stop myself. I'm deriving a certain amount of pleasure from this one-eighty about-face turn.

"My name is not 'woman'. It's Stefanie."

He nods.

"If you ever go out, or are late, I will phone you and check up on you, even if it's two in the morning. If you don't answer, it's over. If I have to wait ten minutes to get hold of you, it's over."

Ha! What a grim expression!

"Okay."

"And I want normal. Gary, you *are* going to take me out for dinner. I am not here to serve you. And it's time you stopped the weird shit. I can't do that anymore. I want love. I want to feel that you love me. If you love me, then make love to me. What we do isn't love, Gary. I need you to give me that."

He nods. He's looking calmer. More confident.

"And tell me you love me."

"Why?"

Oooh, that is so the wrong response. "*Why*?" Grrrr.

My adrenalin has just overpowered the spell of his charisma. I grind out with unrestrained anger, "Because if you love someone, they need to hear it. How can I tell when you're lying to me if you never say it? Because you *didn't* love me when you went behind my back to fuck that teenager!"

"I didn't!"

I glare at him in obvious disbelief and stand up, "I've got to go back to work."

I'm not going to say goodbye because I seriously want to cry. I love this hateful bastard. He was the one that was in the wrong, **not me**. But somehow he can't own up and be a bloody man about it. I can't do this. I just can't.

As I reach the open front door his voice reaches me, "Wait!"

I stare at the freedom waiting for me beyond the door. Blue sky. The sun is out. I hear birds and traffic. I want to claw and cry. I want to give him my grief. I want him to see my pain, but my pride is ingrained. The stiff upper lip. I take a deep breath and swivel to face him. When in doubt, feel anger. It's the only thing holding me together right now.

He's standing, his face alarmed.

"Please believe me. I never got that far with her."

Why do I believe him? Because I want to? Or because he's telling the truth?

He covers the distance between us in three steps. Shit. He's so close I can feel the heat emanating from his body. It's like standing too close to an open flame. You just know you're going to catch fire. And the fire-starter is the only fireman with the equipment to put it out.

"I love you. I didn't think I had to say it. I thought you knew. I try to show you, not tell you. I thought it would mean more that way."

A hand reaches for mine and holds it. It's a gentle hand, imbuing a loving touch. It dissolves my resolve, and my own tears finally escape the prison of my pride. He pulls me into his chest and wraps caressing arms around me. Human fusion. It's basic chemistry. Just as hydrogen wants, and can't help, to bond to oxygen, so my body just bonds with his. I feel home. I feel comfort. I feel that I belong here. It's the only place I want to be. I react to him. He is a catalyst for me, he always has been. From the day I laid my naive eyes on him in a kitchen in a stranger's house, I react to him this way. A catalyst usually induces heat and a chemical reaction. More often than not, an explosion. I wallow in his arms; his scent; his heat. My body is oscillating to the point of dissolving. The carnal pyre is consuming my intelligence.

He pulls away, bends his head and kisses me. It's tantalising and excruciating. I have never experienced such tenderness from Gary. I wrap my arms around his neck and get my fill of body length touching, moulding, melting.

Hot tears smudge my forehead. He's crying again. "Stefanie, I need you."

I need you too, asshole.

Hot breath against my ear, "I love you. I didn't know how much, until you were gone. I can't do this without you."

I mumble, as my composure crumbles, and I finally squeeze him tightly against me, "I love you. Gary, you really hurt me."

Gentle hands caress my hair, "I'm sorry. I know I was wrong."

I pull away and stare up at him, inside his loose encircling arms. His eyelashes are saturated.

His hoarse, convincing, voice tells me what a gullible wench needs to hear, "I'll never do that again. I don't know what came over me. I wasn't myself."

Game, set, match.

I don't get it, do I? He's just won again.

Chapter 17

While he makes me more coffee – (what can I say? I'm revelling in this indulgence) – I comment casually, "If this is going to work, I'll wear whatever I want to and spend my own money."

His eyes swivel to mine, drawing his attention away from the task of dunking his tea-bag, "Okay."

(Get your mind out of the gutter! It's not *the* tea bag; it's him making a cup of tea. Hahaha.)

He must really want me back. Gary is just agreeing to everything I throw at him ... (oh ... and I think I need a Lamborghini Gallardo.)

I sashay back to the sitting room and light myself a new smoke. Exhaling slowly, I examine the room. He's kept this place cleaner than a hospital. Hmm. I am impressed.

He places a steaming mug next to my chair and presses play on the remote. My favourite Feedback infiltrates the room softly. *Oookay*, he's seriously trying here. Even I must be impressed. I've known him for years and in one day I get music, flowers, a soft toy, a mystery box in the shower *and* an apology.

I glance at the window, wondering if it's going to snow. Maybe a tornado? Surely a balance has just been tipped somewhere?

His hand blocks my reverie. I stare at the box.

"Open it."

There is an excited thrill drumming through me. The same feeling you get when you're five years old and it's Christmas morning. I take the box and peek in. Still not completely sure it won't hold a scorpion ready to sting me. Gold. *Oooooooohh!* (Move over Liberace, here comes Stef!) I take out a gold bracelet, examine it with as much disinterest as I can muster and replace it. A smirk is tugging at the corners of my mouth. We need to break up more often.

"Thank you."

I stare at the card, gold bracelet and soft toy. DING. "Who helped you?"

A wry grin morphs his austere expression into, Mr Cute-can-I-just-jump-your-bones, "Kristy and Cindy."

Haha! Yay. You had to drop your pride and ask for help. Now I feel better than Brad Pit when Angelina said yes to having his baby.

His hopeful expression twinges the heart strings. This day has turned it into heart macramé. "Do you like them?"

I smile with genuine warmth back, "Yes." I fall into his eyes with my own, "I know you went to a lot of effort. It means a lot to me." As I melt into his irises, I notice puddles forming beneath them.

"I fucked up. I really fucked up."

I love this endless confessional. Maybe next time we play dress up I should wear a Catholic priest's outfit. Gigglemania. Sweet sigh. I have waited for a day like today for years. I had given up hope. Lesson? Never give up hope.

"Can I make you something to eat?"

My manicured eyebrows divorce my face. "Really?"

He gives me a bone rubberising grin, "I've learned how to cook."

Okay, you win. I'm definitely in.

* * *

At approximately quarter past four that afternoon, he pulls my engagement ring out of his pocket. We've been teasing, joking, laughing and bonding, all afternoon. It's been glorious. But my heart stops for at least three seconds as I stare at the ring he's holding out to me. Suddenly wound tighter than Big Ben, I gulp in apprehension.

"Babes, please wear this. You're my woman."

My gaze moves from the bondage ring to his eyes, "I'm not ready. I think we should date for a while."

Instantly, he looks angry, (just add water). I'm waiting for the tongue lashing. His warm eyes are doused with cold. He puts it down on the coffee table. "Stefanie, I want you back. I'm going to try to respect your wishes."

Phew! My heart is racing. I want him as desperately as he wants me, but I'm just not sure I can face being his slave again.

"Are you moving back?"

Crikey. No. Actually, why the hell should I? Work for this cute ass and my phone voice, Gary. Work for it!

"Not yet. "I smile. I feel better than Bridget Jones

(Haha! He's going to have to cook me at least three meals before I'll even spend the night. And I'm going to be spending like today is my last day.)

Chapter 18

I have to admit the first couple of dates were awkward. If he picked me up from work, everyone stared at him with transparent, undisguised hate. He now knew where Selene lived and she just glared at him every time she saw him. But when it comes to Gary, I am blind. They say that love is blind, and the only thing I cared about was the cane that kept me mobile in the dark. He made me dinner every night. He wanted me and didn't want to share me with another human being. I just thought it was adoration, a man salvaging an old flame with every free moment he had.

He teased, he joked, he made me laugh. On Saturday night he took me out for dinner. He held my hand, and he constantly reiterated that he loved me, needed me, needed me, needed me and wanted me back.

In the elevator on the way to the parking garages, after a good meal at a decent restaurant, he held me close. I leaned against him, enjoying his solid strength and warmth.

"Come home for coffee."

Swoon. I love it when he speaks intimately into my ear that way. Slightly tipsy, I murmur into his neck, "Okay."

The tanned arm around my shoulders tightens and I feel his smile. "My woman." It's a statement laced with pleasure. I sense it and wallow in it.

His possessiveness is flattering. I feel needed, coveted, special, when he says things like that. It feels good to belong.

It's like old times when my body helps to close the front door. A hand on either side of me, pinning me to the door. His fervent kiss flips the switch he installed. My nipples are straining toward him and I can hardly breathe.

Cue: 'When it Comes' ... my life would have no soundtrack if Feedback didn't exist.

My quivering breath betrays me, and he smiles a cocksure smile before swaggering his sexy ass into the kitchen. I lean heavily against the door frame and watch him deftly making coffee. I'm fighting the heat quickening through me. I'm weak and shaky.

His eyes trace my body and he drops the teaspoon. I stand up straight as he covers the space between us and holds my chin, "I want you."

Oh God. My spine is turning into a piece of string. One of his hands covers my left breast and I know he can feel my nipple betraying me.

His stubble scars a trail down my neck, disengaging my brain. "I want to fuck you ... please ...?"

I answer by slipping my hands under his shirt. My body is turning into an electrical storm. Somehow, walking backwards towards our prison called a bedroom, he and I both lose every shred of clothing. It's a bit of a blur. All I am is breathing. Deep, quivering, shaking, tingling, breaths.

I am more nervous than I was as a young, gullible, nineteen year old. My lungs are constricting. Gasping. I need air. I'm horribly self-conscious. I want his approval. I close my eyes. (Please don't reject me now.)

A moan breaks free from me unexpectedly as his hot mouth covers my nipple. I fall freely with him onto the bed and try not to think about who else has been on this bed lately. His knee moves my legs apart. I'm so dizzy with shortness of breath. I'm terrified. I need him, hate him, want him, love him. My warlock spellbinds me with his staff.

Gary's presence, heat, passionate eyes that always contain a measure of mischief, are my aphrodisiacs. We've never done foreplay. We've never needed to. Just thinking about Gary saturates my black lace g-string with anticipation. So, lying naked with him hovering above me, sliding his warm tongue over my skin, I am wanton! I wrap my legs around his. Needing, pulling him closer. Finally I open my eyes and stare into his deep blue ones. Touched, I feel the prickle of tears. Gary masks his feelings. He keeps them close. But the tenderness mingling with passion ... I'm done for.

The universe stops moving. Gary knows the tunnel of love like the back of his hand. And I'm sailing down it in a dreamlike stupor with the sensation overload he's bombarding me with. Coherent thought, speech, logic, all normal nervous system functions just shut down. My body is a mass of nerve endings singing, tingling, exploding. It's disturbingly too close to an out of body experience.

(Am I alive?) It takes me a while for my vision to return. I focus on him. He pouts his lips as he sits back and stares at me. I smile shyly back.

His hands explore my body as his head returns to kiss my lips. Tender kissing. Gentle caressing.

Who are you?

* * *

The thing normal people don't understand, is what it's like being addicted to sex. Many wonder where the addiction lies. I'm going to try to explain it to you. The more frequently you engage in it, the easier you are turned on. The more acute the sensation becomes. If you engage repeatedly with a drink break, smoke break, music change break and go back for another swing in the ring, it happens faster and each pinnacle is better than the last. (The higher the highs.) Until all you are is carnal, savage, instinctual, driven by nerve endings, tastes, smells, sensations. You stop when your legs can no longer hold you up and your arms shake in weakness.

* * *

I am used to silence between myself and Gary. He doesn't use words, he uses actions. I could scream after he takes me down the pleasure ride three more times. Breathless, I force my eyes to focus on him as I link my fingers through his. "What about you?"

"Are you impressed?"

I smile. He's so desperate for approval that I feel stupid for being desperate for his. "No."

I watch the pleasure erase off his face, replaced with anxiety.

I giggle deliriously, "I'm teasing you! How could I not be?"

He leans over me again, my nerve endings react and my breathing wants to shut down, "I know how you did it. Now I can go as long as you want me to."

No. No more. There's only so much my body can handle in one sitting.

I catch him off guard as I flip his body over. I sit on his thighs as I snake my tongue up his torso, "My turn!" His hands reach for me

90

and I grab them and hold them down with all of the energy I can muster.

I returned the carnal pleasure trip. I gave him as many as he gave me, between drinking from his lips, living on his breath, tasting his skin, wallowing in his heat. I'm home. I treasure the gifts. A part of him is inside me. A gift from his body to mine. Am I the only one to think that this is a precious gift? He has showered me with attention, adoration, tenderness, affection and pleasure. I collapse against him and hold on, my cheek against the golden hairs on his chest. I treasure this man. His name is tattooed on my heart.

A languid hand moves my long hair. His voice is velvet. It covers me with affection, keeping me warm, "I love you, Woman."

So, he slipped up. Old habits die hard. I lift my head and meet his eyes. He means it. His despair is obvious. His remorse plain.

"You know I love you. But if you ever smack my ass again, I'll castrate you."

He laughs. I think he's relieved he got away with calling me 'woman'.

I sit up and stare down at him. I'm alive again.

His hands move up me and I'm enjoying feeling owned. He really does have a magical touch.

"Move back. I miss you."

He lifts one of my hands and tugs it to his lips. (Shit! I'm horny again.) I nod. I cannot resist this man. He made love to me. It wasn't a game. It wasn't about power. It was pure bonding.

Smiling, I whisper, "Again."

Chapter 19

Selene was obviously disapproving when I let her know I wouldn't be home.

Sunday morning was the enchanting dance of a couple making breakfast together in the kitchen, for the first time in their long history. Between kisses, smiles and chuckling. The gloating kind. We were both high. I was high on him, he was high on me.

So tell me ... why does that feel so good? We'd just entered the giggly, happy, early stages, all over again. He's so easy to fall for, and I'm falling all over again.

But, I had no idea that when it comes to falling, I'm a novice. *Nooooo* sir! Because, as I sit on the floor after breakfast, rifling through CDs and putting them into the player –(*carte blanche* feels *soooo* groovy)– the doorbell rings.

I mean, come on! I have pouty swollen lips from all the kissing I've been doing. I'm still radiating afterglow from my trip to a location called 'ecstatic delight', closely related to Turkish delight but different, so I guess it's possible that I'm looking alluring.

A man I have never seen before, stands at the open door.

"NEV!"

Gary seems really excited to see him. I keep on stepping in and out of this parallel universe. The twilight zone has my name written all over it. They even have my retina scanned. Who the heck is Nev?

"Woman, this is NEVILLE!"

I'm sitting on the floor in front of the stereo, when Neville takes one step towards me and trips over his own toes. He begins launching at me, and I'm feeling mildly alarmed. This guy is bloody phenomenal. He's like one of those weighted dolls with the round bottom. He tips horizontally and, impossibly, regains upright again, defying every law of gravity I know. He blushes and smiles at me, sticking a hand at my nose.

"Hi!"

I lean back and grasp his hand ... whoa! He's nervous as hell. I shake the slicked hand and smile. I am totally lost and Gary stole my map.

Gary booms with manic enthusiasm, "Nev, this is Stefanie! She's my woman."

Neville has cropped dark brown hair. He's dressed in army browns, he still has vestiges of teenage acne and he's shiny, glowing, with spectacles slipping down his nose, as his cheeks try to outdo each other with his gigantic smile, that he's aiming at me. (Nice teeth.)

It's the oddest sensation. I feel as though he's just aimed a magnifying glass on me and is about to spread my wings before he pins me to a mounting board.

I lean back further for distance and look at Gary helplessly.

Gary ignores me flat out. "What are you doing here? This is rad just **rad**!"

Neville keeps smiling as though he has someone tickling his nether regions, "Just got out! I'm on my way home. I've done my duty and I'm a free man. You're my first stop!"

"You need a beer. Let's celebrate!" With this statement Gary leaves me alone with Neville and moves off to the kitchen.

This is so not cool.

Neville smiles at me, so widely it's unnerving. He stares. Doesn't he know it's rude to stare? He says bugger all. All he does is stand there beaming at me.

Weirdo!

I ignore him and go back to my task of putting the CD shuttle into the player and press play. I've found this band I quite like. So I have a selection of Sisters of Mercy and Surrounded By Idiots doing the shuffle through the speakers.

Nev drops onto the carpet next to me, grinning, "I also like Sisters."

Huh?

"I don't have a sister."

(*And I am not into sisters! Do I look like Katy Perry to you? Yeah, one look and you can tell I'm babe bait. Hello?*)

He points at the CD shuttle and almost impales my nose with his finger; it almost slips into my eye. Flippinheck dude.

He laughs like a giggly teenager and explains for the blonde half-wit, "Sisters! They rock! Sisters of Mercy."

Ping Ping Ping.

93

Riiight! Okay, I am not making a good impression. I guess it's true. Someone can fuck your brains out.

Why do army men all smell the same? Is it the water? Or the soap they use? He is much too close for comfort. I've only just met him and he's gazing at me as though I have a fairy on my left shoulder, the wicked devil on the other and the bluebird of happiness circling my head chirping twit- twit-twit!

Gary intrudes between Nev's fixated stare and me, by hovering a cracked open can of Castle in front of his nose.

I sigh, with relief, as he grabs it, stands up and the two of them smash the cans they're each holding together, "To freedom"

"Wicked!"

I need to find the way out of this worm hole.

"We have to do something. We'll go camping! Rad! How about this weekend? Hey Nev?"

I watch Gary. He's smiling as much as Neville is. I'm dumbfounded. What the hell is going on? Who *is* this man?

"Right **on.** Yeah."

This is so strange; I'm feeling like I've stepped into a hippie camp with a nerd and a stud. (Sounds like one bad joke coming up.)

"Hey, Woman?"

I look at Gary. I'm feeling edgy and mildly unnerved. *Whatever, right?*

"Sure."

Neville beams, but now he has this confused expression he's aiming at me. He looks at Gary and asks with obvious shock, "Woman?"

Gary realises he's slipped up again.

"Yes! My woman! My sweet adorable lady - my little woman!"

(Me man, she woman ... you stand in man's cave ... rwaaaaaarrrrhh!)

I'm watching this with amusement. Gary is scrambling faster than eggs, and Neville obviously doesn't approve. One point awarded to Neville, whose eyes I cannot see because the light from the window reflects off his spectacles. And it's altogether creepy. (I wonder where he's looking?)

When he gets up to leave, he hooks his ankles together again, and naturally falls like a felled log straight at me.)I've heard of someone falling for another, but this is getting ridiculous.) He grabs my shoulders and I stagger slightly under the force of his fall and weight.

He gathers himself, stands straight and beams, "You're FABULOUS."

Erm ... "Thanks."

He stands there, just staring down at me, smiling.

Dude, you are freaking me out!

Gary nudges him, "See you Friday. Legend."

He's in pause mode. Someone forgot to replace his batteries. He's not registering at all. (Control, alt, delete.) Okay, now I'm alarmed.

What's he thinking behind those spectacles? What did he do in the army anyway? Torture people by plucking out their eyelashes? Maybe he's one of those mind-reader types. He's doing the soul searching stare, so deeply, I can feel his gaze at the top of my thigh already.

(Thinks: Nananananana.) God help me, I never want to be alone with this man. He's scaring me spineless.

After a full minute of awkward 'pause' mode, he turns and trips towards the front door, slapping Gary's shoulder as he staggers past him, "Excellent! See you then."

There's a vacuum after he leaves. It's too quiet all of a sudden, too still. I stare at Gary, feeling unnerved.

He grins at me and says quietly, "Shot. He likes you."

I don't care! Who is he? You've never mentioned him to be, Gary. Ever.

"Who was that?"

He gives me the 'How thick are you?' look.

"N-E-V-I-L-L-E."

Exhale slowly. Do not do anything you'll regret. "I know that. How do you know him? You've never mentioned him."

He gives me a shocked stare, "Haven't I?"

"No!"

He flops down into a recliner with a goofy grin, which now reminds me of Neville, "We went to school together. This is soooo raaaaad!"

* * *

Friday night comes and I've moved back in. I pump up Gary's performance daily. High octane stuff. We are both *zinging* with erotic chills. We're both back in the saddle and we missed the ride. I'm open to doing things I normally would not consider. So, I have to take chocolate cake with me to go camping. I know I'm nuts.

But I can't live on alcohol the way everyone else can. And I've just perfected the art of the most exquisite chocolate fudge, chocolate cake. And I am making some to go with us, when Gary walks into the kitchen with his excessively tall friend, Alan.

Gary holds out a plastic bag of ganja to me. "Put some of this in!"

(Oh, what the hell. What can it hurt? Honestly?) I take it and smile.

The two of them leave the kitchen sniggering like two boys that have just successfully pulled off a prank. I have no idea how this stuff works. Do I put in a teaspoon? Two?

So, I'm mixing, and get to the 'add in this stuff' point. It's full. Packed. Like a blown up pool pillow. I put in half and mix it in. Where are they? I need to ask someone what to do.

I can't find them. Oh, what the hell. I dump the rest in, mix, pour them into the tins and bake them. Stuff stinks! It doesn't smell like chocolate cake at all. But I stand in that hot stinky kitchen making the chocolate fudge icing, using Mars bars - (this is very apt because I leave the planet soon.)

Three hours later Gary walks into the kitchen just as I finish icing them. He wraps his arms around me and kisses my neck. *Hmmmmm!*

Holding me against him, he looks around, "Where's the stuff?"

I point at the cake, "In here."

He laughs and spins me to look down into my eyes incredulously, "You used all of it?"

I nod, confused. *Wasn't I meant to? No one gave me instructions and the stuff doesn't come with instructions.*

He chuckles and kisses my forehead, "Oh woman, I love you."

* * *

That night, at a camp fire in Noordhoek, I am starving! All anyone has done is barbecue sausage, drink and smoke. I don't eat *boerewors*, South Africa's special brand of sausage, so I am ravenous.

The tents are up and I am sitting at the fire with Kristy. She's drinking her usual red wine, I have a cider and she's enthusing about how great it is to be back to normal.

Gary staggers over with his entourage. He's holding the sliced up cake, "Woman, this is excellent. You have to try some."

Gosh darn, I am *soooo flippin* hungry the bark wrapped on the nearest tree looks appealing. I'm ignoring the fact he just called me woman as I don't feel like ruining the harmony we've rediscovered.

So, I have some. Kristy takes some. Gary wanders off with Charl, Alan, Neville – clutching a bottle of strawberry Mampoer – and Graham. Gosh, this is yummy. It tastes just like my usual chocolate cake but with a few chewy dry bits in it. The icing is **out** of this world. Mars bars just **make it**.

So what's the big deal with dope anyway? Nothing's changed. I need to pee.

"I'll be right back," I tell Kristy. She's staring off into space, gazing at the entrancing flames of the campfire. (Zoned **out**.)

Whatever. I move to get up and **omigod**. *Holy crap*. I am spatially retarded. Everything is zooming in and out. My head is whirling like a ballerina on crack. *Bugger that*. I think I'll just sit here again for another few minutes. I really should have eaten something. I'm obviously so hungry, I'm hallucinating.

I turn my head to say as much to Kristy, when the world starts spiralling with the movement of my head. Flippinheck, but I am vertically challenged! I lean back in my chair heavily. It's one of those deck chairs that sits about an inch off the ground. I am going to FALL. **Help**. Stop. I want to get off.

Okay, now I'm scared to move at all. I sit and watch the flames, wondering what Kristy finds so mesmerising. I try to focus on the sound of distant waves crashing.

Gary comes bouncing over, "Stef, come look here, babes"

He lurches into my vision. I stare at him, "I can't move."

He laughs as though I just tickled his g-spot.

Waaaaahahahaha, "My woman is stoned! This is *so* rad!"

No, I'm not. I just can't move. Nothing works. Oh lordy, there's bloody breathing in my ear. I can't even turn my head to see who it is. Gary is gone. There's so much brush around us, I'll never find him. They've probably gone off to smoke a joint on the beach.

"Hello!"

That sounds enthusiastic.

I mumble, "Hello."

"Would you like a drink?"

"Yes please."

Hang on, I can't find my hands. **I can't FEEL my hands.**

A cold Savannah is placed between my fingers. I can feel the cold slippery wetness of a bottle. Okay, my hands are still there. Thank God.

Oh look, it's Nev. Yay. I'm still not sure why he instils never-ending enthusiasm with his mere presence in everyone. Oh god, was it his breath in my ear just now? He's doing the manic beam at me.

He trips and falls at my feet, smiling at me. (He's like a cat, this dude. He falls head first, but when he lands, it's gracefully facing the right way as if he planned the whole thing. Bloody bizarre!)

Speaking of which, I guess we all dream of having men fall at our feet. But I didn't picture it like this.

SMASH.

"Cheers!"

Whoa, too fast, slow down dude. *R-e-e-e-e-l-a.a.a.ax.x.x..* (My world has turned into slow motion and his fast-forward gestures turn him into Neo from the Matrix.) His blurring Keanu manoeuvres are making me feel nauseous.

Mumble, "Cheers."

"Did I tell you that you're **fabulous**?"

I nod. **Oh my freaq**! Eeeeeeeeewww ... Lurch ... I think I'm going to be sick. Head spiralling like a Catherine Wheel. Wheeeeeee, nausea ... ugh, I feel like crap. Get *your hand off my leg.* Oh mommy! My head won't stay still. I feel as though I'm lying down but I don't remember lying down. (I can't focus on the hand that I can feel. Everything is blurry. Breathe slo-o-o-w-ly. Fo.o.o.c.u.s. There you are.)

Fuck dude, you are *waaaay* too close. Where the hell is Gary?

Oh look, Nev's lying next to me grinning like a happy camper. (Waaaaaahahaha, sorry I could not resist that one.)

Why does he only smile at me? Go away. I can't move.

"That's the best cake I've ever had. Did you make it?"

Deeeeeelaaaaay ....

"What?"

Get your hand off me.

Want to cry. Mommy! He's rubbing my arm and I can't move away. Running is out of the question. His face is about three inches away from mine and he's still beaming at me. Is he trying to seduce me? Is he mad?

"The cake. I want more."

Oh, I bet you do. Uhm ... Gary would have a hissy if you told him you tasted my cake ... usually I would find that funny, but right now I'm just trying to hold onto consciousness, because if I pass out ... with you ... you fucking scare me dude.

I feel sick.

"Smoke."

Oh jeez. He's just moved his head right up to my nose. I can feel his breath. I was trying to distract him, send him off to get me a smoke because I'm spatio-temporally paralysed. I am legless! Stop **breathing** over me.

"Hmm?"

(It's all flirty. Shudder.)

"Smoke ..." Croak ... head spin ... ugh ... "Please ..."

Phew, he just bounded off out of my vision. PHUCK ME. This is insane.

I think I need some of Gary's starch. I've lost my bones. They've liquidated. I try lifting the drink to my lips. Why is it taking *soooo* long? After what seems like three and a half hours, I feel the cold glass on my bottom lip. Feeling like a toddler, I carefully tip it.

Wow, I am thirsty. I down the whole thing. Damn, I just remembered I need to pee. That's just going to have to wait. Pity I'm not a lizard. I'd just grow some new legs so that I can walk again.

I've turned into the blob. A dizzy blob. I keep myself as still as possible, just waiting for the vertigo to pass. I hate this. I am never doing dope again. Now I know why they call it dope. You have to be a dope to like this! Who needs the date rape drug when you can have chocolate cake? Here have some cake, then you can't run away.

I'm in shit street and Kristy hasn't even registered that I'm being stalked. How can I be fabulous? He's known me for all of five minutes. Am I the only person to find that assessment scary?

... Pause ...

Chapter 20

... Play ...

After three and a half hours I could finally use my body again. And that was the one and only time I was ever stupid enough to eat laced chocolate cake. It was so laced, it put a corset to shame.

It was one of those enlightening weekends. I got to know Neville, vaguely. What I did like about him, is that he's intellectual and philosophical. At last I had someone I could really talk to inside the Gary entourage.

* * *

For two months I was happy. Really happy. Gary used my name more frequently, he made coffee, he even cooked dinner. So when he sat me down on a Saturday afternoon, looking like he'd just swallowed arsenic, I had no idea why he looked so serious.

"There's no easy way to say this."

My eyebrows rise as my stomach clenches.

"I think getting back together was a mistake. I want you to move out."

What. *OMG this isn't happening. You fucking son of a bitch.*

"Why?"

He seems dead serious too. This time he's not joking or messing with my mind.

"It's not working."

*What do you **mean** it's not working? It's never worked **better**.*

I am *not* going to cry another goddam tear over you. I am livid!

PING.

"Who is she?"

"An old friend."

So you're still fucking me around? I HATE you.

I nod and stand up, grabbing my smokes, "Fine. I'll be out by the end of the week."

"I'll help you move, find a place. I feel bad."

I nod. "Great. See you later."

"Where are you going?"

I glare at him, "That's none of your fucking business."

Wow, somehow he still manages to look hurt! He just booted me and *he* has the *cheek* to demand to know my business. Asshole.

He stands up and walks after me, "Woman, wait."

I keep walking.

"Stefanie."

Oh look, my name. **That** I respond to. Swivel and **glare**.

"Yes?"

"I'm sorry."

Sure you are.

You selfish, self-centred, dumb, motherfucking son of a bitch.

I just give him the why-don't-you-go-put-your-head-in-a-furnace stare, then keep on walking. As soon as I'm out of sight, I sit down, light a smoke and phone Selene.

My throat is tickling, my eyes are prickling.

"Hello?"

"He just broke up with me."

"Where are you?"

"Down the road."

"I'm on my way."

I sit and smoke, pondering.

My solar plexus is so constricted, I feel ill. I'm so choked up with anger I can hardly breathe. What the hell did I do?

I stare up at the perfect day. Mocking me. A happy, sunny, blue day; a perfect mountain, in a perfect seaside location. I exhale my smoke and glower. I need to exercise to work off some of this anger. So, I start a brisk walk. He's colder than cryogenics, he is.

I am seething and ranting internally so much that I didn't even notice Selene until she yells "Hey."

Stunned with panic, I stop and stare wildly. Phew! It's Selene.

"Get in."

I get in, and her sympathetic expression just nails me. Now I feel emotional.

She says nothing, she just keeps driving. I laugh at her when we get to the pool bar.

Amen sister. Let's hustle some boys! And I think I'd like a seriously girly drink.

Wow. All it takes is fifteen minutes and I have a man flirting with me and buying me drinks. And I'm kicking his ass at pool. I Am Empowered. I do not need Gary. Maybe I should make that my mantra? I do not need Gary. *I do not need Gary.* **I do not need Gary.**

Selene giggles and gossips. When it's dark and we're starving she says, "Staying at my place tonight?"

I could kiss you!

"I'd love to. Right now I just want to kick him in the nuts so hard they'll look like baubles on a Christmas tree."

She throws her head back and laughs with abandon. Selene has one of those totally infectious laughs. It reverberates and booms and soon we're crying, we're laughing so much.

My laughter chokes. Shit. Everything I own is at his place.

I am telling you this woman is telepathic, "We're the same height. You'll fit into my clothes."

Smile! "I'll buy us dinner."

We're sitting at her kitchen counter, dishing up Chinese, when her home phone rings. She saunters to it and I take over.

"Hello? ... Hang on."

She gives me an austere stare, "It's for you."

"That's impossible. No one knows where I am."

She arches one eyebrow, "I think it's him."

Fuck.

I take a huge inhalation and walk to the phone, suddenly feeling afraid, "Hello?"

"Stef ..."

"Go away!"

"WAIT."

Grrrrrrrrrr! I wait in silence.

"I just wanted to make sure you're okay."

"Don't pretend you give a damn. I am no longer your problem."

Shit. I hate tears. Why do emotions only visit you when you really don't want them to?

"Stef, I'm not sure ..."

"I am! It's over."

Slam.

"Sorry."

(Don't slam your friend's phone, it's not polite.)

103

"How did he get my number?"

I hiss venomously, "He must have gone through my phone book."

Riiinggg.

I glare at the phone. Snatch.

"Hello."

"Are you coming home?"

"Gary, it's not my home. You just kicked me out. REMEMBER?"

"Babes, I'm worried about you."

(You're such a liar! You're just saying that to be p.c. To make yourself feel better. Shagging someone else and then pretending you give a shit.)

"Oh, don't you worry about me. I'm going to be just fine without **you**. I have to go, we're going out tonight. I'll call **you** when I'm ready to pick up my things."

"I can drop them off."

"**You do that.**"

(Dripping scorn. Actually doing an Exorcist with it: I picture scorn hurling over the walls and slowly seeping like slime, down to the floor.)

"When?"

"**How the hell should I know? I'll call you when I'm free.**"

Slam.

Crap, I just did it again.

"Sorry."

"It's cool. I understand. If it rings again, just ignore it."

I nod, "I will. Selene, I'm so sorry to make my shit your problem."

"You didn't. I offered."

I gaze at her aquiline nose and full lips and smile, "I think you're the best friend I've ever had."

She smiles and pushes a plate at me, "Eat! You're going to need it. I think someone's going to be getting shit-faced tonight."

I giggle, "I just might."

Chapter 21

One week later, I moved into my own tiny apartment two roads away from the beast. Naturally, all of my Gary friends were banned from speaking to me or associating with me. (I like the way I get to lose everything, even my friends, because *he* says so.)

I told you he was spawned by the devil. I told you.

Right, so I have my housewarming that weekend. Gary and Alan move my stuff in for me, including my brand new bed, in the morning, and I'm finally free of my shackles by that afternoon. BUT. There is one thing I don't like about my new one-bedroomed hovel: **there is a mirror on the bedroom ceiling!**

Right, so that makes masturbation out of the question. Freaky-freaky-freaky.

But, who cares right now? I'm delirious with freedom overload. All I want to do is **party**.

Oh right. Yeah, I forgot to tell you. My friends? My only friends? That would be the very nice crowd at work. And they're all the best people *ever.* They're all coming tonight.

I don't think my lounge suite will ever be the same. James makes it look like children's furniture. Julie and Frank are as bad as each other when it comes to flirting and drinking. Shayne is the quietest man on the planet. Michelle can really drink for a nerd. (I think Shayne is perfect for her.)

Dianne has a really rubbish boyfriend, but they both pitched up. They like what I call, doof-doof music, the kind that gives you a headache without alcohol ingested.

What I don't get is, she's fall-off-a-bridge-backwards gorgeous. Seriously, this girl makes supermodels look plain and gangly, she could have any man on the planet and she chooses the guy with the cap, hunched shoulders, tattoos and appalling humour. (Check me calling the kettle black. If we were all saints we'd make better choices.)

I, like an idiot, did not eat anything. So, I am totally wasted by two-thirty in the morning, after playing coinage with sherry! (No, it's not a girl named Sherry, it's the fortified wine called sherry. Shakes head vigorously. Learn from my mistakes please.)

Okay, right, so I've figured out what drunk really is. This is the theory. Have you noticed how, the more you drink, the less gravity has an effect on you? And you feel all floaty? Well, that's why we start to feel sick – it's the zero gravity. They say that space travel is like that. That's why the zero gravity plane is affectionately referred to as 'the vomit comet'. You see? I've figured it out.

Aw. James is so sweet. He regularly comes to put his arm around me and check that I'm feeling okay. So sweet. But let's be honest here. When are these people going home? I just want to sleep, now.

Selene leaves with Michelle. Then Shayne leaves, in what I would call a reluctant manner. How often is he ever going to see me this floaty? I think he saw opportunity knocking for thirty-two seconds. Anyway, to cut a long story short, everyone leaves except James. Now he wants to help me clean up. *Nooooooooooooo.* Go away.

He's chucking the flirty hints at me so hard that I feel I'm playing paintball. (**Splat**.) I stare at his gigantic hands and feet and think he'd probably break my brand new bed – and me – in the process. **I - don't - think - so**. I like you, as a person, but I can't ever have a boyfriend as humungous as you. And I'm not into a pity fuck right now from you, either. I will never have sex again as long as the mirror is hovering above my bed! Very, very, very, bad feng shui, dude. Just too much Def Leppard in that mirror.

Three coffees later, at more or less 3:45 a.m, he finally leaves, and I have the relief of passing out, fully clothed, on my new bed draped in fresh, fabulous linen. I dig this. It's the best! For years I've lived a monochrome existence. Now I can have checks! Blue and white. I don't do girly, pink, shiny or frilly, (pretend vomit at the thought). I like the masculine look. I hate fuss, it irritates me. (Like those pathetic extra cushions everyone and her mama has on the sofa! I move them, hate them, wish someone would have a bonfire where I can lose them!)

I watch my world spiralling as I wait for sleep. I hate that mirror, it's stuck on askew.

(Yes, I am a perfectionist. Symmetry is everything.)

I'm on a fun-house ride that refuses to slow down. I'm feeling rather ill to be honest. Lesson learned. Sherry and I are arch enemies and I'll never throw my money at her again. Ever.

* * *

One week later, I get crazy. Do you realise that I'm free? FREE. So, now I'm ready: I'm ready for a shag-fest without guilt. I'm ready to go head-banging with Selene and James. I'm ready to get my own chop (tattoo for the rest of you). And I'm ready to make real friends that Gary can't steal from me when he finds a replacement better than me. Every two months it seems.

Item number one on the agenda: Shag *shag* **shag**. Sorry if you find this offensive but I'm a biological human being. However, things aren't looking so hot because my day's entertainment is Shayne. He's taking me home to show me his fish. (I mentioned I'm interested in marine fish tanks.)

Now, Shayne is a nice guy. He's not a lot taller than me. He's got floppy, flat, straight brown hair. He wears spectacles and dresses like a financial nerd. But, I don't judge people on the way that they look. When it comes to men, I don't do type. I have only two requirements. Confidence, and you have to be stronger than me, and preferably (but not essential), taller than me. Oh dear, there's a flaw here. Okay, I cannot date a man shorter than me either. Who's going to get things off the top shelf if he's shorter than me? Na uh. That doesn't turn me on.

Right, so we've spent the whole day together and I am bored out of my mind now. I cannot speak about fish any more. There is nothing left to say on the subject. So he comes home with me, and I make coffee and chuck on some decent music. *Aaaah*, now you see: even a nerd has merit. Shayne then introduces me to Toto. Wow. What a kick-ass band.

(Where have I been? In a cave? That I've never heard this band ever. Oh wait. Duh! I was stuck in the AC/DC time warp wasn't I? And there was no stepping in or stepping out of it either.)

Now we get that awkward moment where he slides his arm around my shoulders, all casual like. My relaxed happy moment evaporates in a heartbeat, completely.

Just what the hell do you think you're doing?

I arch my eyebrows, "Are you coming on to me?"

He grins shyly, "I was trying to, but you ruined it."

I can't explain this to you, but I react so badly. I feel rage. I shudder at the whole, 'I want to cosy up to you – which could take *hours* thing.

"Shayne, if you want to fuck me just say so. The answer is either going to be yes, or no. I don't do the mating dance. I HATE IT."

Oooohkay! I think I just blew 'ladylike' right out of the stratosphere. Shit. What is wrong with me? Poor dude is stunned into silence.

"I want to fuck you."

I cringe. I honestly didn't mean it like that; it was a bad reaction. It sounds horrible when he says it. So degrading and *eeeewww.*

I stand, staring at him lounging on the chair in my apartment, and think, Oh, what the hell? I have to break the ice, get out of the Gary shackles. It may as well be with you.

BUT, after Mr Crabs, and 'I shag the world' Gary, I have this thing about personal hygiene now.

"Fine! Take a bath and I'll meet you in the bedroom."

Waaaaaahahahaha. I am *sooooo* peculiar: I can tell he's never had such a weird proposition in his life. Look out boys, here's the sad strange ex with 'odd' issues. She'll shag you but you have to wash between your toes first.

I am blushing.

So, I strip off and pull Victoria on while my victim has his bath. My new place does not have a shower, which would have made life a lot easier.

Cutting to the chase. In twenty minutes I have a glowing, squeaky clean, Shayne, lying on my bed, and it's ready to have its virginity popped with my first post-Gary shag.

So I'm working my magic ... doing my thing. You know what my thing is ... a tongue here, a kiss there, a lick, a caress, hair everywhere. Oh, and I have to tell you something. Who knew? This boy is built like an Olympic swimmer. He's beautiful without his clothes. Really!

What the hell am I doing wrong?

How can I have failure? I'm doing everything I can think of, and the bazooka still looks like my lipstick tube. It hasn't changed one iota. So I start asking, probing, questions.

"Do you like this ...?"

"Hmmm."

"Does that feel good ...?"

"Yeah."

Eventually, I sit back and whine, "What am I doing wrong?"

He smiles, "Jesus, would you just sit on me already!"

I am no Jesus, but **sure,** if that will work.

So I slip over him, and do my Asian number. He writhes and moans and ... and ... and ... oh for FUCK'S sake. When will this guy get hard? I'm actually tired, which is saying something.

"Have you come?" I pry.

"Ages ago. You're like a machine!"

What! When? Where the hell was I?

I slip off and stare at the lipstick tube. No way. *No way.*

This poor man. How can nature be so cruel? His cyclops is still eight years old.

He grins at me, obviously pleased with the show. (Show? What show? Where?)

And then! *Then!* **Then**! He says, "You're like a dude."

What? Grrrrooooowl. *What!*

(I think my face conveys this, because, hey presto, he doesn't look so relaxed as he starts explaining.)

"You just want to do it. No fucking around. No kissing, or cuddling. Just get it on. I think I like that."

(Well, that's just great. But loverboy, this will never work. You're the size of my tampon.)

I grab a smoke and light it. Buying time. I never ever thought I'd be one of those shallow women who cared about size. I always thought size didn't matter, only how you used it. I am so shallow. But now I know, to a certain degree, size definitely matters.

I look at his hands, then his feet. So it's true. He's got hands smaller than mine, feet smaller than mine. That does it, I'm staying the hell away from James.

Sigh.

What have I done? I just shagged a boy from work. This is going to be awkward.

Chapter 22

Monday morning Shayne sidles up to me and fiddles with statements on my desk, "I don't want anyone to know. Just keep it between us, okay?"

YAY!

"No problem."

Inside jiggy dance. What a relief. Although secretly I am *aching* to tell Selene; I know what a rabid sex-addict she is. She'd find Shayne's dilemma hilarious. To my credit, I never tell a living soul about him. (Until now that is).

So imagine the thunderous 'Thor is angry' glare I get from him, when James pops over to my desk, squeezes my shoulders –(ouch!)– and sits his mammoth frame on my desk, folding his arms, to smile at me. He also wears spectacles by the way. (Gee, what's going on in my life?)

"Are you busy tonight?"

Where's this going? "No. Why?"

Slap. Ow! My shoulder is cramping now.

"Great, I'll be over at seven. I'm making us dinner."

Weeeell now, how can I say no to that? Gary is *so* yesterday. Not to mention Neanderthal.

I smile, "Okay."

Shayne glowers at me but says nothing.

I stare back and want to telepathically yell, 'Keep your wings on, angel! I'm not going to shag the whole office.'

At seven, James arrives, beaming. Why do men smile at me like that anyway? What does it mean? Is it a secret code for something?

He walks straight into my kitchen, whips out a chardonnay, uncorks it and pours us each a glass.

Clink

"Cheers. Now get out. Go and relax while I cook."

(This is so odd. Why cook here? Why not invite me to your place?)

"Okay."

So I take my black-jeaned ass out of the kitchen and sit down on the couch, sipping wine and indulging in a new smoke. How come none of these men smoke? I thought non-smokers hated smokers?

Twenty minutes later, he produces a plate for me with a flourish, "Tah dah!"

I stare at the huge steak dwarfing the plate. Oh no. "Thanks. This looks fabulous, but I don't eat red meat."

(See? I'm the cheapest date ever. I feel guilty, because I certainly don't mind cooking it for other people. I just don't like it myself. It's like chewing on polystyrene.)

His face is crestfallen. He's horrified. His big surprise just went belly up.

"Darn. It's my speciality. I thought you'd love it."

Oh shit. Life just sucks.

I rub his forearm the size of my thigh, "Thanks; I really, really, appreciate this. I'll try it, if it'll make you feel better?"

"No ... Crap! I didn't know."

I'm squirming for him. This is so awkward. I get up, "It's fine, really. I have loads of meals frozen. I'll just pop something in the microwave."

He masks his chagrin with a rueful grimace, "Are you sure?"

"The wine's great." I give him a reassuring wink.

We go into the kitchen together and I prepare the 'other half' of our meal. I watch his deft movements around the kitchen and am impressed. He's really overdressed though. Black boots, black trousers, black button up shirt: a closet goth cooking in my kitchen. I smile to myself. Spiky dark brown hair. This guy is just huge, it's the only way to describe him. I suppress a giggle as I realise that his hand is bigger than my face.

We eat together and this evening is dragging. It's early but I'm awkward and nervous.

Why is he here? What's his intention exactly?

At nine, after he's washed the dishes (HELLO!), and after at least forty-five minutes of small talk, he suggests, "Should we go out?"

Hell yeah. Anything to get out of this rut.

"Yes!"

"The Corner Bar okay?"

I nod.

Great! Smokes, money and off we go.

This evening is working now. I haven't ever met a man who actually dances. That's what girlfriends are for. He towers over everyone on the dance floor. Now we have something to bond over. Music! I love this place. It's a biker's, head-banger's, delight. It's dim, smoky, and wall-to-wall average dudes and gothic chicks. The men are all earthy and ordinary. Jeans, T-shirts, denim or leather jackets are everywhere. Lots of interesting tattoos, lots of long hair on everyone, I fit right in. The girls all look vampish. So my maneuvers are right at home. No one hits on me. No one harasses me. Wow. The people here respect each other. Don't believe the stereotype rubbish you hear; or maybe it's because I'm with my own personal bouncer?

To make my life complete, we are lucky enough to have one my favourite local bands playing live. Unobtrusively, I lean against the wall, watching Nic James growl out lyrics that I've set my life to. I mean, come on, a girl's allowed to swoon in secret isn't she? I am way too cool to ever do the groupie thing.

Lordy, Gary might have stripped my dignity, but in public I have my pride. Nic James is really tall, his hair is dyed black, and he has electric blue eyes that scythe through the room seductively. Couple that with his, 'I can sing the pants off you' voice and, let's just say, my body likes him very much. A lot of their lyrics are heavy, deep, intellectual. Which is probably why James likes them too .... hmm ... I wonder if James planned this?

I watch their drummer, Marc, strip off his shirt with the suffocating heat in here and am reminded of how groovy it is to be single; and grin at the Feedback CDs stacked on a table, '*Pieces*'. How apt. My life is in smithereens. My heart is smashed to shards. Nic's voice is like Sam Elliot mixed with Chad Kroeger. Just close your eyes and let that voice carry you anywhere you want to go. I think it's time I upgraded to a man.

I fan myself, imagining how awesome it must be to be stuck in a blackout with this crowd. Is it suddenly clammy in here?

That was the night that James and I became friends. He never ever put a move on me. And I respect him for that. We share a love of grungy music. Soon this becomes routine, sometimes including Selene. I like having male friends.

Anyway, so I meet Don at the Corner Bar. Don does tattooing for a living. And who needs Tupperware, when you can have a *tattoo* party? I explain how shy I am. The only tattoo parlour I know of with a good reputation contains two flaws. A gigantic python! And glass windows into the studio. Which means everyone will see me with my pants off! No can do. I pout, plead and manipulate, until Don tells me, "Fine. But make it worth my while. I'll do yours for free if you line up five clients."

So that weekend I have five friends lined up. Don is expected at two in the afternoon, so I wonder what the hell? when my doorbell rings at eleven in the morning.

I look through the peep hole and see a huge man I've never seen before at my door. He rings the doorbell again.

Suspiciously I crack the door open, "Can I help you?"

"Are you Stefanie?" I nod.

He smiles, "Great! I'm at the right place."

Huh?

"Sorry?"

"Hey man, it's breezy out here, aren't you going to let me in?"

I am a dimwit. You can tell. "Um. Why are you here? Who are you?"

"Eddie! Jake sent me."

Jake? Dianne's seedy boyfriend Jake?

"Dianne's boyfriend?"

He nods, looking around as if he's about to score drugs off me and has a guilty conscience. So I let him in.

He walks in, surveys my tiny home, and flops his body-builder's frame onto my sofa, "Got anything to drink?"

"No, you aren't supposed to drink before getting a chop. Don emphasised that he wasn't tatting anyone who's been drinking in the last twenty-four hours."

"Got any coffee then?"

You know what? You are fucking rude. "Yeah, sure."

Paranoia snakes up my spine as I leave a complete stranger alone in my living room while I make him coffee. Feeling jumpier than exploding pumpkin seeds, I light a smoke and sit down opposite him to watch him drink his coffee. We have **hours** to go before Don or anyone else is due to arrive.

"Nice place you've got here."

Whatever. Actually, I'm scared. This man is huge, arrogant and confident. I feel like a ten year old on my seat. Shit. Maybe I should start praying?

Ding Dong.

What? Has someone put up a neon sign saying, 'STEF'S PLACE'?

I get up and move to the door. Eddie gets up too, and stands behind me like my bouncer, as if he's going to protect me or something. Fuckenhell. This is so freaking weird. My life has just become insane.

I look through the peephole and see another complete stranger. I open the door, "Hi?"

"You Stefanie?"

I nod as my stomach arranges itself into a perfect sailor's knot.

"Excellent!" and he pushes past me. Body-builder number two!

"Eddie! Hey man. How's it hanging?"

"I wasn't sure I had the right place."

And the two comrades bounce off my sofa's bonding, relaxing, while I feel completely redundant and alarmed, and go to make more coffee.

I sit and smoke quietly in my corner, with huge frightened eyes. I'm scared. I hate the way they're looking at me. I am feeling very diminutive and 'alone', right now.

Ding ... Dong.

I race to the door. **Please** let that be one of my friends. I need back up. I fling it open.

"Stef!" Jake. Thank God. Who ever thought I'd be happy to see you?

Dianne follows with four more people. No Way. My home is not big enough for the Chippendales. Unlike every other woman on the planet, I don't like bulky boys and this is sawing on my sanity. I grab Dianne and haul her, and their drinks, to the kitchen, while the men all do their macho fist-thumping bonding crap.

"What were you thinking! How can you send complete strangers to my home?"

She giggles, completely unfazed. "Relax man. They're all friends of Jake's." Miss tall, willowy, long straight black hair, high cheekbones and doll perfect skin just winks at me.

"I don't care: that's *not* cool."

"You said you needed five or more people. So shut up and stop complaining."

My house becomes like the subway that afternoon. I get my chop done first. A little Celtic cross on my hip. I'm deep into symbolism. Sometimes we're nailed to that cross; sometimes we're carrying that cross; sometimes we find salvation and peace through that cross. But it's private. I don't want to share it with the world. That's why it's on my hip. But having this party was to ensure my privacy whilst receiving ink. I am alone in my bedroom with Don, nothing but the buzzzzzing of his tattoo thingamajig breaking the reverent silence of an artist at work on a human canvas.

Great. (Major sarcasm in that 'great'.)

In bursts (ew-ew-ew) Eddie and two of these strangers, into my private space – (my bedroom) – and I cannot obviously run away now, can I? I can't cover up my thong either. I cringe and close my eyes as my cheeks flood with heat. Shudder. Don feels it and the buzzing stops as he glares at the intrusion, "What?"

"What's taking so long, man?"

I take a peek through a half-open eye. Oh skin crawling *Gaaaawd*. Get that man's slimy gaze off my naked thigh. This is so wrong on so many levels. Eddie is standing there and he has creep written all over him! No no no no no! Fuck OFF.

Don calmly, but in a fabulously passive-aggressive way, says, "Get out and close the door after you."

They seem stunned, but they comply. When bahm! In bounce two more men. I am going to gut Dianne for this.

"Hi Stef!"

A new, kind of acquaintance, Tim, who is about a foot shorter than me but built like a bull terrier, waltzes over to have a look at my half-finished cross. "Looking sweet, babes."

He holds out a hand to Don, "Hey Don. Thanks for doing this."

Don shakes it with a latex gloved hand and pushes his bandana up to wipe the sweat of concentration off his brow. I am beginning to feel like a specimen all scientists with bulging muscles should come to study. I feel like a piece of meat for the first time in my life. I'm embarrassed by Robert's observation of me, as he's filling my door-frame with his humungous build. He's built like the Rock, to put it into perspective for you. I've known him since I was sixteen. We did bodybuilding together a very long time ago. He has a violent temper. I met him when he was going through his first divorce. I still, to this day, have no idea how old he is. But he still looks exactly the same as the first day I met him. Huge, tanned, brown eyes, cropped brown hair and a great smile. Which is aimed at me, "Hey Stef. I didn't know this was your place?"

(Did I mention he's a TV gladiator too?)

"Hi Rob! Please go away, I'm half naked here!"

He winks at me, "Sure!"

So with a sigh of relief, I know that I at least have two friends here who are male. At last I don't feel quite so vulnerable. If Gary could see me now he'd have a seizure. I relax as Tim and Rob close the door. I know I'll be left alone now, until this rather raw-feeling body art, is complete.

When it's done, I rub the ointment over it to prevent scabbing, carefully pull on my jeans, and call the next victim. I get Don a drink. (He, at least, is allowed to have one.) Oh, and did I mention that people would be talking about this party, for years, at work? This nice sweet girl, that blushes, had a tattoo party. And Dianne tells the world that we were the only girls at it. Nice one!

Well, I'm now a chop that has a chop.

Chapter 23

Friday, two weeks from then, I wake up with an overwhelming feeling of dread. I look outside my blue and white bedroom curtains and see it's a fabulous, beautiful morning. The sun is out, the sky is periwinkle blue, not even a breeze. Why do I feel like this?

I walk to my closet and take out a blue skirt suit, don my pantyhose, pull on my matching court shoes. Brush my hair and my teeth – (I no longer have to wear make-up, do I?) – and walk to my door. As I turn the handle, my stomach knots with tension. I start shaking. I sit down on the closest slate grey sofa to the front door, to catch my breath and try to instill calm.

No. I can't do it. Something very bad is going to happen today. We aren't allowed to take a Friday off work without a doctor's note. I don't care. I have to trust this instinct. I never take off anyway. Even when I'm sick I go to work.

I walk back to my bedroom, take off the suit, hang it back up, and pull on skin tight jeans instead, with Chuck Taylor's. I can't shake this fear creeping all over me.

I sit in the corner of my lounge knitting; I do that in winter to keep my hands warm. I'm deliberately sitting where I can see every window and door, but where I can't be seen if someone tried to peer in. From my view I can see my full, floor to ceiling, bedroom window. I notice a white car rev past noisily. My fear intensifies as the car reverses back into my view, drives up the driveway and stops outside my kitchen window. They could be here for anyone, for anything. But I can barely breathe right now. My lungs are constricting with my stomach, and I slowly lower my knitting onto the couch and keep an eye on the car.

Two young white guys get out, and come straight to my front door. Ding dong! I ignore it. My instincts are screaming at me that opening the door will end badly for me. Ding ding ding ding dong.

Just go away!

I hear a noise. I sneak a peek down the passage to my bedroom. One of them is trying the door to my bedroom. It's a glass door and I am now certifiably terrified. At the same time, I notice the front door handle twisting. **Fuck!** My phone is dead and I don't have a landline.

117

I can't even call for help. I sit back down on the couch with shaking legs, and wonder what the hell to do.

I watch in panther silence as the two of them bang, knock and fiddle with my bedroom door, which faces the street. The two of them presumably decide it's better to try the front door because that is hidden from anyone driving past. And it's glaringly obvious that all of my neighbours are at work.

Thump. Gaboing. (Metal clanging.)

I sneak up to the front door to peek through the spy-hole, and see the two of them up against my new security gate. They are both looking down, concentrating on breaking the lock. Crap. I have to take a stand. Aha! I remember, long ago, I saw a black and white movie with Goldie Hawn, where she uses a knitting needle to poke a man in his eye when he tried to attack her. I sneak back to the couch, and pick up the loose knitting needle. I tiptoe back to the front door with my blood gonging in my ears and my stomach, intestines, kidneys and heart all lodged in my throat. I am so afraid, I feel dizzy.

I know I'm going to have to be quick. The element of surprise and pain have to work in my favour. Silently, I unlock the door, and unlatch the bolt. Planting my feet firmly, I fling the door open and am ready with the needle. Ready to stab the closest eye.

Waaaaahahaha. The looks on their faces! I have never seen anyone turn so white, so fast. They just dropped the file they were using to file through the bolt of the lock, and ran for their car. They reversed with stunning skill, as fast as they could, and took off down the road. I let out a *looooong* sigh of relief. They could have been armed. I took a huge risk. Lucky for me, they simply just wanted to break in. I stare at the file and get my key to unlock the security gate. And I try and I try: the damn thing is now broken. I am locked in!

I sit back down on the couch and breathe, pondering my dilemma. Then I recall the bedroom door. Well, thank God this place has more than one door. The plus and minus factors of an apartment on the ground floor. I give it another hour and a half before I decide they're not coming back. The wild dread has left me. Now I simply feel adrenalised. I have to go and get coffee anyway, so I decide to take my bag and take a quick walk to the mall down the road. This is the one part I hate about living alone. Dealing with drama by myself.

I'm walking with the warm sun heating my limbs, lost in thought. I would almost pin my money on the fact that those boys knew about my place through someone that came to my tattoo party. I don't have insurance yet. If I hadn't been home they would have broken in and left with everything I own. Half of which is on loan from my mom, fridge and TV for instance. I'm now angry that people like that exist in the world. I'm also feeling really chuffed with myself for listening to my instincts, even if it meant a warning at work.

Fuckenhell man! **Watch** where you're driving!

This stupid woman, who can hardly see over her steering wheel, just went onto the wrong side of the road and nearly ran me over! What is going on today? Do I have 'Here I am – come and get me' emitting from me like a radio wave?

I stop and watch the moron park her Fiat and jump out, "I'm so sorry! Are you okay? I wasn't concentrating ..."

I can't believe it. "Cindy, you stupid woman! When are you going to get your bloody license?"

Poetic justice: I have a license and no car. She has a car and no license.

"Stef! Omigod. How **are** you?"

"Been better."

"Come in for coffee. I've really missed you. It's so great to see you!"

I belatedly realise that I am in her road. "Okay."

I sit in her lounge and light a smoke while I wait for her to come out of the kitchen with coffee. She smokes more than I do, so I don't feel bad about this decision. I also feel shaken up. I don't know why I can't join her in the kitchen, but she didn't want me to see it in a mess.

I smile as she sits down opposite me.

"How are you?"

"I'm okay. How are you?"

"Missing you. I wanted to stay friends, but Graham wouldn't let me."

I nod and sip my coffee.

"How's everyone?"

"They're fine. Gary has a new girlfriend. She's very nice."

I nod. Mouth full of teeth.

"Stef, do you know why you guys broke up?"

I shake my head. I'm not saying anything here.

She gives me this accusing stare. A real bitchy glare. And with scorn and disdain dripping off her tongue, she accuses me. "Stef, men need sex. He broke up with you because he wasn't getting any."

I almost gag on my coffee. I had been watching her, not my cup and nearly throw up as I notice the thick white ring edging my cup half way down on the inside. I feel simultaneously ill and angry.

"Is that what he told you?"

Choke.

She leans back in her black velvet chair and glares at me with 'don't you dare deny it' eyes.

"He came to us a couple of weeks ago. He was nearly in tears. He didn't know what to do. He was desperate."

I have read the statistics. 'Normal' couples get laid about twice a week. Gary was getting laid every morning; (he lived by the maxim, 'never waste a hard on'). He was getting laid every night. He had a blow job literally daily. And he's not getting any? FUCKING LIAR.

She sits forward and smiles, her long curly hair almost dipping into her coffee as her cold blue eyes impale me, "We all understood where he was coming from. Stef, you fucked up."

I can't sit here and listen to this shit. Complete and utter **shit**. I stand up and pick up my bag, "Thanks for the coffee. I have to go." And I never, ever, want to see you again. How DARE you judge me?

She gives me a wounded glance. As if she was trying to counsel me, help me see the error of my ways, to get that lying scumbag, back.

I pause at the door on my way out of her lounge, "Cindy, he lied. He was getting plenty."

Her compassionate visage turns icy again. "Bye."

Oh, I'm ready to pop a blood vessel and blow up his face, I am so outraged. He set me up. That lying, conniving, son of a bitch, set me up. He has them all feeling sorry for the poor man that isn't 'getting any'. ANY! That's quite a statement. So, somehow he's managed to visit the friends as the victim. Not knowing what he's going to do with Stef. Stef, who doesn't have a sexual appetite to save her life.

Bitter tears are blurring my footsteps. My pleasure at being outdoors is stripped. I hate you. *I hate you.* **I hate you.**

So they all are backing him. Giving him support when I'm the one who needs it. Lying FUCKER.

I hope you go straight to hell, Gary Fuchs.

Chapter 24

Saturday morning Lindsay from work pops in to see how I am. I tell her about Friday, how it sucked so badly and why I didn't go to work. She works with me, as does her boyfriend Ted. Ted was seeing Deborah, who works in reception; it's a huge office scandal that Lindsay 'stole' him from poor needy Deborah.

She has shoulder length honey-hued hair and huge green eyes. She's fun, pretty, and totally on my side.

"You're coming out with us tonight. I won't take no for an answer."

(She and Ted both smoke. Both she and Julie manage to make sucking on a cigarette look like foreplay and I'm envious of how seductively she's smoking in front of me.)

"Okay."

She stands and winks, "Come, let's go shopping. You need to get out and forget about those people."

I love you!

"Okay."

That evening, I'm sitting at a picnic table outdoors, with candlelight illuminating this dim place. It's dead boring and I'm wondering why we're here.

"Can't we go somewhere else?"

"We're waiting for Marty," Ted explains. He's shorter than Lindsay, with amazing blue eyes. And wow, can he gossip.

I discover that Deborah's only 'experience' came from romance novels. And he could no longer stand her lacerating his back until it bleeds with her false nails when they were 'at it'. I smile. (And Gary thought he had it tough?)

This tall dude, in midnight jeans and a matt navy blue silk shirt, comes striding purposefully toward us. Ted stands and automatically shakes his hand as he reaches us, "Finally!"

He gestures at me, "Marty, this is Stefanie."

He nods at me as his hazel eyes slip down me and back up again, "Hi."

Then he dismisses me and sits down next to Ted, "I need a drink. What a fucking day!"

I feel awkward. I'm definitely the extra wheel here. So, I swivel around and stare at the other patrons as I light a new smoke, and think, *'It's damn cold out here. The music is from the seventies. We're the youngest people here. Why did I agree to this?'*

"Stef! Hey Stef!"

Huh, what?

Embarrassed, I turn back to the three heads staring at me. I have no idea what they want. I wasn't paying attention. Oh look, Marty has a drink.

"Sorry?"

Lindsay gives me a stern glare, "Can we leave you with Marty? Is it okay if he takes you home?"

I stare at Marty. Deep sigh. "Okay. Where are you going?"

"We forgot we have to see Ted's sister tonight. We have to run."

I nod, "Okay. Bye."

Well now, isn't this uncomfortable. I am sitting with a complete stranger who's had a shit day, and the only common connection just abandoned us.

"Should we duck? Are you hungry? I'm starving!"

I observe him as I nod. Food is good. He's about six-foot-two. His hair is so black it looks oily. It's wavy like mine. His eyes are dark right now. His complexion is Mediterranean. Olive toned, I think they call it.

Oh wow, look at that, I have the door opened for me. I get into his SLK, and off we go to a restaurant I have never been to.

It's so awkward. We're sitting outside because we both smoke and he's staring off into the night. Neither of us knows what to say. We're at the top of a long road sitting outdoors at a table lit with a lamp. Italian opera floats faintly over us as I stare absently down into the Waterfront. The sea seems limitless from up here. The black night kissing the ocean, merging seamlessly. Both spattered in twinkles of reflecting light. The sky is wearing her sequinned velvet party dress for this special occasion.

This guy must be loaded. On tenterhooks, I flick my eyes at him. I wonder how Ted and Lindsay know him. And why he agreed to have dinner with a peasant like me.

He stubs out his cigarette and stares hard at me. Gosh, there's some serious chemistry going on here. He fiddles with his clasped hands, leaning on the table, just staring at me. I return the stare, unwavering. (I can stare you down any day, dude.)

His hand reaches over and covers mine. Wow, it's so warm. I'm freezing out here.

"I just want to kiss you. It's all I can think about."

My hair feels like it's standing up with static, I'm feeling so charged. His eyes are beautiful. They're so hypnotic. Mysterious. His mouth is full; he missed a spot when he shaved. It makes me smile as I look at the tufty patch on his chin. My heart is **bounding** like a kangaroo. The biological signs are all there. I'm hot for this guy and we've only just met. But I like to keep it cool. I've always tried to hide my real depth of feeling. I turn everything into a game so that I don't feel stupid if I'm alone in my perceptions.

"So do it then."

Gauntlet thrown down. Challenge issued.

He leans across and without touching me, places his warm lips on mine.

Zing! Ooh. Moreish. More. Totally yummy. Man, he's the hottest kisser I've ever had the luck to kiss. A hand behind my head pulling me closer. Oh my god. YES! I could kiss him **forever.**

Soft pliable lips, sucking, pressing, warm, *oooh,* this feels, *hmmmmmm!*

"Excuse me!"

Kissing, *oooh,* flirty tongue, you taste nice, you smell nice. Don't stop.

"Sir?"

He pulls away with a wicked grin as the waiter tries to put a huge plate of butternut ravioli drenched in formaggio sauce down in front of him. I have the same, but mine's the half portion. As soon as the plates are down he leans over, slides his hand into my hair again and continues where he left off. My body just turns into an amoeba. I am *aching* for him. I just want to fuck him like a bunny, a playboy bunny! Love right now has nothing to do with it. It's pure, unadulterated, primal chemistry.

He pulls away and pops a square of ravioli into his mouth. I grin and do the same. We've hardly said two words to each other. He leans over and slips his tongue in the corner of my mouth, teasing, "You messed your sauce."

You're going to be messing your sauce, if I have anything to do with it.

He chuckles. Oh swoon. His voice is deep and velvet. He's like a vampire seducer. And hey, I don't care. I'm falling for it. In fact, he has that untouchable vibe about him. He seems aloof and unobtainable. His posture, regal. I wonder about him. He's enigmatic and it's a complete turn on.

How we managed to eat anything, I have no idea. Between each mouthful he kissed me as if a nuclear blast had just detonated in the harbour, and this was the last moment on earth alive.

Passion took over my body. I had such a deep ache of longing that I could hardly walk as he threaded his long fingers through mine and tugged me out of my chair, against his side, wrapping an arm around me, (wow he's so warm), and down the stairs to his car.

He slips in behind the wheel, leans over and kisses me further. His hand finds my nipple and he knows what is going on inside me. Unexpectedly he jerks away, and grips the steering wheel before running his hand through his sleek black hair, "Come home with me."

YEEEEEEEEEESSSSSSSSS!

"Okay."

The smile that he then shoots at me, with his fathomless eyes, is so happy and pleased, my heart feels like someone just thumped it hard. I am so used to games, having a man openly reveal his joy, his lust, to me – (because of me) – I find I have a weird sadness mingling with pleasure.

The engine purrs into life and I feel a thrill of excitement as I do what a good girl would *never* do. I have been set up. Ted and Lindsay set this up. But the chemistry, it's mind numbing. And I'm going home with a complete stranger I met about three hours ago. And I don't care!

The wild thumping of my excited heartbeat blurred the ethereal drive through avenues of ancient oaks, to his expansive home in Constantia. As I suspected, this guy probably doesn't live on a budget like mine. However, my body was so busy trying to split the atom, most of this only occurred to me later.

I feel like laughing, telling you this because it was so choreographed. There should have been a camera and a script. It was the classic Hollywood passion scene. Clothes were being ripped off in a frenzy the minute his front door closed. All the while trying to keep our lips and tongues glued together. I lost all of my clothing, as did he, before we'd even travelled down the passage to his bedroom. The rooms were **huge**.

He just picked me up and I wrapped my legs around him, as he carried me against his warm silky skin, in the dark to a room. He flipped the switch, and a gigantic bed in a vast room was revealed. Bohemian throws adorned the walls. I stared at him with renewed interest. Exotic and mysterious. Now I'm wondering if his colouring comes from an Arabian line. He lets me stand and I look around with curiosity.

He trips me and I fall backward onto ... oh my ... this bed is just *sooo* cosy. He falls over me and starts raining hot kisses on me and I'm ready to rape him if he doesn't do something *soon*. He chuckles again. It's deep and seductive. Throaty and flirtatious. This guy should bottle charisma. He'd make a killing. He fumbles in a drawer and rips open a wet suit.

Stop breathing. I am spasming with pleasure. The Marty-lucky-packet rocks. Fuckenhell! Yes! *Yes!* **Yes!** I stare up into inky eyes, and smile back at the dimples cornering his mouth. He seems very pleased with himself. His physique is smooth. Nothing like the Chippendales who bombarded my home. He's got long muscles to match his long arms. Whoa! He flips me up to sit on him as if I'm a plastic bobble-head and weigh nothing. I entwine my arms around his neck and smother him with tasting, tempting, kisses, as I shimmy up and down on 'Mr Ever Ready'.

Sharp indrawn breath as he picks me up, and walks with me attached to him to the kitchen. It's a huge room, cold and breezy, with haunting moonlight flooding in over the sink. He takes me straight to that sink, pushes my shoulders back and blasts me with ice cold water from the tap. Cold. *Cold.* **Cold.** I am covered in an all-over nipple stand. Actually, this is hectic fun. It works! His laughter fills the room and I fall back into his hypnotic spell, mesmerised as he rides me against the kitchen sink with water spewing everywhere. He's so vocal I'm finding it delicious.

We are both soaking, and giggling. Man, this ride is awesome. He walks with me like that, back to the bedroom, where he carefully disengages and flips me over. Onto my knees, as I hear a new wet suit package ripping open. *AAAAAAAAAAHHHHHHHH fuck.*

I have that hot and cold sensation rippling up and down my spine as my body covers in tiny bumps. My nipples, frigidly hard with the unexplainable sensation of being nailed fervently from behind. My cheeks are glowing with the exercise. The minute I feel him explode, I withdraw and wrench his arm, making him fall, as I sit on his legs and hold him down. Sucking, tasting his skin from his shoulder down. Holding his hands with his fingers laced through mine. Straining, he pushes back, and I watch his muscles outlining, his stomach rack hardening. We are taking sex to Olympic level as we strain in a wrestlemania style against each other. Each of us winning bouts, giggling, breathless, screwing endlessly. Again and again and again.

Finally we fall together with arms resting peacefully. Relaxed, he moves my hair away from my face, and tenderly puts his lips on mine. Gentle nuzzling. Delicate pressure.

I move my eyes up to meet his, and smile. I think I've just found the perfect man for me. He's fabulous.

"Thirsty?"

I nod.

Caught off guard, he picks me up and carries me squirming, into the shower, as he blasts me with cold water, "There, there's plenty of water in there."

SQUUUEEEEEEEAAAAALL.

I'm shrieking, my body's relaxed stupor is annihilated rudely as he chuckles, and we slip and slide, chasing each other down the wide passage. Dripping like bedraggled rats caught in a thunderstorm. His arm swoops around my waist and he hoists me into the kitchen, "Coffee or alcohol?"

Hmmm coffee.

"Coffee." I smile as I lick my lips. I feel like a voyeur in the best zone ever as I watch him confidently stalk around the kitchen with long legs, stark naked, making me coffee.

Can I stay? Please can I keep you? Please?

Chapter 25

I woke numerous times with him wrapping an arm around me, pulling me closer, kissing my neck, my temple, tucking me tightly up against him every time I moved away during slumber. And each time, I smiled. I felt so cherished. He is comforting, his heat reassuring. I'm just wallowing in his soothing ambience. He's the magic potion I've been missing. Gary could just never compare with my vampire seducer. This man is perfect. And when I say perfect, I mean flawless.

When at last I wake up and stretch lazily, I can see daylight trying to peek around the drapes. I turn to Marty and discover he's missing. I feel his side of the mammoth bed and it's cold.

Crap. What time is it? How can he have no bedside alarm clock?

I sneak out of bed and tiptoe to the open door. The passage is wide, the ceilings everywhere are high. The passage runs right from one side of the house to the other. I haven't even seen the rest of his home. I look at last night's clothing crumpled on the floor and banish that idea.

It's quite chilly actually. I'm sure he won't mind if I borrow a T-shirt to waltz around in. I flick the light switch and open his closet doors. Un-fucking-believable. This man doesn't own a single T-shirt. Button up shirts only. Sigh. Reluctantly, I pull my clothes on, which are somehow all collected together in the bedroom, run a cursory hand through my hair, and walk to the bathroom. I brush my teeth with my finger, wash my face, and go in search of the man.

I love the way he reacted to the huge mess we made last night with the water. "It's just water, let it dry on its own." Wow! He's Gary's polar opposite. These rooms are gigantic. Everything is so simplistic. A mixture of Spartan and Japanese from a non-clutter perspective. He has those huge Bedouin type throws on the walls in every room, even the ginormous entrance hall. There's a faint waft of incense. Who is this guy?

Voices? Mumbling. Who's he talking to so softly?

I keep walking until I reach the very last door. It's the only one closed. Softly, I push it open.

Wow.

The room is flooded with sunlight. The doors are open to a balcony. This is his very own pool room with a pool table dominating the space! The table is covered with scattered pool balls, their numbers as shy as me, half hidden from my perusal.

Ted gives me a brilliant smile, "Have a good night then?"

Now I'm really bloody pleased I put my clothes on.

Sheepish grin, "Hi, Ted."

He chuckles and takes his next shot. I smile at Marty and he gives me an austere expression back. Not smiling, just shooting me a fleeting wink. Well. That's a huge difference from last night.

Lindsay gives me 'the look'. Wowzah. Okay then. That look says, 'Hey! What the hell are you doing here girlfriend?'

I'm feeling mild vertigo. What changed? I give her the 'Whaaaaat?' look back.

Then oddly, just as fast as the vibe got weird and strained, everyone's back to normal. Last night was fun, but right now I'd give my push up bra to be at home. Lindsay obviously feels the same way.

"Come on Ted, we're going."

He gives her the 'Oh come on, don't be such a medieval slave driver and let a guy have some fun' dog-box look.

It almost works, because she finally cracks a smile, but insists, "Now."

Ted and Marty exchange the 'uh oh' glance.

I feel as though I interrupted something, like an intruder that isn't welcome.

Ted thumps Marty's shoulder, "Later."

Then he gives me his 'you bad *bad* girl' grin, and a quick wink, before dropping the wicked mischief to stare woefully at Lindsay.

She stares pointedly in my direction, "Coming? We'll take you home."

Jeez! What are you? My wicked stepmother?

Marty towers over Lindsay and quite assertively tells her, "I'll take her home."

This is freaky! It's like a silent power struggle over me. What the hell did I miss?

Lindsay looks at me again, obviously willing me to go with them. Why? Is there something I should know? Is he married or something? I don't want to go with her. She's in a foul mood.

I smile demurely, "Thanks for the offer, but I'm good."

Oooooh! Wrong answer obviously. She's scowling at me now and Ted almost looks apologetic.

Crikey. Work on Monday is going to be really bad at this rate.

She walks out. Ted blows me a kiss secretly and follows her. Marty follows them out of the room to show them out, and seems so serious. I'm not sure what to think. Am I the bad news, or is he? Are they trying to protect him from me, or me from him? Then what was last night about? I thought they did it deliberately.

A weighted, happy-bubble-destroying sigh leaves me as I stare out at the glorious day. Now I'm worried. I have tension grinding into my stomach lining and feel like somehow I'm in trouble.

I jump as arms wrap around me and Mr Perfect kisses my neck.

"Good morning, beautiful."

Oh melt me, why don't you? This guy's voice was made to seduce. I turn and face him. The warmth is back. Was he getting a grilling from Lindsay? I return the succulent smile he's loving me with. I am so screwed. This man is addictive. "What was that about?"

He looks out at the day highlighting his secluded mini forest of a garden, way above my height, "Nothing."

I envy tall people. They get to hide their eyes just because they're so tall and their vantage point is so elevated.

He lifts my hand and kisses it, "Coffee?"

I shake my head. I really want to escape. I'm feeling unsettled. "Home."

His hazel eyes hone on me swiftly and I read confusion there. Shit. He thinks that I see this as just a one-nighter. And I was just getting that vibe myself.

He nods. "Okay."

He turns and leaves me there. Wow, long legs must rock! Imagine crossing a room and out the door in four strides. I'm really feeling lost. I don't know what would be appropriate. So I wander back out of the room and down the wide passage. Curiously I dawdle past huge rooms and peer in nonchalantly.

I spy him striding out of the farthest room, his bedroom, keys in hand, sunglasses propped perfectly on his head. Casually, "Have you got everything?"

I scramble. He doesn't mess around. Straight to business. I dash into his room and grab my smokes and lighter. I hurry to meet him back in the entrance hall. My eyes savouring the moment of a tall, hot man, in black jeans watching me. He could even be a model, he's got the build and the height. I still don't know anything about him. As I reach him, he slips an arm around my waist, holding me tightly against him for a moment, before guiding me with strange familiarity out of the front door and down the steps to his waiting car.

That small gesture lets me know we're okay. That whatever happened earlier wasn't my fault, or affecting him and how he feels about me. I smile, thrilled as the door is opened for me. I stare at the sunglasses and wish I could see his eyes. I can't define the drive home. He was withdrawn. Quiet. It still feels stilted and awkward.

I reason that what's done is done. I'll probably never see him again. No point in making anyone feel uncomfortable. He halts the vehicle in front of my door and I unclip the safety-belt and smile at the sunglasses, perfectly outlining an aristocratic nose poised above delectable sensual lips. I smirk slightly at the stubble. Somehow, he doesn't do scruffy.

"Thanks."

I don't try to kiss him, or touch him, or make false promises. As I turn to open the door, his hand shoots out and grabs mine. I pause and watch him, guarded. He slips the sunglasses onto his head and stares hard at me.

He kisses my hand, holds onto it, "I had fun."

I smile back, "Me too." I step out and whisper, "Bye."

I don't wait for a response. I shut the door and walk to my front door. I unlock it, walk through it, raise my hand at the hunkamasaurous staring at me through an open window, sunglasses back in place, wave briefly and shut the door.

I slide down it and sit on the carpet, wondering what the hell I've just done. I want to jump with unrestrained joy at finding Mr Perfect. But Lindsay and Ted just ruined it all. Now I'm completely unsure and I just know that Lindsay will have my head on the office block tomorrow. But why? Why introduce me to Marty, leave me alone with him, if she didn't want us to ever hook up? Surely it was a possibility?

Tired, I walk straight to the bathroom and start running a bath. It's time to wash off his kisses.

* * *

I'm listening to music, SBI have the perfect song – the candles lit, feeling relaxed and safe, when my doorbell sounds at exactly seven o'clock. I look through the spy hole and whoever it is, is tall. I can't see who it is because the light bulb is obviously gone outside the door.

Worried, I open it. Instantaneously my heart is in my throat, a happy smile lighting up my face, my eyes glowing at a mischievously smiling Marty on the other side of my repaired security gate.

Sweet lust-dust this man is uncut temptation begging to be shot straight into my veins. He's lounging casually against the wall, a tub of ice-cream in each hand. He exudes 'cool cat'. He holds up one hand, then the other, "I didn't know if you preferred vanilla or chocolate, so I got both."

A laugh bubbles up out of me, as I unlock the gate and let him in. My heart is bouncing off the walls like a squash ball at this unexpected surprise.

He pauses in front of me and lowers his head. No resistance here. I kiss him back eagerly. Hmmmm, he doesn't stop. He just follows hot breath and warm lips with more warm lips and pressure. Each kiss longer than the last. He's still holding ice-cream in each hand but wow, whatever kissing class he went to, he got his Master's degree: Professor Kiss. He could conquer the world with his kisses. Maybe he's a Casanova? My laugh ruins the moment. He grins at me, his eyes dancing with dark mystery as he nudges his head at my kitchen, "In here?"

I nod, and watch his suave stroll into the room close to the front door. Those jeans just suction over his derriére like ganache on twin cupcakes. Yummy doesn't do him justice. I lock the door and gate, and move to wrap my arms around his waist, my head tilting back as

I join him in my tiny kitchen a fifth the size of his. "This is a nice surprise."

His happy smile just warms me to my toes, melting my nervous system on its way down. He's teasing as he lowers his nose closer to mine, a smile dancing at the corners of his mouth, "Good thing you were home."

Oh slurp! He wraps his arms around me and just lifts me right up off the floor to kiss me. I can't describe it to you. But his embrace, the way I feel with him, the way I respond just to his presence, before he's even touched me, I feel home. He makes me believe in soul mates and happy endings. Gary was never like this. I never, ever, felt this happy or safe, with Gary. I didn't react this way to Gary. Marty has a gentleness inside him. He's tender and warm whilst simultaneously being reassuring and confident. I let him prop me against the counter top to rain kisses down my neck, his hands already feel familiar. I know it's early but I swear I'm feeling love for this man.

He pulls away, smiling at me. I can't help but react in kind. He fumbles through the drawer next to my leg and pulls out two spoons. "Chocolate or vanilla?"

I shake my long hair across my shoulders as my head moves in disbelief, "Chocolate."

He grins and lifts me off the counter with one arm. Go Mr Perfect! He laces his long fingers through mine and picks up the chocolate tub and walks me back to the lounge. It's as if he's always known me. He manages to make himself perfectly at home. He flops down onto the carpet, reaching his long arm up, hooking my hand and tugging me down to join him. He says nothing. His eyes warm, flirtatious, naughty, playful. He pops the lid off the tub and dips a spoon into it. Chuckling, he wipes the cold wet chocolate across my mouth, holding me down with one hand, he starts kissing and licking the chocolate off my lips.

I collapse, relaxed next to him, giggling happily as I let Mr Perfect make chocolate ice-cream instantly, and forever, a memorable experience. It didn't take him long to find out I was ticklish. Lying on the floor looking up into his dark reflecting eyes, happy to just be with him, my wavy blond hair splayed around me, he starts tickling my knees, then my waist and hip bone. I am squealing and laughing a belly laugh so loud I'm sure the neighbours can hear me. He is just **scrumptious.** I'm squirming to get away from his hands, he's laughing at my giggling, the two of us making a real ruckus, when my bloody doorbell ding-dong's an intrusion into perfection.

Breathless, I crawl away from his hands on my blue jeaned knees, before standing up, cheeks flushed, a happy smile smirking across my face, I open the door without looking first. My heart instantly plummets as I stare into the disapproving faces of Graham and Cindy. I swallow heavily, my breathing has vanished as I stare at the past invading my future, waiting to be let in. How the hell do they know where I live?

Graham looks past me, to Marty lying with his shoes kicked off, still sprawling on my floor, watching him with unfeigned interest. Graham's grey eyes swivel to mine, "Hello, Stefanie."

He could have been the schoolmaster and me the naughty child with that tone. Marty notices and sits up, pulling his shoes back towards him, as I nod woodenly and look to Cindy, who's now glaring at me.

"We thought we'd come over to say hi. We were worried about you being all alone."

Graham adds coldly, "But you aren't alone. That didn't take you long."

"Aren't you going to invite us in?"

I look at Cindy and sigh heavily. *Fuck.* Here goes nothing.

I unlock the gate and stand aside, "Come on in."

I look to Marty, who's giving me his 'I sense all' reassuring warm glances, sensing my discomfort and their disapproval.

"Marty, this is Cindy and Graham." Then to them "Guys, this is my friend Marty."

What the hell am I going to say? He isn't my boyfriend yet. I'm not sure if we're even dating. But a friend, yes, I think so.

Graham squares up, he's thick set but much shorter than Marty, he shakes Marty's hand, "Hi."

Cindy just shoots him the once over and comments sarcastically, "Nice to meet you."

I stare at them, they are unwelcome. "We were busy, I wasn't expecting company."

Cindy doesn't mess around, she flicks her long curly blonde hair a-la-bitch mode and stares at me. "So, is this your new boyfriend?"

I look at Marty, I want to laugh so badly. He grins at me and shrugs. I look back down at the impertinent haughtiness confronting me, "I hope so."

Well, that just snapped something in Graham, he shoves a finger into Marty's chest, "Who the hell are you? Couldn't wait?"

He glares at me then, "I never figured you were such a slut." He grabs Cindy's hand, "Come on, we're leaving."

I'm appalled, embarrassed. Somehow they have ruined a delightful evening.

Marty shoots me a wink, "Don't bother. I should go." He smiles at me, "I'll call you."

Before I can say three "ums" he's gone. I stare at Cindy and Graham and I am livid.

Cue song: Andrew Chester, 'Understand'.

"Who the hell do you think you are? Gary can date, but I can't?"

Graham glares down his nose at me, "Gary did well to get rid of you. Now I understand his problem perfectly. Cindy insisted that we had it all wrong. But you aren't pining over Gary one bit. Slut."

I feel as if he slapped me. *Fuck you.*

"Just go."

Cindy stares coldly through me, "**Fine**. I thought you needed a friend. I can see I was wrong. GOOD BYE, STEFANIE."

And, self-righteous and pompous, she struts out of the still open door.

The vacuum after this awful confrontation just sucks the joy out of my home as the quiet pervades. I slide down the closed door, wondering how I'm always the one to blame? I stare at the two spoons and the open tub of chocolate ice-cream sitting, waiting, in the middle of the room. I smile. Then I start crying. Did they ruin it? Will he run from me now knowing that kind of baggage is just waiting to jump on us?

I lost track of time. I was sitting in the half dark, smoking moodily, feeling depressed, when thumping started again on my front door. What now?

I drag myself off the sofa and fling open the door.

"Neville?"

"Thank God!"

"What?"

"Open this door!"

I unlock the gate and he pounces in, looking half mad and deranged. He looks around behind himself nervously before shutting and locking the door.

He grabs my hand and squeezes it, "Are you okay?"

Adrenalin starts coursing through me. "Yes. Why?"

"Gary is furious!"

What?

"Why?"

"Stefanie, you can't stay here. He wants you dead. *Tonight.*"

My legs lose their rigidity and I wobble weakly to a sitting position, looking up at Neville seeming terrified, wild and insistent.

He leans over me and emphasises, "He's taken a hit out on you."

My heart is racing as fast as my thoughts. I'm afraid, scared, angry, everything all at once.

"Pack things! Quickly! You're coming home with me."

Oh no! No fucking way.

I shake my head. I'd do anything, in fact I'd rather be dead than be alone with Neville.

"What happened?"

He stares at me as though my head is sprouting carrots, "Cindy and Graham left here and went straight to Gary's. I was there. You have to leave. NOW."

I hate that little snitch bitch. Some friend! I could SCREEEEEAAAM.

Shaking my head, "Thanks for worrying Neville, but I'm not leaving. I've got work tomorrow and I'm done being afraid of Gary. I won't let him control my life any longer."

He falls to his knees, grabbing both my hands in his, pleading, "Pleeeease Stefanie. I can't lose you. I only just found you."

Oh fuuuuuuuuuck. Shivers of revulsion charge my spine.

"You should go. If he finds you here, all hell will break loose."

He stares at me in disbelief. "Do have a death wish? Aren't you hearing me?"

Sigh. I'm drained, exhaustion claiming my rationale.

"Neville, **fuck** Gary. I'm not afraid of him. And I'm sleeping in my own bed tonight."

He grabs me and engulfs me in a suffocating hug against his cold, black, leather jacket. He pulls away and I can see tears unshed, glistening his eyes. He's really worried. He believes Gary will do it.

He stands and pulls me up with him. His hand holding onto mine. He whispers, "I love you."

Oh God. No. Don't **do** this to me.

I smile and pat his hand patronisingly, "I know. Now go."

He kisses the top of my head, hugging me again as though I'm already a corpse. "Please be careful."

It was a faint pleading whisper.

I nod, showing him to the door insistently, "I will. Thanks for the warning."

He pauses outside my door as if in two minds about leaving.

I take charge, "Goodnight Neville."

I shut the gate and lock it. Then smile sadly at him. He looks as though someone just grabbed him by the throat and started squeezing. I close the door and lock it.

Shaking, I switch off the lights and move to my bedroom with my smokes and an ashtray.

I huddle on my bed, light a smoke and start crying uncontrollably.

Chapter 26

Nothing happened. I sat through the night, sleeping with one eye, and one ear, open. The longer I pondered it, the more convinced I became that Gary was going to have me bumped off the planet. And if he was going to have it done, being afraid wouldn't change that fact. So, by the time I arrived at work, I had resigned myself to an early death, taken with a double, and neat, helping of paranoia.

"You look ill. Are you okay?"

Tired, I smile at Selene, "I didn't sleep well. Gary drama."

That gets her undivided attention and she drops the cards in her hand that she was about to file, and gives me a piercing brown-eyed stare, "What happened?"

Briefly I outline the course of events to her.

She leans back with a smirk flirting over her lips, "Stuff Lindsay. It's about time you found someone else."

I love her. Girl power support is just what I need. I'm dreading seeing Lindsay.

"Problem is, I don't even have his phone number."

Shaking her head, Selene chuckles. "How blonde are you?"

I'm embarrassed, and grin back stupidly. Ted and Lindsay arrive together.

She throws a cool glance my way, sans greeting, but Ted chuckles evilly as he deliberately saunters past my chair. Pausing briefly to murmur into my ear, "Good weekend?"

He doesn't wait for an answer as he swaggers to his desk, throws himself into his chair and casts an infuriating and knowing smile at me.

Does that mean he's spoken to Professor Kiss and knows? Did he say good things for me to have Ted's transparent approval? I push it from my mind. Work is work and I'm tired, and have a long payday ahead of me.

Just after lunch my phone rings.

"Stefanie speaking, how may I help you?"

"Well, that all depends on how far you're willing to go."

"Pardon?" *Who is this?*

"Don't play shy with me. I'm missing you."

My heart speeds by increments as I wonder if this is Mr Perfect. People sound so different on the phone. "Are you?" *I'm playing it safe.*

"We were interrupted and I wasn't finished with you or the ice-cream."

My heart bungee jumps across the office, "So when can I expect the next rendezvous?"

"We'll see. I like surprises."

I have an awfully mortifying blonde moment, "How do you have my number? I don't have yours."

Silence.

Hmm, not good.

"You're joking, right? Ted and Lindsay work with you."

My cheeks flood bright pomegranate, "Just teasing."

Ted starts laughing as my cheeks begin radiating. Belatedly, I realise that he put the call through to me.

"Later babes."

And just like that, he's gone. And I **still** don't have Mr Perfect's phone number.

Shayne sits opposite Ted, and he's been watching the silent interaction. God! I overhear him speaking to Ted.

"What's going on with you two?"

Oooh, Mr Suspicious is on duty.

Ted laughs and pretends to shuffle papers. Finally he stares with unfeigned "fuck off Shayne" written across his face, "It's a private joke."

Shayne pushes up his spectacles and scrutinises me. Great. Now he thinks I'm screwing Ted as well. I stare back, feeling cheaper than chewing gum, as he flicks his gaze to Lindsay, and thinks he understands why she didn't greet me. *Go on! Jump to conclusions. You know you can't help it.*

I sigh heavily. When will this day end? Maybe a bullet with my name on it is a godsend and not a curse. Being stalked by the angel of death is tiring. I just want to go home. Bullet or no bullet.

One thing I do, now that I'm Gary-free, is treat myself. I pass up the lift home from Selene in order to go to the florist on my way home. I buy St Joseph's lilies every payday. Or tulips. Sometimes both. I don't have a garden to grow my own bulbs, so I buy these as a

139

treat. Call me a hypocrite. After purchasing my flowers, I take a languid stroll home past Rondebosch common, savouring the waning day. Each time I do this, I get a knot in my stomach when I have to pass Gary's garage and his road.

I've got droplet-forming, hot Chinese takeaway in a stretching plastic bag in one hand. A bouquet of stunning flowers in the other, but I hesitate as I reach his road and carefully peer around a tree to see if he's home, before walking down to my road. My heart stops as I voyeur like a cheap thrill-seeker, as fate kicks me in the heart. His car is poised at the front door. And he's opening the door on the passenger side for someone. I squeeze myself behind the tree and hold my breath, almost afraid that he will sense me with his preternatural vibe sensors. I watch tentatively, as he helps a girl about my height out of the car. She's voluptuous, with very blonde hair. Without equivocation, the hate resurfaces.

Fucker. Why do men do that? Open doors for women, if it won't last? He never ever opened my door for me. Not once. Scowling, I feel tears splintering my eyeballs with cactus-like prickles, as I watch him wrap a sexy arm around her waist and pull her close. Intimately they stroll inside together. GASP. I hadn't realised I was still holding my breath.

My anger gauge reaches close to warp pressure as I stalk into the road and storm home.

Why? Why does he want me dead if he's obviously moved on? He's the one who dumped me, for 'an old friend'. But now that I'm anywhere close to happiness, I must die? That's so unfair. It's deranged.

... Pause ...

How long will it take me to accept that he's a psychopath?

... Play ...

The pleasure of the flowers, not cooking and the prospect of a surprise visit is lost as I reach my home. Every parked car is cause for paranoia. All traffic meandering nearby makes me hold my breath; my eyes focus unwaveringly, until the threat has passed. I almost run to my door and fling myself inside, hands shaking, fumbling with the keys to lock the security gate behind me.

Slamming the door in rage, fear, trepidation and relief, my eyes sting as I allow what I just witnessed, to fully hit me. I don't want him but it still hurts like Russian eye-drop torture, to see him with another me.

I hate you!

I fling the flowers onto the closest sofa, kick off my shoes, determined to reach for red wine and a cigarette. Instead, I form a human puddle of misery as I sink to the floor and allow myself to feel the pain of betrayal.

Sob.

From now on I'm calling Gary, Fuhquim.

Fuhquim. *Fuhquim.* **Fuhquim.**

Chapter 27

BANG BANG BANG BANG! THUMP!

I jump, jolted rudely from my miserable reverie as my front door threatens to leap out of the frame. Night has fallen, and I creep with anxiety to the door and sneak a swift glance through the peep hole. *Damn.* I forgot to buy a bulb and it's so dark out there, it could be anyone.

Taking a deep breath, I brace myself to face the Mob. Some huge, shaved, bald man, with a gun and a silencer, probably already lined up to the spy hole to shoot me clean in the eye, through the brain, dead. I unlock the door, ready for the release of emotional torture, called life. I take a last deep breath, tears left unshed, causing my eyes to sparkle, and open the door.

"THANK GOD."

Sigh.

"Hi, Neville."

He still seems frantic. Waiting with obvious impatience for me to unlock the security gate, which I do. He bolts through it, locks it swiftly, and slams the door behind him.

I stare at him in the enveloping anticlimax of silence.

He runs a hand down my arm. "I was so worried. I couldn't drive here fast enough after work."

Death is overrated. Who cares if I die? And why does this male always have to *touch* me.

"Neville, stop worrying about me. I'm fine. Gary's probably just stuffing with my mind. He knew one of you would tell me. He's probably getting a diabolical kick out of this."

I am so good at pretending to be in control and fine.

Cue song: Feedback. 'Fallen'.

Neville notices my food, cold, still in a bag on the floor next to the couch. He sees the flowers, follows the shoes, my bag; he scowls.

"I'm not stupid. I can see you're upset."

He flicks the lounge light on, blinding me momentarily, and before I can sidestep him, he's fucking hugging me again.

SHOVE.

"Would you like some coffee?" I query casually as I use the momentum to walk into the kitchen.

"No. Stefanie, tell me you're okay."

Repulsive shiver as he slides his hand down my spine. He always stands too bloody close to me. I feel suffocated and step back, away, towards the fridge.

"I'm fine. I just had a crap day, that's all."

"What happened? Did he phone you?"

Yes, he did. Mr Perfect did phone me. Secretive smug grin. But I know he's referring to Fuhquim.

"No. Why would he?"

I stare at Neville, wondering just how bright he is anyway. "Neville, you don't seriously think Gary's going to phone me and say, 'Hey ex, I hate you. You're going to die for dating'?"

Those chipmunk cheeks expand as he realises how stupid that sounds. He chuckles and wraps an arm around me, "Yeah, I suppose you're right."

Stop *touching* me.

I move away and start boiling the kettle. Moving as much as possible so he can't get a hold on me. He's like a leech. If he could he'd tapeworm me and be a permanent parasite.

"I think I will have coffee. So, how are you?"

Then he smiles the predator smile and suggestively mumbles, "Hmmmm?" as he 'affectionately' runs his hand down my arm again, lingering the hand in my waist.

An uncontrollable spasm of repugnance runs through me. His eyes alight, misreading it for eager anticipation. He steps closer, breathing all over me as he looks down at me suggestively.

I can't do this. This is **not** happening.

I step away, "Please stop touching me."

Scowl, as he folds his arms.

Inwardly, I sigh and roll my eyes. Why do I always attract the fuckheads? Do I seem desperate? I loathe being alone with guys who give me the creeps. Of all of them, Neville is the one who chooses to defy Fuhquim and stay friends with me. Just my luck.

"I appreciate the concern Neville, but you don't have to keep reassuring yourself that I'm alive. As you can see, I am fine!"

I storm around making coffee, wishing he'd just **go**.

Ding Dong

He moves before I can, and answers my door, looking at me as he opens it, "You should replace this light bulb out here."

Like I don't **know** that? Thanks for implying I'm an idiot and possibly retarded.

Oooh! A dreamy voice floats into the kitchen, "Er. Hi! Is Stefanie home?"

I get the daggers glare from Neville as he picks the gate key up to let Professor Kiss in.

YAY. My hero! Rescuing me from being alone with Mr Creepy.

Neville does the alpha male thing, blocking Marty's entrance into my modest home, extending a hand in passive aggression, assuming the 'I'd like to disembowel you' stance, "I'm Neville. You are?"

Marty smiles, looking down on shorter Neville; I'm watching it all from the kitchen, my innards leaping with glee like trampoline girls, "Marty!"

He says nothing else, but shakes Neville's hand, then catches my eye. I can see that he's finding this funny and I beam back at him, which causes Neville's cheeks to infuse with a dark angry red.

Neville pushes for information, "I'm an old friend of Stef's."

Marty doesn't indulge him. "Nice to meet you." He strides past Neville into the kitchen, and swoops me off the floor, my legs dangling in a bear hug. I whisper quickly into his ear, "Please don't leave me alone."

He lets my feet touch the ground, leans a hand onto the kitchen counter, and mentions casually, "Why aren't you ready yet? We're going to be late."

My blood cells run amok in silent rioting as I play along. "What time is it? I forgot. I won't be two secs. I'm just going to put jeans on."

And I flee, hiding my smile, into my bedroom where I close the door and flip on the light switch. After closing the curtains, I strip off my work clothes and hastily pull on charcoal skinny jeans and a black and white shirt. I'm thrilled that I'm wearing phenomenally sexy black undies, spritz on my perfume (I have expensive taste, but don't tell anyone or they might run for the hills screaming), and slide my feet into flat black pumps. I pull out my hair clip and let tendrils of long waves cascade around me, I check my reflection and dash back out before bloodshed ruins my carpet.

I smile at Marty and sidle up to him, slipping my hand into his, "Ready."

Then I smile at Neville. "Thanks for stopping by to check on me."

I want to laugh as Marty takes control of the awkward moment, leading me by the hand as he picks up my keys on his way out the door. He stands and waits at the gate, staring pointedly at Neville, "We're in a bit of a hurry."

Neville is obviously reluctant, but walks out, stops and stares down at me. I can't read the expression he's giving me. He takes my free hand, holding it, "I worry about you."

He shoots a quick glance at Marty who is now pointedly clanging the gate shut and locking it, but watching him all the same.

"Have a good evening." And he's gone.

But I do notice that he's waiting for proof that we're leaving. I so badly want to burst out laughing. There's a laugh-fest just screaming around in wild dorm-party mode in my chest, but with immaculate composure and restraint, I walk sedately with Marty to his car, let him open the door for me, pause and loooong kiss, hmmmm, such a fantasy-fest! And I settle into the car which has, thank God, tinted windows, so the spy can't see what we're doing in here at night.

Marty stares, contemplative, out of the window at Neville's car after he settles into the driver's seat. He turns and smiles that "'Can your heart feel this?' smile at me, running an elegant hand up my thigh. Hmm, he smells nice. I see he shaved just for the occasion too.

"My place?"

I smile back, "Sure, if you're up to it. Sorry but ..."

"I don't need an explanation." The ignition turns and his car purrs with affection back at him. He looks at me as he puts it into first gear, gifting me with a wink, before deliberately accelerating too close past Neville's waiting car, down into the darkness of the street, "Just have to get two things on our way."

"What do you need?"

Mr Melt smiles at me again, wickedly, "Ice-cream and smokes."

He has a knee repelling smile. One smile from him, with the twinkle of mischief from his eyes, just makes female knees repel each other. Hmmm, I wish I had a smile with that much power.

Cue song: SBI 'Seeing Stars'.

Chapter 28

I couldn't take it. After two weeks of intense observation of every single person walking towards me, driving past me, parking in my road, I was close to cracking. I couldn't take the tension any longer and decided to get crazy.

I waited until the office was almost deserted at lunch time when I picked up the phone and dialed Fuhquim.

"Hello."

"If you want me dead, just do it."

Strangled with mental anguish, my throat closes and I cringe at how pathetic I sound.

"What the fuck are you on about, woman?"

"Gary, someone told me you'd taken out a hit on me. I can't handle it. Just tell me where to be and I'll be there."

He starts laughing in my ear.

"I wouldn't waste the money on you."

I choke, in denial, angry at what I'm hearing.

"Woman, I derive far too much pleasure waiting for you to fuck up your life. You can't handle life on your own. Don't call me again."

Click.

The sheer relief overwhelms me. I fumble for my cigarettes and take an accelerated Charlie Chaplin walk straight outside. I hide on the steps, smoking, wanting to cry with desperate relief that my life has been hell for two weeks. For nothing.

Thank the stars I have a reason to get rid of Neville dogging me closer than my own flipping shadow. Five tears avalanche down my face before I rein in my emotions. I still have half a day of work to go before I can indulge in some relief wallowing. I think going out, getting shamefully drunk, and not wearing a bra doing it, is in order.

Selene is my number one groupie. Followed by James. We are closer than fingers. And tonight, my people are taking me out. I'm going to be irresponsible and I'm going to love it.

The thing is, Mr Melt is a photographer, often away on assignments. Most weeks I am free, and spend my weekends with him. We squeeze in as much time together as we can. He's not the jealous, possessive type. I guess my adoration and Professor Kiss worship is transparent.

That, and the fact that he often surprises me with his spies, Ted and Lindsay. Lindsay finally got over whatever issue it was. All it took was her seductive smile to break the ice. We laughed at each other, without either of us having to explain, or apologise, for whatever it was we'd done.

(See? Men think it's them only that have these issues with women. I still don't know what I've done. But yes, I'd be willing to apologise to kiss and make up.) We're back to normal, and I'm relieved. It has been two weeks of tension that could support a tightrope walker.

That night, I get very, *very*, **very** tipsy. But I feel safe with James. And Selene is almost as bad as Michelle when it comes to being the evil eye that keeps the predators away. Finally my life is back to perfect. Back on track, the roller coaster magnets are on full throttle. Perfect.

* * *

Perfect, for two whole months. I've found Nirvana and it's incarnated as Mr Melt. But then Mr Melt drops me on a Saturday. In a space as tight as a book and its binding, we are perfect.

We have a routine, I'm so in love I am already thinking marriage, when he picks me up on a Saturday morning, takes me home, covers my skin in kisses and nibbles, takes me for a scenic tour of the outer galaxy, lays back down next to me and tells me, "I'm leaving the country the day after tomorrow."

An invisible force has my throat and I'm struggling for breath. Someone is going to make haggis with my innards and they've started gutting me without my permission, and without a body I can see. I can feel the pain ripping through me. I can't breathe. I've suddenly become asthmatic.

Why?

Marty sits up and looks down into my face, propped on his elbow. He reads my eyes like an iridologist and starts kissing me. Deeply. As if somehow this can give me air. My flame is snuffing out, my heart just stopped, no kiss in the world can restart what has just been stolen from me. He's trying to love my hurt away and all I can think is, Why? *Why?* **Why** no warning? Why surprise me with it two days before he leaves? I'm hoping I am misunderstanding him and gasp.

"For how long?"

Please let it be an assignment. *Please!* I've done nothing wrong. I've given him all the freedom he needs. I've never demanded anything from him. How can he not feel what I'm feeling? He seeks me out. He's so tender and warm with me.

I've seen him with other people and his eyes are so different when he surveys the world. But when they catch my gaze, they soften, shooting celestial sparkles at me. You can't fake that. What did I do to chase him away?

"Years. Permanently probably."

He hasn't packed. His house still looks the same. I'm wondering if he's lying.

"What about your stuff?"

"I'm packing it all tomorrow. The movers will be here on Monday morning to collect everything."

"Where are you going?"

"Spain."

"Why?"

"I got a permanent job there and I have family there."

I stare up into his beautiful eyes, feeling robbed. I should be savouring every second but I can't, because I'm feeling so bereft. The grieving has already started. I don't get out of that bed. I stay in it, keeping him with me, trying to squeeze in a lifetime supply of Marty before he takes me home.

When he leaves my home, we kiss. It's the longest, most heartbreaking kiss I have ever endured. I love him. I keep the tenuous hold on my tears until he leaves me. The final good-bye; the last fingertip touch.

I wait for him to drive away and begin dissolving like ice-cream in a thunderstorm. I cried for the rest of the weekend. It was the last time Lindsay, Ted or I ever heard from Marty.

I never ever said, 'I love you' to him. But I did. He was, and always will be, Mr Perfect.

Cue song: SBI : 'Like Rain ... I miss you like rain ...'

... Pause ...
... Play ...

There is nothing here for me now. Nothing. I can no longer handle living close to the devil's spawn, Fuhquim. I sell everything I own, after giving in my notice at work. It's time for this little sparrow to fly.

I've put my clothes into storage, and have a job lined up in the big wide U.S. of A. as an au-pair. I love my friends but without love, without him, something went with him when he left. An essential part of me disappeared: the part that knew how to derive pleasure and joy from life. I can't find it anywhere. And I've decided to go looking for it. I'm taking a leap. I have nothing to lose.

The build up at work is traumatic. The girls burst into tears walking past my desk. Selene has an address book she's made everyone write in for me to stay in touch. It's an affectionate and aorta-tugging farewell.

Our usual crowd go out for ladies' night. But the magic is missing. The gloom of my impending disappearance mars the festivities.

Instead, we all just end up recklessly drunk together, crying, telling each other how much we love and will miss each other.

Only one more day of work and my days here are done. The following day I'm due to go to the embassy to fetch my visa, flight out is the following day.

It's been three long months, without a word from Marty. I've stopped hoping. He was the longest one night stand I've ever had. I don't regret it. For those months I was truly and vibrantly alive. More than I have ever been, or will be. Oh, what the heck, I'm not trying to get you to understand. You won't. Just take my word for it.

I have the hangover from Hades and I'm not the only one. The office is subdued. My shoulders slump further as my phone rings.

"Stefanie speaking, how may I help you?"

"I want to meet for coffee. I need to see you one last time before you go."

I'm going to hurl.

"Why?"

"Please?"

Long pause as I think about why the hell I should.

Another soft, plaintive, "*Please* Stef?"

Closure? Is this finally closure?

"When? Where?"

"My place. After work." I swallow with difficulty.

I hate him. I only hate him because I will always love him and he makes me nervous as a flat-lining heartbeat.

"Okay."

Whispered, "Thank you."

Click.

My heart has somehow split into two halves. One half in each ankle. It's an odd and painful sensation. It also means that my brain can't function. I feel blindfolded and as if I'm now running only on instinct and I need a smoke.

I stand up, "Smoke break."

My eyes don't want to focus. My adrenalin is surging and my heartbeat is racing to catch up with the speed of light.

"Are you okay?"

I mumble back to Selene, "No."

"I'll cover for you."

I nod my thanks, snatch my smokes out of my drawer and head outside. Once out there I lean heavily against the stairwell wall.

Just breathe ...

Chapter 29

With my stomach clogging my throat, I knock on his door. It swings open and I'm graced with a winsome smile.

"Glad you made it. I wasn't so sure you'd come."

I incline my head slightly, still not sure this is the best idea I've ever had, and walk in. I swivel my eyes, looking for clues, and quickly decide that the place is still the same. Everything but the new, black leather, lounge suite. I wait to follow him into it, sit down, and watch him smile smugly.

"Do you like it?"

"The lounge suite?"

He nods, "Yes."

I think it's too hard and uncomfortable. "It's okay."

I refuse to be impressed by his material acquisitions.

He leans back and stretches jean-clad legs out, hooking his ankles, reclining, his eyes slide over a more slender me. "It's good to see you. How are you?"

Why am I here, Gary? "I'm fine. Excited to be leaving."

"What made you decide to go?"

I'm sending out feelers, trying to sense why he's suddenly being so friendly after being such a jerk.

"Too many reasons to list."

Blue eyes penetrate mine, "I missed you."

Sure you did. You missed me like fire misses water.

I dig in my bag and unearth my smokes. I light one without asking permission. Exhaling, I stare at him bitterly through the haze. I hate being close to him. My body duels with my mind when it comes to Gary. He excites me, but my mind knows that he's a snake just waiting to strike, with enough venom to disable my nervous system and induce brain death.

"Is that so."

"You don't believe me?"

Incredulous, I stare coldly back, "No."

"Why not?"

"Well for starters, you said you wanted me dead."

"That was a joke!"

"Oh really?"

"**Yes**."

He leans forward, causing his arm muscles to leap out in definition, "Stefanie, you can't believe a word that lying bitch tells you."

Hmmm. So he thinks Cindy told me. "Why not?"

"She's jealous, and has been trying to break us up for years."

"Jealous? She's married, Gary."

"She hates to see me happy. I blame her for our break up!"

Crap. "Why?"

"She got inside my head. Made me think you were bad for me. I regretted it."

Sure you did. "Then what was the bullshit about 'an old friend' when you kicked me out?"

He leans back again. I'm amazed that his abs are still so flat and defined. He's closing in on thirty and still looking hot.

"It was a mistake. It's all fucked up. I should never have let you go."

Gary, shut up. Don't do this to me. "Well you did. So, who was she?"

"I'd rather not mention her. Anyway it's history. I've been single for months."

Liar. Who was the blond I saw you with? "I find that hard to believe."

His eyes focus sharply on mine, he seems intent that I believe him.

"I dated, but none of them came close to you."

You are such a convincing liar. I continue smoking. Time to switch subject. "So, why'd you want to see me?"

Well, that just changed the vibe in here. He's staring at me with such a perturbed expression. I watch him release the tension by standing and wandering sexily over to the window, staring out thoughtfully. I wish he wouldn't wear knitted shirts that cling to his shoulders. He's so fucking hot he should get fined for breaking a law. Stop thinking that; he's looking at you again. I stare at his captivating blues defined by dark, haughty eyebrows and long eyelashes.

"I needed to tell you something."

153

Like what? You have AIDS? And I might too?

"I'm listening."

"It's hard for me to say."

You are making me nervous! How bad can it be? I'll kill you if you've given me some life threatening disease.

I stare.

He walks back, and sits down on the coffee table. His knees an inch away from mine. He puts one self-assured hand on my knee, stares deep into my eyes and tells me, "I love you."

I recoil from him. *No. No. **No.** Gary, don't you dare fuck with my head and my heart again! Why must you torment me like this?*

The hand tightens, "Stefanie, listen to me. I'm not trying to hurt you. I just don't want you to leave without knowing how much I love you."

No! My mind is screaming in denial. My ears want to block to shut it out. *Why now?* "Why are you telling me this?"

"Because I don't want to lose you."

You have already. When you kicked me out for an old friend. I shove the hand off my knee, feeling angry, "Gary, I'm not a toy. You can't keep on dumping me and then change your mind."

He looks like he's going to cry again. *No. Oh, please don't cry!*

His hand, which he's returned to my knee, starts trembling. "Stefanie, goddammit. Do you think this is easy for me? You forced my hand by leaving. I wanted more time, to do it properly. To do it right."

Gary, your hand is hurting me.

"Please stay. I need more time with you. I'm not ready to lose you."

SNAP.

"No!"

SHOVE. Stand. Glare down into those throat constricting eyes, "Fuck you, Gary. You are such a liar. I've sold everything. I have no job. I'm due to leave in just over twenty-four hours, and **now** you decide to pull this shit on me? Why the hell would I ever want to come back to you?"

"Because you love me. I know you do."

You've got me there. I loathe myself, because I can feel emotion rushing up to overflow.

"And then? Then what? I become your victim again by being your housewife?" I grimace at him, resisting, and argue, "And give up on my dreams, for you? What makes you think you're worth that? I won't, Gary. I won't. I'm doing this for ME."

"Postpone it."

Why am I wanting to? Why are you so irresistible to me? "And then what?"

"Give me the time to resign at work, so that I can come with you."

He stands up and looks down into my eyes. Wrapping his arms around me, he implores, "Please, Stefanie. I'd do anything to keep you. I'll give up everything here and come with you. Just give me the time I need to sell this place."

I'm broken. All I ever wanted was to be loved and cherished. But delicious men keep on dumping me without warning.

"Gary, plane tickets don't grow on trees. I'll lose that money. This is seriously impractical."

His arms tighten as his mouth gets closer to my ear, "I'll give you the money to replace it. It's perfect, don't you see? You've got your stuff sorted out, now we just have to sort out mine."

My knees are weakening, as I coat his body with mine when he starts kissing my neck.

"I love you. I need you. Please, Stefanie, stay with me."

God, his voice is a salve, adoring and seductive. My mind is telling me no. But his argument is logical. And my body craves him. I drop my head weakly against his chest. "Gary, if you hurt me again, it will destroy me."

His kisses feel so good that I can feel my nipples hardening.

A throaty whisper in my ear, "I promise I won't." He tilts my head back, staring into my turbulent eyes, "I need you."

His lips cover mine, all of the old desires resurface. He knows my weakness. *He* is my weakness.

His hands roam, find home. He rests one on my throat as he lifts his head, "Will you stay?"

I nod. Knowing it's insane. His smile could melt the polar caps as a hand slips under my shirt to play with my nipple, "I missed you so much!"

I resist with a mammoth effort. Pulling away, I play hard ball. "One condition."

155

"Anything."

"You tell me who she was."

He looks fearful, but obviously is sincere because he gives me the answer, "Lesley."

WHO!

Chapter 30

... Pause ...

LESLEY! That hurtles my mind into the wall and smashes it in disgust. Of all the people on the planet, he dumped me for the biggest slut in my school. (I know you don't think this is a big deal but for me, it's huge. No comprendo?)

You see, Lesley and I just never got on at school. I was a good girl and totally disapproved of going to bars (underage), and sucking dicks to get free drinks from bartenders. Which Lesley did without conscience. In fact, every horny male frequenting the place knew she'd blow him for a cigarette – she was the best thing to hit the local pool hall. She spent half of her school life on her back or on her knees, instead of getting an education. I deplore everything she stands for. That girl doesn't have standards. She has none. There is nothing and nobody she won't screw. It's not a compliment at all that he went off to fuck *that*. I know how he met her though. He met her through Adelle.

Lesley *Bedspread* is shorter than me and five times heftier. She has boobs that hang past her belly button and has hideous acne scars on her face. This forces me to deduce that the only thing going for her is her mouth and how she can use it, because I know for a fact that she doesn't have beauty or brains, and after the sheer numbers of boys – (and teachers) – she screwed at school. I doubt very much she's 'untouched and glove-like' in the other department. Lesley. I'm gonna be sick.

Remember I told you about the girls who used to phone him when we were dating? The ones with balls? SHE IS ONE OF THEM. She was my biggest competition in landing Fuhquim? And now all I can think about is how long has this jerk been nailing her behind my back? It's been years since high school, but I can't get rid of her. To be honest, there's absolutely nothing to say to him. I am so disgusted he'd screw that truck. He dropped me for *that*. Not something cute like baby girl. **That** I could understand. No, instead he betrayed me. That is a state line he's just not allowed to cross.

... Play...

GASP!

"Sorry Gary, but there's nothing left between us. Gross!"

He looks like he's either going to hit something or cry. I have never witnessed him looking so unnerved.

"No, Stefanie." His voice morphs into whiny pleading, "Stefanie, please, you don't understand."

"I understand perfectly. You dropped me so you could fuck her. Which you already have. If that's what you like, then we aren't compatible at all."

"It was a MISTAKE. **Please**. God woman, how many times must I tell you that I made a huge mistake letting you go. I let that little bitch fuck with my mind and convince me I'd be happier with Lesley. She was wrong! I need you. Lesley is history."

I cannot believe that Cindy would condone, or instigate, him getting together with Lesley. Cindy does not socialise with Lesley at all. I know this is all Gary. He found her, or she found him, or they never let each other go all those years ago, and have been laughing at my naive expense for years.

Glaring at him, oozing disgust, "You are despicable!"

I grab my bag and start heading for the door. I pull it open, my heart pounding in my chest. I can't believe how much this knowledge hurts. This is a whole new low, even for Gary. How desperate was he for a shag, that her name came up in the black-book-Russian-roulette.

Almost choking on tears, I yank the door. I did everything, *everything*, **everything** he ever asked of me. I denied him *nothing*. But somehow that slug got my man. I hate him and wish someone would give *her* a bullet to suck on.

SLAM.

In shock, I recoil from the hand that slammed the door from behind me. It grips me, tight, by my upper arm. "THAT'S WHY I DIDN'T WANT TO TELL YOU. I knew you'd react like this. I knew you'd think I loved her instead of you. I knew you'd think it was a match made in heaven because of my history with her. **And it wasn't like that.** We got together briefly. We had a couple of drinks together. Yes, I fucked her, Twice, if you have to know. But it was just out of curiosity. The minute I did it I knew I'd made a mistake. I knew there'd be no going back with you if you ever found out. Why the hell do you think I tried so hard to hide it?"

I am fighting with his fingers, desperately trying to uncoil them from my arm before I burst into tears and give him the satisfaction of knowing he's hurt me. Twice? What? He wasn't sure the first time? He had to give it another bash?

SHAKE!

"Dammit, Stef, listen to me, *please*. I can't lose you, you're the only thing in my life that matters. I was so stubborn, I insisted I didn't need you. After less than a week I got rid of Lesley and haven't spoken to her since. I hate that bitch Cindy for screwing up my life. I hate myself for falling for her lies! Stefanie, please baby, come on, you know I'm telling you the truth. I knew the risk of telling you, but I did, I'm being honest. I'm giving you full disclosure. I tried dating, but they're all so annoying and full of shit. I missed you like hell. Baby, come on, please? Stay?"

His arms close around me and I'm sandwiched between Gary's muscular body and the solid wood front door.

Fuck. Don't cry, Stefanie. No! Not now. Shit.

My shoulders start shaking and a voice drops honey tones into my ear, "I love you, babes. I'm sorry I hurt you."

He starts caressing my back and I believe him. I need a new brain, because he's convinced me. He did know the risk. And it's blatant that he knows me and my reactions better than I do. He knew I'd bolt and reject him. But he told the truth anyway. I don't really have a reason to doubt him, do I? Is this the new leaf we needed?

The sheer anxiety that he might never see me again was a catalyst for the truth? Can we really have the dream? I know he's a magician. He conjures up things in me very few have been able to achieve. In a room full of men, I'd choose Gary over all others.

I'll never have Marty, and Gary did come first. Marty was perfect. We never had a disagreement or an altercation. But Gary is worth fighting for. I'll be damned if that bitch gets my man. She knows I love him. She's always known. And she just thrives on dropping her acid into perfection to watch what happens. Me walking away is exactly what she'd want. No. I'm staying.

I nod.

Finally, he lets me go and examines my face streaked with emotional pain. He kisses me so tenderly that it almost undoes my feeble self control.

"I'll make you coffee. Let's catch up. What have you been up to?"

And just like that, he changes gears, makes me feel normal, attractive, special, interesting.

... Pause ...

... Play ...

Three hours later as I'm sitting on the floor next to a black leather couch,(yes the floor is more comfortable), he starts to interrogate me about the real issue.

"Did you have sex with anyone?"

I nod. His eyes turn into icicles and he unleashes the demon.

"Who is he?"

"No one you know."

"But ... Shit, Stefanie. I didn't think you'd be like that. I thought you'd wait."

Why are you such an egotistical asshole, anyway?

With a voice saturated in scorn, "What? Gary, *fuck* you. You dumped me for another woman and you expected me to wait for you? You gave me no reason to hope for that. I moved on. Yes, I did have sex. You aren't the only person to get away with having a body and using it."

He's charged. I can sense the tension.

"How many men did you fuck?"

My eyebrows arch. I don't know why but I'm scared the truth will send him away from me back to megaslut. So I lie, "One."

"The moron Graham and Cindy saw you with?"

I nod uncomfortably. Mercury is settling in my stomach and it's getting heavier.

He bolts out of his chair and stalks to the window, "Jesus, Stefanie! I never thought you'd screw an Arab!"

He swivels and glares at me, "I don't think we can do this."

You racist prick! I never asked him what ethnic group he got his colouring from. It didn't matter to me!

I nod, feeling tears threatening again. I'm better off without him anyway. I don't respond and stand swiftly, making a hasty escape.

"Wait!"

I pause, with my hand on the door handle.

"I'll get over it. I need you more."

I slowly turn and examine his face with my cautious gaze.

"You promise it was only one. You're not lying to me are you?"

Yes, I am. And I know you can sniff it out with your supernatural super-sense, but there's no way I'm changing my story now.

"Promise"

Burn in hell, liar, the flames want you.

He nods, "Stefanie, I love you."

I'm stunned. This is already an emotional roller-coaster ride.

He nudges his head, "Come here."

Cellular memory kicks in and my legs respond to his command before my mind has a chance to challenge my emotions.

Lips trail down my neck, "Now I have to have you. You're mine."

Yep, you have to mark your territory with your scent. I don't care. When you do it, I am transformed.

... and like a lamb to the slaughter, I let him strip me of my dignity and clothing. Again ...

... Pause ...

... Play ...

The next day at approximately three in the afternoon, his phone rings. We've just fallen back into step with each other. We are both comfortable and 'home' with one another. I don't feel like a stranger in this place and answer the phone without compunction, "Hello?"

A throaty, gushy voice, exhales into my ear, "Hello, is Gary there?"

Office Stefanie kicks into gear, "Yes he is, who shall I say is calling?"

"Lesley."

My heart splinters into needle-like daggers, piercing my body in every direction. It's not too late to leave.

"One moment, and I'll get him."

But he panicked when he heard the phone ring and ran like Kali was after his skull for her belt. He's standing here looking more nervous than I've ever seen him. Ever.

I hand the phone to him, "It's for you."

His expression is transparent. I just caught the Master of Lies lying to me. Red handed asshole!

The phone, you see, is still right next to the door. My bag is on the table right next to the door. I pick up my bag, throw open the door in a flounce, and stalk away from him, forever.

Chapter 31

Okay, so forever lasted a whole fifteen steps at a brisk pace. My heart is pounding so fervently with outrage, that it hurts. It feels as though it's doubled in size. Since when did I give my heart to McDonald's to supersize it anyway? Maybe a supersized heart would help me. Get more blood flowing to my brain and injecting the dormant brain cells with much needed oxygen to see the big picture and WAKE UP.

A hand grips my arm and spins me around. The fright completely shuts out sound as blood pounds past ear membranes. Good lord, he's pale. He looks panicked.

Suck it up, asshole.

His voice filters in, gaining in volume, as my heart decides to abruptly deflate back to caged size.

"I promise that was a sheer coincidence!"

"Hmmm mmm." I purse my lips in total disbelief. They say there's a thin line between love and hate and it's true. I waver between the two constantly with Gary.

"*Please*, Stefanie."

Oh look, it sounds like he's begging. Wow. Gary pleading with me for a change? Not some doe-eyed baby girl. Oh shame, he's getting all choked up. Bet he never thought I'd have the strength, or self-esteem, to choose to walk away the minute he slips up.

Who's desperate now, dipshit? Looks like it's you for a change. After all the times I stood in those shoes, I feel sorry for you. Mistake number one for me.

"You *have* to believe me. I told her to go to hell and hung up. I'm doomed! I swear I haven't heard from her in months. It was just really bad timing."

Tears begin. Sigh.

"*Please, Stefanie*, don't go." All choked up and heart wrenching.

It's strange the way I'm feeling so detached to this right now. As if I'm a voyeur on my own life. Disjointed. Victims of trauma do that don't they? When they can't handle any more emotional pain, they disengage in order to cope. Is that what I'm doing?

He tugs my hand, "Come back. You have to finish your coffee. You can't just leave. God Stefanie, I'm *fucking* cursed."

And so, like the imbecile that I am, I let him lead me back into his lair. Unresisting. I have a soft spot for him. I believe every lie he tells me. I'm positive I believe him because he's telling the truth. But a huge part of me is always on guard, never completely fooled.

Not any longer. Although the sheer transparency of his emotional duress is going a long way to convincing me that he really loves me and doesn't want to lose me.

"What did she want?"

"She just called to see how I was doing. And to find out about you."

Yeah right! "Is that so."

He reaches with trembling fingers for his smokes, lighting one before staring at me with more tears highlighting his incredible eyes, "I told her when I made the mistake that I wanted to get you back. Of all the times to call me, she chose now, to find out if I managed to get it right."

"I'm sure she really cares about that. She's just checking to see if you're still available." Just call me Sarcastic Stefanie.

He turns from me and walks away, staring fixedly out of the window. I don't know why I'm being so cold when he's so distraught.

Eventually he turns to face me. I'm sitting down again, nonchalantly finishing my coffee, pondering whether I'm strong enough to handle the Gary ride again. He looks broken. *Oh no.* My heart aches just looking at his expression.

There's something about him being vulnerable and needy that just sucks me right in.

... Pause ...

... Play ...

I fell for it. I had to move back in with him because my lease had ended on my place. I no longer had an income, but was led to believe that it wouldn't take longer than two months for him to sell his home, give notice at work, and we'd be off on a huge adventure together.

To be honest, I was excited. I couldn't believe how lucky I was to be anticipating travelling the world with Gary. I was more than happy to do nothing while I waited those two months.

But I was no longer stay-at-home Stefanie. I couldn't be. I had friends. And this time I wasn't going to lose them. So imagine his surprise when the moment of truth came calling.

"Is it okay if I go out with the lads tonight?"

I'm impressed he considers asking me still. "What are you up to?"

"Just off to shoot some pool."

I nod and grin, "That's fine."

His face illuminates with an effervescent smile. I smile back and pry discreetly, "What time? Are you having dinner here?"

"Seven. Nah, I think we'll just grab something there."

Mental happy dance! It's Thursday night! Ladies night! I am *so* going out now.

"Great. I'll phone Selene and go out with them tonight."

Oh look, he's grumpy. Mr dissolve-your-pants-with-my-smile looks decidedly grumpy.

"What for?"

What the hell is that supposed to mean? I have fun with the girls. There is no way I'm staying home while *you* go out! The fire ignites in my eyes and I'm so ready to take a stand.

"Gary, I'm not sitting at home twiddling my thumbs while you go out!"

"Where are you going?"

"I don't know yet! I haven't called her."

He glares, "I don't like this."

Too fucking bad. I glare straight back, "If you don't want me to go, then *you* can't go."

What's good for the goose is good for the gander.

Gary hasn't heard the word 'can't' from me, ever. This is a whole new educational experience for him. I want to smirk so badly as I watch his internal struggle.

After interminable silence, making me wonder how he's going to react, finally he exhales "Fine. But I want to know where you're going, and who with."

I nod and grin, "Fine." I stretch my legs and strut to the phone. Making a point. Dialling Selene.

... Pause ...

... Play ...

I am dressed in my tight black jeans and a loose shirt. I'm wearing my Doc's, my hair is down, I have just enough make-up on to accentuate what I have that works. Pure Poison by Dior, and a smile hot enough to smelt titanium, I'm good to go.

I skip down the stairs with my bag and get into Michelle's car which is already packed with girls from work. I smile at Selene, Michelle, Julie, Lindsay and Terry.

"Hi!"

Selene smirks wickedly, "I never thought I'd see this day."

I wink back, "Me neither!"

Michelle interrogates, "So are we getting drunk tonight?"

The interior of the vehicle explodes with a chorus of 'Yes!' We smell like a bouquet of flowers. We all look stunning. I am delighted that at last I am in a normal relationship, with normal boundaries.

The first thing that happens once you are in the door, is the free drink. Which we down. It's our ritual. We then take turns buying rounds of drinks in quick succession. Within an hour my head is foggy. My ears are deafening and shutting down from the insane base pumping at us.

I get a mild kick out of watching Julie's shameless flirting. She's looks like a movie star, naturally. Couple this with those teeny-tiny heels she's wearing and second-skin jeans and she is a source of endless amusement. I watch the men behind her accidentally bumping into each other as they're captivated by her writhing form.

Selene is on my left, Terry on my right, we're all smoking and giggling. I am totally oblivious, I'm relishing the moment with my friends so much. I watch Terry's eyes light up as some tall guy starts walking towards her. He squeezes between us and talks to her, then kisses her.

Oh, this is interesting. She tugs my arm and yells, "This is John! He's my boyfriend!"

I smile at him and offer my hand, "Hi John. I'm Stef."

He leans his dark haired head down to my level, "Sorry, what was that?"

"I'm Stef! Pleased to meet you!"

He lifts his head somewhat and shoots a melting smile at me, "JOHN." And he shakes my hand.

I continue dancing and lean over to Selene to tell her who the guy next to me is. Terry is chatting away into his other ear. The loud music forcing us all to speak intimately into each others ears. Not that I mind, as it's La Paz from Scotland.

"So how do you know Terry?"

Be still my heart. I was so zoned out he gave me a fright. Smiling politely, I speak into his ear. He's so tall, he really has to bend down to hear me, "We used to work together."

He shoots me another cute grin, "Oh right! Yes, she told me that." He rubs a hand over my shoulder in a friendly fashion and queries by bending down, "Can I get you another drink?"

I nod and yell, "Yes please!"

After a quick query around the circle, Terry and John go off to acquire refills.

"He's cute!"

I grin at Selene, "He is."

We continue gossiping, dancing, giggling, eyeing out the talent at Stones, and I do feel very bad for John, as he's the only man here on a ladies night out. I make an effort to make him feel welcome by yelling up, "So where are your friends?"

He shoots the cute smile down at me, "Working late." He checks his watch and scouts the perimeter, and the bar, with his gaze, before yelling, "Actually, they should be here now!"

I nod. Not knowing what to say.

"You don't look like this kind of place is your scene!"

I arch an eyebrow, surprised it's that obvious, "It's not. I usually go to the Swinging Door!"

His face beams with recognition and it finally hits me between the eyes that he's dressed only in black, "Me too. I can't believe I let Terry talk me into this!"

He turns to talk to Terry and I give Selene a covert smile, eyeing out the heroin addict-looking guy who just sauntered in. Black leather pants, a laced up white shirt with long straight black hair like a Cherokee. I nudge her, "He looks like your type!"

She laughs, "You know me too well!"

A tap on my shoulder returns my attention to John. Two more tall guys are standing with him, one looking a tad too interested in me to be honest, "These are my friends! André and Sam!"

I smile at each, and shake hands. Then return back to my circle of friends, suddenly feeling awkward.

"See you later. It was nice meeting you!" He yells into my ear, drawing my attention back to him.

I nod and smile, giving a brief wave good-bye to his friends too. I exhale a sigh of relief at being just us girls.

... Pause ...

... Play ...

I can't hear anything as I try, as quietly as possible, to open the front door. I am much later than I thought I'd be home. It's just after two and I'm hoping Gary is still out.

My ears are humming from the sudden silence after all the noise. I have had far too much alcohol and am definitely drunk. I'm also really happy. I let myself in and slip my shoes off at the door. Softly, I close the door behind me, when the lights flip on, exposing me.

"WHERE THE HELL HAVE YOU BEEN?"

I don't know why, but I feel guilty. "Out with the girls. I told you where we were going."

"WHO WAS THAT MAN YOU WERE WITH?"

Chapter 32

GULP.

Jeeez! Fuckenhell, what's your problem?

"What man?"

He looks really angry. His face is pinched with rage.

Just look at you. Sitting in a chair, right at the door in the dark, waiting to be my killjoy the minute I get home. I've never done this to you, you know.

And in all of our years together, this is the first time I've gone out with my friends without you. So why the hell are you being so bloody anally retentive about it? How dare you spy on me, you asshole?

Annoyance rises in me as he stands up to look down his nose at me, "I'm not stupid. You're fucking me around!"

Lifting my chin, I glare back, I wish my ears would stop buzzing, "I am **not** fucking you around."

He grabs my arm in a death grip and jeers into my face, "WHAT IS HIS NAME!"

Seriously, I don't know who he's referring to. He saw me talking to someone. But who? The guy I said 'excuse me' to, as I squeezed past him into the Ladies? Or the guy at the bar that tried to chat me up when I was buying a round? Fuck it.

"Gary, I don't know what the hell you're talking about!"

He thrusts me away from him in disgust, causing me to collide with the kitchen door frame, "Lying bitch."

He has just robbed me of every single shred of joy I walked into this home with. I can feel the hurt stinging my eyes as I rub my arm.

"Gary, explain to me what you saw, so that I can answer you."

And why the hell were you spying on me?

With a clenched jaw he forces out, "The tall guy you spent your night dancing and flirting with. I SAW you together. **Don't deny it.**"

His eyes shout whore at me, without him saying a word.

Relief floods through me at the misunderstanding. I smile and sag, "Oh *him*. That's John. Terry's boyfriend."

He leans over me again and inches his nose close to mine, "Do I look stupid to you?" He stands up straight and scowls down at me, "If you're going to lie, at least try and make it sound convincing."

I'm so appalled. I watch as he marches away from me into the dark of the home. I stand alone, the cold of the tiles seeping into my feet. Deflated and hurt, I'm not sure what to do.

I spy him storming back with a pillow and a blanket, which he throws with amazing precision onto the couch, "You're sleeping there tonight."

You know what? I'm very angry myself now. *How dare you assume I'm guilty.*

"Gary, stop being such an asshole. I did nothing wrong. It's not my fault that Terry brought her man to ladies night. I didn't do anything with him ..."

"You TOUCHED him. You had your hand on his arm! I SAW you!"

I flinch at the sudden shouting in the quiet of the early morning, and argue back, "Gary, did you see how tall he was? I had to stand on tiptoes to talk to him. I touched his arm to keep my balance. I was being polite. I felt sorry for him being stuck with us because of Terry."

Oh God, he looks like he's going to hit me. I keep a wary eye on his fists clenching and unclenching at his sides. Without warning, my body floods with fear. Maybe I should just leave it and let him persecute me for something I didn't do.

I wait and watch him, convinced he's just gutted me and my entrails are falling out. I'm weak and shaky. We're right back in hell again. Hello misery. How nice of you to come back and find me. I didn't miss you.

He looks like he's going to say something, but then turns and stalks away, slamming the bedroom door, leaving me alone in a cold twilight of an entrance hall. I sigh, and tiptoe to go and brush my teeth.

After that, I couldn't sleep. I felt so cold and uncomfortable. This leather is freezing, the chair hard and unyielding. I've become a bit of a bony wench, which isn't helping. I wriggle onto my back and stare up in the dark at the ceiling.

John was with us for, at the maximum, half an hour. Did Gary spy on me the whole night? Or did he just show up in time to see John with us, and assume it was the whole night?

The mental playback reveals John rubbing my shoulder when he offered me a drink. Gagging on tears as I realise that it did look bad. But why couldn't he have confronted me right there and then? It could all have been cleared up. But no. Instead he has to do this to me. Now, when I have no security. No home of my own. No job. Now, he's trying to destroy my life again.

I flop onto my side and begin sobbing. I feel so desolate and lonely, that I pray for death. The reunion of Gary and Stefanie just lost all the joy.

Bitterly, I realise that it's already been more than a month and he hasn't even tried to sell his house. And he just went back to the way things were when he owned my money. I buy the groceries.

He has his friends around every weekend as usual. I'm catering crates of beer and for food I don't eat, all out of my savings. I have to do something.

I wake up with a gaze burning a hole of hatred into my shoulder blades. I turn and survey Gary sitting in an adjoining chair, glaring at me, his mouth tight with disapproval.

"You look like a slut."

Good morning to you too.

"How can you go out dressed like that?"

I sit up and sleepily observe my wicked master, "I am wearing jeans, Gary. I'd hardly call this a slutty outfit."

My mind instantly jumps to Selene's dress that she had me wear from the Robert Palmer video, and I smile accidentally. *You'd snap your aorta if you saw me in that.*

"So, you think this is funny? Coming up with a plan, abusing my trust, so you can fuck me around with other men?"

I keep quiet and fold my arms. *Go on. Get it all out of your system.*

"I knew it! Your guilt keeping you quiet? Worried you'll dig yourself in deeper?"

I sigh heavily and examine my hands.

"You are never going out with that bunch of slags again! **Do you hear me?"**

171

My heartbeat just accelerated. I have to fight for this freedom. He can't take this joy away from me. "Yes, I will."

"No, you WON'T."

"Yes, I WILL."

"Then get out! Fucking *SLUT*."

He stands, his face flushing with anger, he yells louder than I've ever heard him, "**GET OUT.**"

Oh look, he's pointing at the door as if I don't know where it is. My logic kicks into action. "Where am I going to go?"

"I don't fucking care."

"Gary, you fucked up my plans, and you expect me to just instantly have a reserve plan? I am here because you *PROMISED* not to hurt me. I am here because you told me you *LOVE* me. You haven't done *ANYTHING* you said you would. I am *NOT* leaving until I am good and bloody ready to"

He glares at me and spits out, "If you stay here, then you are getting rid of the tramp stamp! You were never a whore. Three months without me and just *look* at you! You are pathetic! I wouldn't fuck you now if you paid me to."

Ouch.

Good, because I don't particularly want you anywhere near me either.

I argue back, "You have a tattoo. How come it doesn't make you trash, but it makes me trash? I'll have mine removed when you have yours removed."

"Fuck you."

" No, *fuck* you."

He grimaces maliciously, "Not if you paid me for it, darlin.'"

I glare and reach for my box of smokes. My hands are shaking violently from the adrenalin surging through me. Survival instinct is at full throttle.

I take one out and light it, exhaling the smoke in his direction with as much disdain as I can muster without my morning coffee.

He leers toward me again, "If you stay here, that's going to stop."

What's going to stop?

He reaches over and picks up my smokes, crushing the box in one hand. "Enjoy that. You've just stopped smoking."

What? No! I've smoked since you met me. How dare you!

172

I stand up, now shaking with vicious tremors, "You can't do that."

"Watch me." He looks so triumphant, I feel like decking him.

"The smoking in this house ends right now. Look at you. You look like such a cheap piece of shit. Dressed like a slut, a fag hanging out your mouth. Throwing yourself at men."

If looks were actions, he just slapped me and spat at me. "Only cheap slags suck on fags. I'm not having cheap trash in this house! If you want to stay here, then you have to stop your whore habits. It's my house. If you don't like my rules get out now."

Final insult.

"I don't know what I ever saw in you."

He scrunches up the smokes effortlessly and drops them on the carpet. "Clean this place up. If you want lodging, it's time you fucking worked for it."

He turns and stalks out the front door.

Leaving me stunned, appalled, heartbroken, and as crushed as my cigarettes. My legs, weak, dissolve underneath me, and I collapse back onto the chair I slept in; a sob pulls out of me like a ghoul with a get-out-of-purgatory-free card.

Oh god.

Chapter 33

In a rage, I go and wash my face and brush my teeth. Angrily, I pull on my Doc's, lace them and stalk outside, slamming the door behind me. It takes me less than five minutes to get to the twenty-four hour service station to purchase a whole new box.

I am going to defy him. Yes, I AM.

Before I get home I already have one lit. I am so angry that I don't even feel like me. I know why I'm angry. It's because it's the only thing preventing me from crying.

The minute I walk in the door, I flounce into a chair next to the phone at the door and dial Selene. I tell her the entire drama in an unconscious stream of despair.

"Fuck him. We're going out again this Thursday too now. You can't keep on taking this shit."

Knowing I have her support somehow gives me calm. Yes, a plan was just what I needed.

"I'll organise for all the girls to join us. Stef, you have to be normal. That guy isn't normal."

Despite preferring not to, I acknowledge this. I am so jealous of girls like Terry whose boyfriends are so secure, and even want to join her when she goes out. Gary despises everyone I call a friend.

"Thanks, Selene. I need this so badly." Tears well up and I suddenly can't speak.

"We are here for you. I'm here for you."

I nod, too choked up to speak.

"Stef?"

A keen escapes my throat as I fan my face, struggling to respond, "Mmm..."

"Oh god. Are you okay?"

I clear my throat awkwardly, "I will be. Thanks. Have to go ..."

"Okay. Call me if you need anything."

I nod again, my face screwing up, tight, *tight*, **tight**, as I try to fight the anguish overwhelming me, "Okay."

"Bye."

"Bye."

I hang up and curl up into a foetal ball hugging my knees. I cry uncontrollably until I feel numb.

The automaton I have become cleans up the crushed cigarettes. I polish the tables, working systematically around the house cleaning, until I have nothing left to do but contemplate my box of smokes.

I sit down with a fresh cup of coffee on the floor in the lounge, all of the windows open, and I smoke five cigarettes in a row. Actually, now I feel quite ill. I haven't eaten anything since lunch yesterday. Unwillingly I take myself into the kitchen. I am loath to make a mess. I know he'll find fault with something and persecute me for another night. He's going to get the shock of his life next Thursday.

Dinner is ready and waiting when he stalks in the door, moody, pulling his tie off in rough jerks. He pauses in the doorway of the kitchen and glares at me.

"That smells good. I didn't think you'd still be here."

Why? Are you expecting megaslut to come and show you a good time, already?

"You know I have nowhere to go." I feel as though I've imposed on Selene enough and am reluctant to run to her haven. I know she'd understand, but Gary is the reason why I'm even here now. This *should* be his problem.

He stands there, silent, surveying my unhappy face. He knows when he's destroyed me. He's done it before. There's no hiding the fact that I've been crying.

"Good to see you've cleaned up."

Nice to have your slave back, fuckhead? I shrug in response. What was I going to do? I have nothing else *to* do. I don't even have a book to read. My life is in boxes in storage. And I'll be damned if I'm suddenly going to start reading his collection of Hustler to while away my days.

He continues walking beyond my line of sight and my shoulders sag as I exhale a relief sigh.

He sits down at the table and picks up his beer as he looks at the plate waiting for him. I'm picking at my food, my stomach and throat too tight to consider eating much at all.

His eyes stay trained on me as he takes a long swig from the glass. Unstrung, I watch the blue eyes and wait for the beast.

175

"Look, Stef. I don't enjoy fighting with you. But a man has to have boundaries. I don't approve of this new you."

I stare back, too afraid to answer.

He pats my thigh, "It's better this way."

Sure it is. Better for you. "Thanks for trusting me." I swallow the bile that accompanies this.

He leans back, and surveys me with a thunderous expression marring his amazing features. "What the fuck is that supposed to mean?"

I swallow the lump in my throat. "You couldn't trust me for one night."

"And my instincts were RIGHT."

I stare in disbelief. I can feel my bottom lip trembling, "Nothing happened."

"Only because he was more interested in your friend than you. You couldn't have tried any harder if you'd taken your clothes off right there."

His insult strips me of my humanity. My instinct is to cry. Distraught, I leap from my chair and dash to lock myself in the bathroom. Tight-lipped, tears threatening to drown me.

I stay there, until I hear him leave. I knew he would. I've been in here for at least an hour. He's gone off to play and I'm stuck here with myself, alone, again.

I unlock the door and venture out, carefully approaching the dinner table. His plate is cleared of food. I can smell his lingering scent and ache with longing and hatred. Miserably, I sit down and force myself to swallow my cold dinner, between sobs. I don't think I've ever been this unhappy. I feel so powerless.

... Pause ...

... Play ...

I have been living for Thursday. It's the only thing keeping me mobile, and preventing me from slitting my wrists. He hardly speaks to me. When he does look at me it's with anger and distaste. I count on him going out with the lads on Thursdays. I become agitated as he prolongs leaving.

His fucking sixth sense is in overdrive. He knows. How he knows, I'll never fathom. But he knows. The girls are due to pick me up at seven-thirty. He's usually long gone by now. And I haven't had a chance to phone Selene to get her to come later, because he's been oddly omnipresent.

I can't wait any longer and miserably go to the bedroom. I lock the door and get ready, studiously ignoring him with all of my might when I emerge. He's ignored me for a week. Well, two can play that game. Living separate lives.

I hear the car arrive, and the laughter floats in through the window. I pick up my bag which now hides a secret cigarette stash, some money, my ID and keys, and walk through to the front door.

"Where the fuck do you think you're going?"

"Out."

"Oh no you're not."

With great effort, I meet his eyes, as my legs linger undecided, halfway between him and the front door. The doorbell rings and I turn to it.

"Stefanie, I'm speaking to you!"

"I know. I'm not deaf."

He aggressively advances toward me, rage evident in his demeanour and expression.

"What are you doing, Stefanie?"

"I'm going out with the girls. You get to go out. I'm going out."

Laughter bursts out from the other side of the door and the girls sit on the doorbell. Ding-dong ding-dong ding-dong.

He's comes closer, looking livid and ready to destroy me. "NO YOU ARE NOT!"

I am torn. I'm afraid. Plain and simple.

The girls start banging on the door and yelling, "Hellooo! Stefanie!"

I swallow with difficulty. Terrified. I know that this is going to be very, very, bad.

He stalks past me and yanks open the door. He glares at Selene, "WHAT?"

Julie giggles as if she's already tipsy, "Hello. We're here to collect Stefanie."

Selene looks past him to me. She can see I'm ready to go, and she can tell by my expression that I'm in the middle of an awkward situation.

177

"Come on, Stefanie. Let's go!" All bravado, her gaze swivels to challenge Gary's.

Gary turns to me and warns, "You are not going out with that, that, *thing*!" His finger wavering behind him from his extended arm at Selene.

What have I got to lose?

"Yes, I am."

Julie looks like she's suddenly sobered up. I start walking towards them until I'm on the threshold.

"If you walk out of that door, DON'T think you can come back!"

I pause. My stomach is so tight I feel like I'm going to be ill. This is taking more courage than I have right now. I turn back and look at his face, reading absolute sincerity in it. He means this. I know he means it. He's the man that's told me to get out of his car in the middle of nowhere before. Gary doesn't mess around when he threatens someone.

"Come on, Stef. Let's get out of here."

I swivel and look at Selene.

"Stefanie, I MEAN it."

I turn and walk out to my girlfriends. Terry has said nothing. Her eyes are trying to overpower her face they're so large.

"God, is he always like that?"

I nod. Too choked up to speak. I get halfway to the car when the dread hits me. "I don't think I can go."

Julie immediately reassures me, "Of course you can."

I shake my head, "You don't understand. I have to come back here. You don't."

Selene wheedles, "Come on, Stef. You can't give in now."

I'm too upset to speak. I shake my head and my balled fist smothers my mouth to kill a sob.

"Sorry. I'm sorry you came all this way for nothing. Have fun!"

And I turn and hurry back to my cage.

I hear their voices calling after me. They even wait to see if I'll change my mind. But I don't. All it took was one look at Gary's face and I knew, I was never going out unchaperoned ever again.

Glare, as his voice barks, "Good! Finally you show some sense."

My eyes glisten as I stare back in silence.

"I never want those bitches near this house again. I am telling you this once. If I ever see them near you, we are over!"

We're already over. You hardly acknowledge me.

He grabs his pool cue once he knows they're gone, and the music is too loud for anyone to hear their phone ring. He leaves in victory, as I descend into the darkest mental despair I've yet encountered.

Looking beautiful, I sink onto the floor in the lounge and defiantly light a cigarette.

One tiny victory for Stefanie.

Chapter 34

I haven't spoken to a female, or been in the presence of one, for four months. Gary's life has not altered. His male friends pop in every weekend. None of them bring their female partners. I am beginning to think that I'm a secret. He doesn't speak to me unless it is absolutely necessary. The only person who can sense something is wrong is Neville.

Being alone so much has given me plenty of time to contemplate my predicament. Because of Gary, I have been too embarrassed to stay in contact with the crew from work. I am so humiliated. I know the entire office will have heard about what happened. For this reason alone, I haven't gone back and applied for my old job. I know I can't go out, and feel like such a loser, so maintain the briefest amount of contact with Selene as possible. I am ashamed. I am.

Gary despises me with every breath he inhales. His eyes are flat and hard when they encounter me. He constantly seems on the verge of violence. He always appears to be seething. I am so miserable that I can hardly force myself to eat and am wasting away rapidly. This is a spill-over, childhood residue. It's a habit I just can't seem to break, even though I am fully aware that I am stressing my body.

I am fast running out of money and can see no options open to me without a work wardrobe to wear, to apply for new work. My plans of going anywhere have gone out the window like stale smoke.

I have no conversation. Gary does not touch me at all. Which is saying something. Yet he is the most convincing actor I have ever witnessed. When Neville, Charl or Alan pop in, he laughs and smiles. He treats me normally as though we are in a happy relationship. I, on the other hand, can't fake it. And they all pick up on my less than enthusiastic attempts at smiling. I am on the verge of tears, permanently. I am so unhappy that I can barely function.

... Pause ...

... Play ...

"We're going away this long weekend."

I glance at Gary, sullen. "I'm not going."

"Yes, you are."

I suppress a sigh. He throws a pamphlet at me and tells me, "I'm paying for the food, you're paying for the accommodation."

I look at the cost and hate him. This will deplete my account completely. "I don't want to go."

"I don't care. You're going, because I said so."

I watch him, filled with bitterness. He stands towering over me, curled up in the corner of the lounge with a book I've borrowed from a neighbour. We ended up chatting when we coincidentally washed our windows on the same side, at the same time. She'd started bitching about a woman's work is never done. I couldn't agree more. And so we have struck up a polite acquaintance, and she lets me borrow books to read.

All I've had to read in this house is Hustler and Playboy, which Gary keeps piled up in pride of place on the coffee table. He thinks reading is for nerds. The only movies he owns are pornographic, which doesn't exactly entertain me. I am grateful for this neighbour. One small act of kindness has helped to keep me sane.

"I'm waiting."

In a huff, I unfurl myself and get my purse. I give him the money and interrogate, "Who's going?"

Because I know he doesn't do anything without his adoring entourage there to praise him for his wit, success, charm, and for being the hottest in their crowd.

"The usual."

I groan inwardly. Time for female scorn to add to Gary's persecution. "That bitch is going. I'd better not catch you talking to her."

He must be referring to Cindy.

"Who *am* I allowed to speak to?"

"Just watch what you say. I don't want any of them knowing my business."

So let me stay home. "Fine."

... Pause ...

... Play ...

The worst part of this ordeal, is that we're not going in Gary's super fast car. Oh no. Gary arranged to have his car stolen through some dodgy connection he has, so that he can claim from insurance and replace the car with a two litre something or other. I have been sworn to secrecy, possibly death, if I tell anyone.

None of his friends know. Poor Gary, such a poor victim of crime. So I am stuck in the back seat of Charl's car, with Gary. Charl has a new girlfriend. She's just horrid. She's built like a potato, loud, condescending, bleached white blonde, really vain and opinionated, and wears enough make-up for the entire Miss Universe line up. She reeks of crappy perfume and cackles so loudly, in her fake seductive way, every single time either Gary, or Charl, say anything.

I've brought a new book along, and pretend to be engrossed as they chatter loudly over Gary's selection of music. Before long we have Alan and Kristy trailing us, behind them we have Cindy, Neville and Graham. Everyone seems shocked to see me, but no one has yet said anything to me, other than hello.

It's a long drive from Cape Town to Mpumalanga. The joy of Cape Town is that the sun is so bright that it's reminiscent of Mykonos. The beaches are clean, wide and powder soft, with perfect cream sand. I love it. My heart belongs to those mountains and beaches. Driving inland depresses me. The scene flattens as we drive through the vineyards, before climbing the mountains. It's lush and green with fynbos. Proteas in full splendour flirt on the edge of the highway. Give me a surfboard and the beach over where we're going, any day.

Mpumalanga is home to the Kruger National Park. It's known for dry grass, thorn trees, and wild game, in a very hot and dry climate. Luckily, where we're headed isn't a malaria hotspot. Wretched, I watch the natural heritage of South Africa whiz past my window. Stunning wild eagles are overpowered by blaring heavy metal. Why do these people have to ruin the drive? The natural beauty and the way the scents change through my window, are devoured by suffocating clouds of cigarette smoke, fake laughter and music too loud and unnatural.

We arrive at a house in the middle of a macadamia farm. It's a glorified shack. Probably an old outhouse, given a fresh lick of white PVA, with its shining corrugated metal roof. We all choose bedrooms in the sparse hovel, put the supplies and belongings in their places. Off the guys go to explore. Naturally I am left alone with Cindy, Kristy and Trish the potato.

The vibe has been less than friendly, so I excuse myself quickly to go back to my room under the false pretence of wanting to finish my book. The bedroom door opens onto the lounge-kitchenette area. I haven't smoked for months. Yes, I am a wimp. So the thought of being with a bunch of girls drinking, bitching and smoking, sickens me and intensifies my misery. I flop onto my military styled bed, and open my book.

"What's her problem?"

"She's mentally unstable. Gary thinks she's sick in the head."

Oh really.

"She's so thin!"

No I'm not, I'm just not fat like you.

"Probably bulimic."

"I think she's anorexic!"

Why don't you two go get fucked!

"What does Gary see in her?"

"Well, we heard rumours she used to be quite wild in bed."

It's not a rumour, it's a fact. And Kristy, you aren't a saint yourself so shut the fuck up.

"But?"

"Gary doesn't ever mention her, so maybe things aren't looking so good."

Yeah, because he's an unstable prick who won't let me be normal.

"He's better off without a nutcase like her."

"He's so hot! How did he end up with a girl like that?"

He is so hot, but that's all he is. Keep dreaming Miss Portly Potato, he's never gonna go near you. I've seen his girlfriends, you haven't.

"Maybe he was desperate at the time?"

He was, to get me back.

"When did they get back together?"

"Alan said he took pity on her when she lost her job."

I lost my job? What the fuck!

"He's such a nice guy. I feel so sorry for him stuck looking after such a leech. And she never smiles. He's so jovial. How does he cope?" Trish says.

The twisting in my stomach is so severe I feel sick with rage. How DARE they judge me? And they're talking about me when I'm close enough to catch them at it too. That does it. I'm not wasting a second of my time with any of them. Fuck them.

"Shh, she's coming."

"Hahahahahaaa! Oh Trish, you're so witty. Would you like some more wine?"

"Oh, hello Stefanie, wine?"

I stare at Kristy being a bitch, "No thanks."

And I stalk past and escape outside. I walk blindly, not knowing where I'm going to go. I just know I have to get away.

Not far, I find a river. I jump onto a rock in the river, sit down crossing my legs, and continue reading in the blinding sunlight. I'm so hurt I feel like crying, but stoically maintain my composure, and pretend this is the best book I've ever read. I have no intention of going back in there. I'm staying right here.

I don't wear a watch, and I have no idea how long I've been gone, when Neville shows up on the river bank.

"Hey Stef! You coming for lunch?"

No fucking way. "No thanks." I fake a smile, "I'm not really hungry."

He shoots me an encouraging grin, "Aw, come on. We're missing you!"

No one is missing me, of that I can completely assure you. The only person missing me is you.

"No thanks, Neville." And I keep on reading to dismiss him.

"What are you reading?"

"Nothing."

"Oh come on, it's me, not some stranger. Don't be shy, what are you reading?"

I sigh, and show him the cover.

"Awesome. We should chat later. I have some books you might enjoy!"

As I said, nerds read. One thing Neville definitely qualifies as is a nerd.

I smile back. "Sure. See you later! And I continue reading, shielding my eyes.

He stands there looking pensive for at least a further five minutes, only leaving when he hears Gary's voice drifting over, summoning him back. Obediently, he turns to comply. That's the thing with Neville. He feels like the outcast in the cool kid group. He tries far too hard to please the cool kids. Not knowing how much they ridicule him when he's not present. This is one of the few reasons that I like Neville. I hate Gary for treating Neville with the same flagrant contempt as he treats me. The only difference is, Neville can't see it.

... Pause ...

... Play ...

As the sun starts sinking, Gary appears where Neville once stood. "Get inside and help with the food."

I glare back at his despising eyes, "What for?"

Oooh, he looks so enraged.

"Stefanie, for fuck's sake, must *always* make a scene?"

Is this for my benefit or for theirs? I stand up, feeling sore and achy from sitting on the hard rock for so long. I jump across and, with a mouth as dry as the furnace at the crematorium; I walk back to the den of disdain.

I overhear Gary complain to Alan somewhere outside, "She's such a goddam drama queen. If she's not the centre of attention she's like this. Do you see what I have to live with?"

I plaster a fake smile on my face and address Kristy, "Hi, can I help with anything?"

Trish, who is shorter than I am, lifts her chin so that she can look down her nose at me, responds, "Oh, you made sure you were too late to actually do any work. Did you think we didn't notice?"

Fuck you too. "Oh, I'm sorry. Well goodnight, I'm off to bed."

And I flee the suffocating attitudes by dashing to the bedroom, grabbing a blanket and covering myself. Fully dressed. I'll do anything to avoid this persecution. I am so thirsty, I haven't had anything since my morning cup of coffee. And now I'm not eating either, so I can't be accused of pitching up to enjoy others' hard work, being a lazy, good for nothing, anorexic, bitch.

"Where's Stefanie?"

Well, at least Neville notices.

"She's gone to bed."

"What?"

Mumble mumble.

I close my eyes when I hear the bedroom door open three minutes later.

"Get up and socialise with them."

I open my eyes and flinch at Gary's hate, plastered all over his face.

"I've got a headache. I'm going to sleep."

He leans over me and whispers in spitting anger, "You are making this very hard for me. Stop it. Stop being so fucking childish."

I close my eyes and ignore him.

Just for the record. That was the longest weekend of my life. And purgatory welcomed me with open arms. My misery was only just beginning.

Chapter 35

I haven't been allowed to consume alcohol either, since Gary made his new rules. Drunk women are cheap. Wow. So the man who regularly plied me with enough liquor for a frat party, now has a new view on me drinking or smoking.

Naturally, he's allowed to do both. He's allowed out. He has freedom, and I have dawdled to the brink of mental ruin by living inside his four walls without any normal anything.

I get up just before dawn and sneak to the kitchen and have a long drink from the kitchen tap. Hoping that's enough water to sustain me for the day. Quietly I slip out of the door and start walking.

I walk until I'm totally lost, in the middle of a field, far away from them. I sit down on the dusty dry earth with the ants and beetles, and start reading my book, but can't focus. My eyes are blurring with pain. I hate this place.

The sand is almost red, like iron oxide. It's hard, and dry, unlike the fertile black soil at home. There's no moisture in the air, despite the knowledge that there is a river close by.

It's fairly flat, the eye can see a panorama for miles. And all I'm staring at is long dry grass, and a smattering of trees on the land. The only nice things here are the few frangipani trees that line the drive in front of the hovel I paid a fortune to stay in, against my will.

It's hell being stuck in a bedroom with Gary. I haven't let him see me naked for months, and now he wants me to pretend to be a loving partner, sleeping in the same bed? Knowing him, he'll take advantage of the moment with a house full of people, all on his side. I have no idea where we are.

It's so isolated that there's no way I can even hitch home, if I even knew which direction to take. I cry for as long as I dare. Then I continue reading, praying for time to accelerate, so that I can get the hell away from them, and him.

I can't go on like this. I have no idea where I'm going, but I have to get out. I feel so stifled and persecuted, my anguish has become unbearable. I cannot endure any more.

Only once, in the distance, I saw Gary, Alan and Neville, wandering along a path chattering noisily and laughing sporadically. The sound of him laughing fills me with more bitterness. I lay back in the long grass to hide until I could no longer hear them.

I would love to brush my teeth. Maybe get something to drink. But to be honest, I'm wondering if Gary ever cared for me. Is he even vaguely worried that something has happened to me? Out here, in the middle of nowhere? If I'd been bitten by a poisonous snake I'd be long dead before anyone found me. His complete lack of interest exhumes heartache I believed I was beyond.

Skittishly, I survey sun blackened rocks. Lizards roam in paradise, here. Shocking yellow and electric blue lizards. If there are lizards, there must be snakes. I mean come on, this is me we're talking about.

Hiking up Table Mountain I was confronted with a yellow king cobra. Hiking the Drakensberg, my best friend stood on a berg adder. I am not known for my luck out in the bush. Do I need a better reason to prefer the ocean and flat white beach?

A part of me wanted him to come looking for me. For once, I'd like to see him smile at me. Possibly say a kind word. My heart aches with constricting pain when I think about how Gary makes me feel now.

He ruined my life. He clipped my wings just as I was about to fly. He wasted my time just long enough to burn every bridge, and then switched. He became the monster I now know: the one who has reduced me to nothing. I am not even worthy of his time.

I stayed there all day, and continued to sit there until darkness had slipped cold tendrils around me for at least two hours. I sigh heavily, wipe my eyes, and trudge slowly and quietly toward the only light in the darkness. That must be the house we're staying in. The cicadas are so loud, they are almost deafening. Good thing I'm not scared of bugs or bats.

As I get closer, I can see and hear them, but because of the absolute dark, they can't see me out here watching them. I'm loathe to return. I'd rather wait until they go to bed.

Kristy comes out onto the steps and calls Gary from the fire, where the men are barbecuing together, smoking a joint in jovial camaraderie.

"Gary, I think it's time you went to look for Stefanie."

I can't hear his reply because of his deep baritone.

"Gary, she's been missing all day!"

This response I definitely hear.

"I don't give a fuck."

And just like that, by accident, I got the answer to the question that's plagued me all day. Does Gary love me? Did he ever love me? Obviously not. I stagger backwards, a wounded yelp sneaking past my lips.

I stumble through trees, trying to put as much distance between myself and him as I can. I'm cold. I'm tired. I'm hungry and thirsty. And I'm so alone.

My hold on composure, and possibly even my sanity, is fragile. It hurts. It really bloody hurts. How many years did I give to him alone? I never cheated once, yet he did. Was it just to own me? Why?

Broken I cry, curled up on the hard earth at the base of a tree. There's nothing left on earth for me. No friends, no job, no home, no love, nothing. I am wracked, broken and I despise life.

I hate living. All it's given me is endless pain. Right now, I want to die more than anything else in the world. In fact, that's exactly what I'm going to do. The minute I get back home, I'm going to go down to the park and end it. Anything to stop this pain.

I fall asleep curled up against the cold. Shattered, inside a body still whole, despite massive neglect.

... Pause ...

... Play ...

I am jubilant when I return and they're all packing the cars. YAY! We're leaving. Neville rushes to me, putting a warm hand on my aching arm, "Stef. Jesus I've been worried sick about you."

I dredge out a smile, "Thanks."

Gary is glaring at me with undisguised hatred now. He doesn't care who sees him loathing me. What? I didn't speak to anyone. Wasn't that one of the rules for the weekend?

He stalks past me and hisses, "When we get home ..."

Another threat. I almost want to smile back. When we get home I'm going to kill myself. And I'll finally be free of you.

I get into the back seat with my book and start reading it all over again. I don't care what anyone says, I am ignoring them all. I just have to hold on to my ragged edges for a few more hours. Just a few more hours of hell, and I can run.

Except the devil is watching. And he's looking after his spawn.

My heart sinks when I hear Gary and Charl talking, on the drive.

"Let's stop and say hi to Adam."

God no! I hate Adam. And I can't keep hanging on.

Gary is so excited that for a nanosecond he forgets he hates me, "Hey woman? Wouldn't that be rad?"

I shake my head and whisper, "No."

I can't. I just can't keep a hold on my agony for as long as they decide to put me through even worse hell with Adam, Gary's druggie, lunatic friend. He's the kind of guy that would bump you off the planet as a favour to an old friend.

Gary's eyes narrow, "What did you say?"

Trish is relishing this stand-off, and turns in her seat to watch the spectacle with obvious glee.

"I want to go home. I don't want to go to Adam."

"You have to fuck up everything, don't you? What the fuck is your problem?"

SNAP

I slap his arm, hard.

"YOU'RE MY FUCKING PROBLEM!"

And just like that I lose it, like a ricocheting bungee cord I start raining bitch slaps all over Gary. He's looking so angry, embarrassed and shocked, he seems alarmed.

I have never snapped. Never. I've let him degrade me, shame me, cheat on me, lie to me, molest me, torture me, punish me and, not once through it all, have I ever retaliated. But I can't take anymore. I just am so hurt that I *need* to hurt him. He hits me back and I feel pain lance though my cheek as the burning spreads.

Wild, crazed, I start clawing and screaming, "I hate you. I *hate you*! **I HATE YOU!**"

Charl hits the brakes hard. Causing me to brace myself and stop hitting Gary. Charl turns in his seat, and points a finger at my nose, yelling at me like I'm his bastard three-year-old son, "HEY - HEY - HEY!" In a disciplinary tone he shouts at me, "You stop this shit right now!"

I slap his finger away, "I fucking hate you too."

190

Trish is outraged and reaches over to slap me again, "Don't you talk to him like that." She makes contact too.

I am crazed with anger and am ready to kill her. I thrust my door open and stalk around the car, yanking at her locked door. "GET OUT. Come on you coward! You've been bitching about me all weekend without ever having met me. I've heard you. If you have so much to say then get out here and face me fair and square."

Gary dives out of the car and locks his arms around me. Lifting me off my feet, "Woman, stop it. Please, stop it."

The cars with the groupies have stopped behind us. Everyone is gawping at me and Gary. Trish yells out of the top of her window, "Crazy bitch!"

I scream back, "Get out here. I'll fucking kill you!"

"Jesus, woman, what the hell is wrong with you?" Gary, naturally, has to defend the potato bitch.

He carries me in a human straitjacket off to a safe distance before putting me on the ground, gripping my shoulders so hard it hurts. Forcing me to face him.

Whispering, in a shaking voice, he demands, "What the hell? Stefanie, I've never seen you like this."

I can't take any more. I disintegrate. My shoulders fold forward as I start sobbing hysterically, "Gary why? Why did you do this to me?"

"What? I haven't done anything to you. You're the one doing this to *me*."

I shake my head as sobs and wretched howls escape from the solitary confinement Gary has made my my wounded life. "Why? Why did you date me? Why did you choose me? I can't do this any more, Gary. It hurts too much."

"Because I could. You were a challenge."

And just like that, the water stops flowing. The anger courses strength back into my bones. I slap him with all of my might, before turning on my heel and starting to walk home.

I have no idea where the fuck I am. But I'm not getting back into that car with that woman, because I want to KILL her. I am not going to Adam's house for more hours of misery. I'll take my chances.

I don't care if it takes me three weeks to walk home. I'm not spending another moment with that bunch of hypocritical, back stabbing, assholes.

He runs after me, "Woman, what are you doing?"

"Leaving."

"You can't leave."

"Watch me."

"Stefanie, come on. Be reasonable. You're miles from anywhere."

I pause, my voice screeching out of me, "*I. Don't. Care.*"

He grips my arm, forcing me to stop, "Woman! Stop this shit right NOW."

With my free hand, I shoot my arm up to slap him again. He catches my wrist. His strength biting into my bones, I'm so painfully thin.

"STOP IT!"

Through clenched teeth, I hiss back, "Fuck you. Thank you very much for fucking up my life, you fucking liar!"

"Me? What the hell did **I** do?"

I wrench my hands free and start battering him again, "WHAT DID YOU DO? ***WHAT DID YOU DOOOOOO?***"

Sobs start falling out of me. The agony seeping out like puss. Rancid, putrid, oozing wounds, kept locked up quietly in silence for so long.

"You promised. ***You fucking promised!***"

Gary starts crying. "Woman, stop it. I love you."

"***NO YOU DON'T.***" I shriek, wounded, howling. "I HEARD YOU TELL KRISTY, YOU DON'T GIVE A FUCK!"

"I didn't mean it. What was I going to say? You made me look bad."

I punch his arm with all my feeble might, "You don't love me. You never did. All you wanted to do was make me a prisoner and fuck up my life. You took away ***EVERYTHING*** that made me happy. I HATE YOU."

He's shaken. I can see him trembling. He looks quite frightful.

I sob, shoving my hand over my mouth, and continue storming down the road. Anything rather than go back there. NO MORE.

... Pause ...

... Play ...

The friends had a meeting as I stormed down the road toward the sign that announced the direction to White River. It was decided that for Trish's safety, Gary and I would travel back with Alan. Kristy, not taking any chances, would travel with Trish and Charl. And, thank God, we are skipping going to Adam's.

I can hardly wait to get home. This is the longest journey of my life. I see Trish and Kristy gossiping about the drama. They keep turning around in their seats to look into this vehicle at me. Every time they do, I defiantly salute them with my middle fingers. And every time I do, upset Gary is gaining in anger. Oh yeah, when we get home, Armageddon is going to look tame.

His face is a postcard for Judgement Day.

Chapter 36

As the car stopped outside Gary's, I bolted. I had my key ready. There was no way I was sticking around for goodbyes. No one knew my side of the story. And none of them wanted to. Isn't it easier to believe the fake victim, over the real one? Let's be frank for a second, by blowing up in front of his entire entourage, I probably gave them all the proof they needed to believe every lie he's ever told them.

While they are at the back unpacking cars, and offering sympathy to Gary, I let myself inside. Grab a jacket, because I am freezing, shove my ID into my pocket so that whoever finds my body will be able to identify me, grab a coke from the fridge because I am so parched, and make a dash out the front, where none of them can see me leave.

In under five minutes I've escaped. As if I'd vanished into thin air. When I left, I carefully placed my keys on the table where he'd see them, and I released the catch so the door locks behind me. I have no intention of ever coming back.

I cover the distance to the park rapidly, and take cover beyond the high hedges with relief. Finally I am alone. I wonder over to a large rock and sit on it, suddenly struck with the beauty and serenity of the natural surrounds.

There's something about contemplating death that makes you appreciate the world around you. When you're looking at it to say good-bye, the magnificence of nature causes tears to well in your jaded eyes. My heart pounds with a sharp pang of remorse.

The grass is perfect. It's lush and green. The trees sway with carefree abandon as a frame for the beauty. It's quiet. The only sound - birds twittering. I lay back and stare at the perfect blue sky. It's just beautiful.

Bitterness struggles to engulf me. Honestly, I just want this pain inside me to stop. It's all I've ever known. The joys have been so short lived.

Marty was a whole three months. My friendships are always cut short far too soon, before they really get a chance to flourish. I love to dance, but haven't been able to do so with relish because of the rule makers I let in to my life.

I wanted to completely immerse myself in the experiences offered on this planet. But I live in fear of judgement. My family would never be happy knowing I'd tattooed my body, drank alcohol, or smoked. They wouldn't ever approve of the music I listen to. Nor the clothes I prefer.

I've never ever felt completely loved, accepted or worthy. I've never been good enough. The only time there is no drama, is when I do what everyone else wants me to do. No one cares what I want or what makes me happy. It's because of this, that I can never go to them.

My mother has an insane need to control everything in her life, including her children. She loses her sanity sometimes, and you can't reason with her. And when she's angered, she likes to make you suffer: weeks of torturous silence, scathing bitchiness every time she talks to you. Literally making you feel despicable for breathing and taking up space.

There is no way in hell, or earth, that I would ever run to her for help. When I started dating after I left school and started working, she still scolded me as though I was ten. And she hated Gary for taking her reins, for dominating my time with hikes, holidays, dinners and movies.

And nothing could get me to ever turn to my dad. He's just as scary. Give him a drink and watch the dark side come out. I can't run away to family in my hour of need. Because of their scorn and judgements. I am here, alone, desperate.

That's what I tell myself anyway. In the back of my mind I know that I chose to return to him. I wanted to believe that happy endings are possible with your first true love. He was special and once was wonderful. I learned this lesson the hard way. Too late.

I have no money and don't want to go home to my parents. I gave him all the power and it's backed me up to a ravine. It's broken my will and my mental resilience. I thought he was good to me, considering mom and dad's volatile marriage.

But the truth is, I traded one victim role for another. I chose to stay a victim instead of acting on the signs that were there to make me run from him. Instead, the self-blame game that victims play had me running right back to him.

Why take responsibility for your own life when you can just hand it over to someone else and then wonder why they can't respect you? This is my fault as much as it is his. But that doesn't change the current stalemate or how desperate I feel. I've lost all hope and have nothing left to live for.

I sit up and unscrew the cap and take angry gulps. My last drink on planet earth. I brought the bottle deliberately. I intend smashing it on this rock when I'm done. And then I'm going to slice my flesh open and bleed to death over this rock. It will be such a welcome release. I almost can't wait to initiate my exit.

Unbidden, words come floating back to me, now that I have time to contemplate.

"He took her in when she lost her job."

Why does he do that? Why can't he ever say, "I love her, okay. I didn't want to lose her, so I fucked up her life instead."

"She's anorexic."

No darling. I'm just desperately miserable. I have to be happy to maintain an appetite.

"He's so jovial."

No, he's not. He's mean and vindictive. He has stolen every ounce of security and dignity I ever possessed. He did it systematically, over a period of years. Love is so very blind. I had to lose absolutely everything, before I lost the hope that things could get better.

I suppose it's true. You never get over your first love. Gary was my first true love. And that made him precious. As much as I truly despise him right now, it only hurts because of how deeply I love him.

Gary jovial? Oh no. He wears a mask every day. I am the only one who's witnessed that mask off. And when he's not wearing it, the beautiful man he seems falls away to reveal a cruel and detached monster. A man who does not care what he has to do to get his desires met.

It doesn't matter who he hurts or uses along the way. Gary has a hole inside of him that will never be filled. The first thing he speaks of in the morning when he wakes, is money.

He eats like a glutton, has sex like a glutton, consumes everything in his path, as a glutton. He's consumed me as a glutton, and all that's left now is this skinny shell. He's depleted me so effectively, that I feel constantly worthless.

He has persecuted me emotionally and psychologically for so long, that I don't even know who I am anymore.

I stare at the empty bottle, aware now that my time has come. I have a weak feeling in my lower body. I am overwhelmed with acute despair and remorse.

His words come back to taunt me. 'Only cowards commit suicide. Fucking losers.'

So, I'm a loser. I am. I've lost everything. This is the final sacrifice. But it's the only one that can set me free from this excruciating inner pain. Tears are cascading past my nose, as I stand up and jump off the rock.

I'm not a coward. The choice is easy. Death is easier than life. I am not afraid of death. It takes courage to live. So maybe I am a coward because I want to anaesthetise this pain. I want to kill it. Please God, stop this pain!

I turn to the rock with the bottle firmly in my hand. I've seen this on TV a thousand times, so think I know what to expect. With a fair amount of force I smash the bottle into the rock.

Ow!

Fuckenhell, this bottle is stronger than it looks. I massage my jarred wrist. That hurt. Anyone watching this would be laughing now. I am so pathetic I can't even smash a Coke bottle. I pick it up from where it bounced out of my hands, with the impact jarring my hand and wrist.

The pain caused me to let it go, and it bounced quite a distance. Angry with it, I launch it with all that I have, swinging down at the rock.

Fuck me!

I want to cry with the pain in my elbow and hand. Tears of frustration rise up. Why is this happening to me? Why can't I even break a fucking bottle? I pick it up and launch it, yelling with an outraged scream of frustration, this time not caring, JUST BREAK DAMMIT.

It shatters into huge chunks of glass. Wow, the glass is a lot thicker than it looks.

Feeling a faint thread of satisfaction, I pick up a large shard and seat myself back on my pity rock. I've had enough, I really have. Everything in my life is this difficult. Illustrated perfectly with a stupid Coke bottle.

Anger flushes my cheeks as I push my sleeves up. You see, I've had three hours to contemplate how I'm going to do this. I'm a blood donor, and know exactly how to find a vein.

I can't see the wrist thing being effective, to be honest. I've also considered the fact that someone might find me before I'm dead. And then I'll have visible scars that I can't hide, for the rest of my life.

This has just accelerated my inner agony. I've proven that I have a high pain threshold internally. How much fun has this life been? I thought it would get better, when I could run away from home.

Love? What the hell is that? Does it even exist? A deprecating laugh runs free from my throat. Am I bitter? Hell yes. You'd better believe I'm more acerbic than cactus juice on a good day.

Sobbing, I take the shard and shove the point into my elbow, where the almost green vein is always prominent. And I push and push. No. *No.* **No.** Goddammit, let me fucking DIE.

PLEASE.

I look at the thin skin and can't believe how resilient it is. I can see the vein. For heaven's sake does anyone have a piece of paper handy? A paper cut is more effective at drawing blood.

Determined, I start jabbing into the inner elbow. It hurts, I won't lie, it hurts. But I'm not stopping now. I want to die.

I swivel the shard, pushing the glass as hard as I can into my elbow, until finally I have a gaping hole. I pull the glass away and watch the blood come gushing out, baptising my leg and the rock.

Fuck, this bloody hurts like a son of a bitch. But I feel triumphant. I gave up control of my life, but I intend to choose how I leave it. This is the only thing I seem to have any power over.

It's flowing fast, and I'm unprepared for the sudden pounding of my heart.

It feels laboured.

Soon, every beat begins to hurt.

Well, this is apt.

Then the veins right through my body start to burn. Why am I burning?

I collapse backwards, smacking my head, staring dazed at the waning blue of the sky above me. I close my eyes, and wait for the peace of death to embrace me.

Cue song: Feedback. 'Powder'

Chapter 37

I regain wakeful alertness and am horribly disappointed that I'm not dead. Instead I'm covered in ants. They're crawling all over me. Little fuckers couldn't even wait for me to die before coming to clean up my mess. That sums up life right there. It continues around me, with gusto, oblivious to my pain, going so far as to smother me because of my painful spillage.

Fuck.

I sit up, my arm really hurts. I can't bend it. But, determined, I gash my arm open again. This time I keep a watchful eye on it. Night has closed in, but I can see, thanks to the illumination of a street light wearing an angelic halo.

This is disastrous, it stops bleeding quickly. I try to hold the glass in my other hand, to slash again into my unharmed arm. But I have no strength. I can't clasp it. Bitterness engulfs my mouth, suffusing a wretched aftertaste. Anguished sobbing begins, as I thrust the glass deeper and deeper into the arm, to resurrect my demise.

It's too bloody cold.

My blood just clots and mocks me. With my mouth twisting dramatically like the tragedy mask, I have to face the unthinkable.

I can't stay here. It didn't work. I failed at leaving. The devil isn't letting me off that easy. Ever greedy, he's feeding off my pain. I forgot he was an angel. He can probably manipulate situations just like this. Oh how gleeful he's going to be when I have to knock on Gary's door to be let in.

He's probably not even there. He's probably gone off to be pampered by his staunch supporters. Poor Gary. Such a good guy. How did he ever end up with mentally deranged Stefanie.

There was nothing wrong with me when Gary got hold of me. I was full of energy, hope, anticipation and joy. I was old enough to look forward to leaving home. To determine my own fate. But then, the dashing prince of darkness crossed my path.

Sighing heavily, I force my legs to slide off the rock. I am so dreadfully tired and cold. I'm aching everywhere. Darn, I even have blood in my hair. I really hope I don't bump into anybody. I don't know how to explain this.

Eight minutes later, I ring his doorbell, standing before it in defeat. My blood has soaked the entire left side of my body. My jacket and jeans are covered in bright red stains of pain, the edges already darkening. But the cold wetness of it strips me of the meagre energy I have left, after not consuming any fuel for three days. I'd kill for a cigarette now.

I stop breathing as the door swings open, and a refreshed and drop dead gorgeous Gary stands confronting me, with a haughty expression.

I'm ready for the scorn. Just waiting for "Loser! Coward!" to come lashing into my mutilated heart.

I glare at him and hiss, "I don't want to hear it, okay."

I storm past him, straight to the bathroom where I strip my body of the cold damp jeans and remove my jacket. Bundling them up I stuff them in the bottom of the laundry basket. Systematically, I wash the blood off me, and glare at the pathetic puncture in my elbow, causing my entire arm so much discomfort.

I put a plaster over it, brush my teeth and head for the bedroom, pulling on stretch pants and a long-sleeved T-shirt.

He appears, like the god of wrath, in the doorway.

"What happened to you?"

"Nothing."

"Jesus, Stefanie. Where's the blood from?"

I had a voodoo ceremony to curse you. I had to seal it with my blood and slaughter a chicken. "None of your fucking business. I'm just sleeping here tonight. I'll be gone tomorrow and I promise you, I'll never bother you again."

I almost want to laugh and say, "I said I was going to kill her, didn't I?"

He stares at me in silence. Then disappears. I wait until I hear the front door close. Launching out of bed I head straight for the kitchen where I pour myself a huge glass of water, grab the only tablets in the house and head straight back to the bedroom. I swallow as many of the headache tablets as I can. Until I just can't face swallowing another one. I'm feeling so weak, that all I want to do is close my eyes.

I replace the lid on the now half-empty bottle, pull the blanket over myself and pass out.

201

* * *

I'm woken by ice cold hands shaking me, "STEFANIE!"

I force my drowsy eyes open, and stare up into his mother's face.

I smile at the kind woman. She's the best member of his family. Maybe Gary's adopted.

"Sit up, love. Are you all right?"

"I'm fine."

Just play act the way Gary does. Lie your way out of your hell. Why won't anyone just leave me alone to die in peace?

"Gary's worried."

Sure he is. You lot will swallow anything. I smile with conviction, "I'm just really tired. I have such a headache."

"Stand up."

I sigh inwardly. Here goes. She was a nurse in her day. I'm about to get busted and have to go to a real straitjacket. Within the next hour, I'll be assessed mentally unfit to be allowed in society. The population is safer without me. Lock me away and lose the key. Set it in concrete and throw it into the ocean above the Bermuda Triangle. That should work.

I stand, and let her manhandle me. She pushes my sleeves up which thankfully bunch at the elbows, and examines my wrists. She even checks my thighs. Yes I know, I thought of using that vein too. Now I'm glad I didn't.

Satisfied I haven't tried to harm myself, she smoothes a worried hand over my face. "Darling, what happened?"

I can never tell you. But your caring is shredding my heart. I want to cry with abandon now. Why couldn't he be more like you?

"I just had a bad weekend, and am exhausted. Do you mind if I go back to bed? I'm very tired."

She hugs me tightly to her, "Sure. Okay." She holds me at arms length, tracing her hands down my arms to squeeze my fingers, "Call me if you need anything. We're all very worried about you."

I nod, "Thanks." I force another smile. I've grown to love this woman. I wish I could keep her.

I climb back into bed. These tablets really work as a sedative. My head is spinning, and I pass out as soon as my head hits the pillow.

* * *

"You're seriously fucked up, you know that?"

Goddam. I'm still not fucking dead! Oh yippeefuckingkayay. I look at Gary standing next to me, staring down at my slumbering form. I'm awake now. I resolve to keep quiet.

"I want you gone. You hear me? I'm not having some fucked-up bitch hanging around here to screw up my life. You're fucked up!"

I heard you. Yes, I am fucked up. Astute assessment, Doctor Fuchs. I pronounce the patient, fucked up. There is no medication available at this time for fucked up. Like a leper, she must be excommunicated as quickly as possible. Outcasts are not welcome here. We must keep the mask in perfect alignment. The impression we make is paramount. All fucked-up individuals must be swiftly removed, for the sake of our pristine appearance to the world around us.

I almost want to smile as I imagine introducing myself at my next job interview, "How do you do, I'm Fucked Up. And you are?"

"STEFANIE? Do you hear me?"

"Yes."

Cue: Feedback: Hero ... 'I'm a perfect stain, on your perfect name, and there's no comfort here at all, for your hurtful shame ... You pass the blame ... make me go insane ... forever hold off the cause of this stupid game ...'

He seems frustrated as he stomps from the room. Within moments, I hear the resounding slam of the front door.

I lay there for some time. Seeking a solution. Finally I find one. Cindy and Graham are moving. In fact, if memory serves me well, they have already left, this morning. On assignment, out of the country, for two years. I found this out when I spoke to Cindy's sister a while back. Out of everyone, at least she still speaks to me. They'll be renting their house out. I walked past it just the other day, and it was empty. Maybe I can call Cindy's mom, and get her to let me stay there for a week or two, while I apply for work? I just need a place to stay.

Chapter 38

You know what? I've just about had enough of this heathen's attitude for one lifetime. Seriously! Hurling back the duvet, I stomp to the phone and snatch the handset, punching Selene's number hard enough to jam the buttons.

"I have to get out, **now**. Please can I stay at your place?"

"So miracles do happen. Sure. My brother has a spare key and he's not working today. I'll get him to pick you up."

"I owe you more than I can ever repay."

"Seeing you leave that backwards prick is enough payment. See you later."

"Selene?"

"Hmm?"

"Ask Sinclaire if I can have my old job back?"

"Yeah, okay."

"I love you girlfriend."

"I know. You owe me a roast chicken!"

"Done!"

"Bye."

"Bye."

Yanking on clothes, I bolt to the twenty-four hour service station on the corner, purchasing smokes and withdrawing some of my dwindling funds. Rather pleased with myself, I return to Gary's home to prepare for my exodus.

Stalking into the kitchen, I unearth the clean ashtrays, plonk myself down in the lounge, and light three. Smoking one, I then leave one in each of the other ashtrays to burn themselves out, with all the windows closed. Just call me Shirley. I Shirley *will* do everything you told me not to.

Deliberately ashing on the tiles on my way to the fridge, I unpack all of the ciders into my cooler box. Rifling through the wine collection, I help myself to half. Actually, fuck that. Feeling like a fishwife with a smoke dangling from my lip, I use both hands to unpack the wine rack into packets; they're coming with me. How can I celebrate freedom from slavery without enough booze for a frat party? He'll only waste this stuff seducing other victims, so I may as well try and save them any way I can, starting with removing the ammunition from the corked shotgun.

Systematically I help myself to supplies, including the chicken that Selene will have waiting for her with potatoes and all the trimmings when she gets home from work today. Only people who love me will get to eat my cooking from now on. My newly discovered malicious streak is tempting me to leave the freezer door open. I battle it for a few minutes while I get packed; eventually integrity wins and I close the blasted thing.

With much pleasure I switch off the geyser. I wonder how long it will take him to figure out why there's no hot water? Giggle. I then take an entire box of tampons, unwrap them, and dump them one by one into his toilet. A little reminder of a woman scorned and messed with for the last time. Moving to my hairbrush, I remove all of the long hair wrapped into it, and stuff it into the shower outlet, running some cold water to secure it in there.

While I wait for Selene's brother, I sit and smoke another cigarette in the bedroom, on a deliberately unmade bed. Call me pathetic, but I'm thoroughly enjoying this rebellion, which in my opinion is about three years overdue.

It's a gorgeous day. The sky is such a perfect shade of periwinkle, not even a suggestion of a cloud anywhere, it seems such a waste smogging up Gary's passion pit for revenge. Grabbing my packed cases, I wheel them outside and stack up everything else I'm taking with me. I bought the groceries, so I own them and they leave with me. Selene and I will at least eat well for a month. I need some retail therapy, a great night out, and some cold-hearted flirting. It dawns on me as I sit waiting on my suitcase, that for years I've followed the worst example set for me. My parents had an explosive marriage, the kind where my mom always lost the war. We lived in the trenches, self pity and hardship became comfortable blankets in that kind of environment. But, one day she snapped, pretty much the way I did yesterday. I remember that day as clearly as if it happened this morning. Then finally she left him, taking us with her. She showed us how to take a chance, stand up for yourself, and how not to be a victim, so what the hell was I thinking?

Jarred out of my reverie, a dude with shocking blond hair down to his chin touches my shoulder. I give him my 'drop dead asshole' glare.

"You Stefanie?"

Lordy, this can't be her brother, it's just not possible. "Yes."

"I'm Lucas, Selene's brother."

Okay, now I know Selene has never introduced us before. She likes to lead a life her family has no access to, which includes her friends. I also know that her brother is at least five years older, but I am telling you, this boy does not look five years older, and he's damn delicious eye bling. I offer him a hand, warming up from my Arctic freeze.

"Stef. It's great to finally meet you." We shake on the introduction.

"This your stuff?"

No it's the neighbours, I'm just sitting it for her while she shags her boyfriend. "Um, yes."

My final insult, is flicking my cigarette butt into Gary's postbox. Oh I really do hope someone is witnessing this. I would love to see his face when he's told some hot man-popsicle picked me up and we drove off into a Doris Day morning, never to be heard from again. It would drive him to distraction trying to figure out how long I've been cheating on him with a new blonde-hot-sexilicious replacement. Trading up darling, this guy has a better view out his window. Actually, the car's a bit formal isn't it? A Volvo isn't exactly my idea of vogue. Haha! This may be even better, Gary can surmise I'm off to be a kept woman.

Yes I know, my imagination is in full pantomime mode. Anyway, so I'm helping Lucas pack my stuff into this car with enough space to hide the entire mafia and their cement clad victims, the spaciousness just pings the hollow in my heart with a sad echo. My life doesn't even fill a car's boot. It's super nice when he opens my door for me, and oooh, look at that, a hand on my waist that lingered far too long to be appropriate. I grin at him and wonder if Selene will turn him into a eunuch if I encourage this.

After securing my seat-belt, I lean back, stretch out my legs, and give Lucas a shy smile.

"Sorry I took so long, my phone was on charge."

You didn't take long at all. "No problem."

Ten minutes later, thanks to the absence of traffic at this time of the morning, we stop outside Selene's home up on her Prince Charming hill. Joining Lucas with the unpacking I ask, "Do you live nearby?"

He points up the hill, "End of the road."

You have got to be kidding me! How is it that I've never known this? How often has he seen me, and I've not even known he was here? I guess my face betrays me, because he starts explaining.

"I'm away on business a lot. Selene keeps an eye on the place for me. It was easier for me being closer to her for convenience."

Well I can see a huge drawbridge lowering down waiting to be crossed. "Would you like to join us for dinner?"

He stops with the key in his hand, pausing before pushing the door open, looking regretful, "I can't. I have a date."

Oh right. Don't I just feel stupid. Of course you have a date. Heck, you probably have every weekend booked until the day you turn fifty.

"Not a problem, I just thought I could repay your kindness."

He pauses outside her kitchen where he deposits my cases, while I place the groceries on the kitchen counter, telling me, "Selene doesn't like me talking to her friends. You're kind of off limits."

That sounds like Selene. She takes paranoia to Illuminati level. If he knew what I know about her, she'd probably get locked up in her parent's basement until she's seventy-five.

"That's cool." I'm trying to give the vibe that it's not any of my business and I don't want to get involved.

"Anyway, if you need anything before she gets home, I'm at number twenty-four."

I nod, feeling awkward, but offer him a smile,"Thanks a lot for rescuing me."

He shrugs, stuffing a hand into his left front pocket, "That's what friends do." He shuffles the toe of a foot into the other, staring down, mumbling, "See you round." Looking up, for the first time I get a really good look into his eyes. They're clear and sensitive. It's so odd, but I get the impression that he's shy around me. "It was nice meeting you. I've heard a lot about you."

Oh god! None of it can be good. "It was very nice meeting you too."

He smiles. Perfect teeth, great skin, gentle light blue eyes that most Husky's wish they owned. How can they be so different? Her colouring is completely opposite to his.

I walk with him to the door, locking it behind him. Standing at the window, I watch him drive away and pull into his garage farther up the road, the door closing behind him. He must have a door from there going into his house. Wow! I wish Selene had introduced me to him. But knowing me, she probably thought I'd be too wild for such a sweet guy. Sighing heavily, I go straight to the kitchen counter and unearth a bottle of red wine. I haven't had a drink in forever, and dammit, I'm fucking old enough to drink. I've lived with Gary's demented rules for so long, as if I was something to be controlled and restrained.

Uncorking it, I pour half of the bottle into one of Selene's gigantic glasses. Picking up my smokes, I walk back out the door, locking it behind me, walking around to the mountain to stare at her view. Settling myself on the same old pity rock, I lean back, letting the sun thaw the tundra inside me, rebelliously drinking red wine before noon on a work day, and lighting a smoke that makes my lungs ache.

I'm sad. I'm angry. I'm also lost. I don't want to stay here with Selene, I want independence. I have to make that happen, but first I need employment. I'm starting all over again at the ripe old age of twenty-five. The problem is, I don't know if men can be trusted. Look at the carnage of my love-life. I've had a series of dismal failures. What does this say about me? Am I not worthy of love? Sighing heavily, I succumb to my emotions, fuelling the tears with sad memories. Will I ever find another Marty?

Chapter 39

I spent the afternoon cooking the perfect meal for the best friend any girl could wish for. Selene has rescued me from my mistakes more times than I can count. The drama merry-go-round with Gary is so old, she must be sick of it and sick of me being on it and always running to her. I've organised for my clothes to be delivered out of storage, but pretty much sold up everything else I owned to get money to take abroad with me. Somehow, I'll find a way to get back on my feet without breaking this friendship in the process. At least with my work clothes back in my closet, I'll be able to apply for real jobs that pay real money.

* * *

Well hallelujah. Sinclaire gave me my old job back. I've decided men are bad news, and have started wearing a wedding ring when I go out, so the buggers will leave me alone. Selene is enjoying having me cooking in her house, and the wine, and Luke is off limits apparently. Just as well, we all know that good looking men spell disaster. Don't suppose you know where the ugly guys hang out? I was thinking that if I need someone to go to the movies with, or a wedding, it might be nice to have a plain old chap as back up.

Oh, I forgot to tell you, Selene has a boyfriend. He's super dishy and nice. Seriously, this dude is an ex-personal trainer with broad shoulders and a wicked sense of humour. He gives me hope that there are men out there who aren't messed up, and who won't mess the woman they're with up either. His name is Zeke, and he's my hero. Weirdest turn of events. Zeke lives up the road and needs a room-mate to stay in his spare room so that his money can go further. Damn strange, but his new roomie is going to be me. I'm beginning to think that the top of this hill is the place to find sweet hotties hiding from the world. It's the best kept secret in Cape Town.

Returning to work was like coming home after a year in the army. It was the best decision I made to swallow my pride and Gary-shame and get that employment back. Frank, James, Shayne, Julie,

Michelle, Lindsay, Ted, Dianne, just everyone really, wanted to celebrate and return right back to where we left off.

So guess who's going out to the Swinging Door tonight? Yep, you guessed right – me and Selene, Zeke and his friend Tom, and the gang from work. This gives me just two hours to go shopping after work to get myself a killer outfit. I'm planning on doing plenty of flirting, but this time, my heart's staying out of it.

Window shopping is fine. Even testing, like a free sample, or spraying a hint of perfume to decide if you like it, is okay. You didn't get that did you? Dancing, kissing, hugging, that's what I'm talking about, and of course accepting drinks is on the acceptable list, just no serious dating, not for a very long time; but, I don't think I'm ready for anyone new. Can't a girl just go out with her friends and not have to play the gender game?

...Pause ...

... Play ...

I'm alive! What is it about dancing that is so life validating? I'm wearing boots, and a strappy black dress to show off my new tramp stamp. Did I or did I not say, I Shirley, will? My body, my life, Fuhquim! Anyway, so this is fun, not to mention the interested stares coming my way. My esteem is finding this good ego-medicine. My mojo is coming back.

That does it. Relationships and me are like phosphorous and water, we don't mix well at all, therefore I deduce I will be a very happy single girl until I meet someone plain and sweet, about a hundred years from now. Right, so, would someone please tell that to Mr-Tall-and-Fabulous walking towards me.

Deliberately I smooth my hair behind my shoulder with the hand wearing the fake wedding ring, currently on loan from Selene until I buy my own.

"Hi."

I smile back. "Hi." He's been eying me out all night from the other side of the dance floor. And he's tall enough to see right over everyone's heads. How tall is that exactly? About six-foot-four? Dayam, go away, you are far too drool-worthy to be good for me.

"I'm Richard."

That would make him a Dick. It takes all of my self-control not to laugh in his face. "Shirley."

Yes, you heard me, I don't want to know men hot enough to blister my lips with their eyes, thank-you-very-much. If he doesn't know my name, we can't manifest an attachment.

"Can I buy you a drink?"

I offer him an apologetic smile, "No thanks." Waving finger in his face, "I'm married." And for the record I only take drinks from ugly boys and friends at this point.

"That's too bad. He's one lucky guy."

Bugger! How is it that a man can manage to snap the cartilage in your knees with one sentence and a strong chin combined with velcro, soft brown eyes? I don't think mine can hold me up any longer. He seems so sweet. None of the usual arrogance or attitude coming off this dude at all.

"Thanks," I reply, watching him turn and shrug sadly to his friends.

Zeke walks over and does the 'my broad shoulders can protect my woman and her friends from anything' step in. Blocking my view of Mr Smooshy walking away.

"Everything okay? He's not bothering you, is he?"

Aw, how sweet is Zeke? Okay, hang on a sec! Where did all the nice men come from? Why now? Why, when I want to hate every single last one of you, do I suddenly have a Zeke and a James watching my back. Oh and look, Zeke's back-up in the form of Tom has just arrived on my other side. Two personal trainers with the muscles to prove it. I feel famous, as if this is my bouncer squad. Tom glares over to where I can't see Mr Smooshy, also known as Dick. Waaaahahahaha.

"I'm fine, thanks." I reassure the goon squad. I'm not used to being protected, I'm used to being stomped on.

Tom offers me a businesslike smile, "Need a drink?"

Well now that you mention it, "Yes please."

As Tom moves away, attaching himself to my elbow and carving a path through the dance floor to lead me with him to the bar, I catch Richard's stare. He points at Tom and mouths, "Is that your husband?"

I shake my head in response, smiling at the guy's balls. They put Texas to shame they're so big. Do men not care that you're married? Or am I just a really bad liar?

Hours later, I'm tired and sitting upstairs watching my friends still dancing. Quietly having a smoke with my feet propped on the bars that make up the railing overlooking the dance floor, when heat arrives next to me, and Mr Smooshy sits down next to me with his drink, which is a Coke and something.

Glancing at him, I'm stuck in his velcro eyes again. One look and you're burred. You can't look away.

"Shirley..."

"Yes."

"How come your friends call you Stef?"

"It's an inside joke." Finally I unhook my gaze and stare back at my friends, wondering if I'm going to need help. Where's James?

"How long have you been married?"

Um, fuck. That's a good question. "A while." I can do this. Play it by ear.

"You used to come here all the time."

Ow, I think I just pulled the tendon in my neck when I Linda Blaire'd him with that comment.

"Yes, I used to."

"I was chuffed to catch you tonight. I've been working up the courage to talk to you for about two years."

No fucking way! "Oh really? Why?" I mean, come on, am I that scary?

"Hot girls make me nervous."

Oh, so I'm hot am I? Are you kidding me? You're bloody walking chocolate, and you think I'm hot? Girls probably stalk you.

"You're much too kind," I say. What an overused saying, but he's obviously forgotten to wear his contacts tonight.

"Pity you left and got married."

Okay, now I'm staring. He seems really sincere, and all heartbroken. His expression would look good on a "I'm so sorry I fucked up" card from Hallmark. Your timing really sucks, Dick. Pfffft! I'm going to laugh again. DON'T LAUGH! You can't laugh when he's just stuck his vulnerabilities out far enough for the entire club to notice. He's actually totally adorable. Fuck it, you know, maybe this is the universe finally taking pity on my sorry ass.

"I'm not married, I just wear it so guys will leave me alone."

212

Oh crap. He looks like I slapped him twice and kneed him in the nuts.

"God. I'm doomed." He runs a hand through his short brown hair as he ducks his head to stare at his foot propped next to mine. Standing, he backs away as he says, "I'm sorry I bothered you."

And he backs straight into Tom. Tom gives him the second bouncer glare of the night. Richard shoots me another, 'Would you mind explaining who this guy is?' stare, before disappearing into the black hole that is the stairwell going downstairs.

Tom replaces Dick's presence next to me, leaning elbows on knees to stare down to where Zeke is being all romantic with Selene. "That guy just won't leave you alone."

"Nope." I'm looking for him to reappear back with his friends. I'm feeling just horrid.

"Well at least we have each other while those two make you want to puke."

Casting a quick glance at the love-birds, I nod, "Yep."

"So I heard you're staying with Zeke?"

Where is he?

"Yep."

"So we'll be seeing a lot of each other."

Red flag! Sirens! What the hell is he saying? Stopping my search for Mr Smooshy, I stare at Tom. He's a player, you can tell. "Probably."

"Good, I like you."

Generic smile. He's a nice enough guy, as Zeke's friend. I'm not sure how to respond, but he clarifies for me.

"I mean, it's good that we'll get along. It'd suck if I thought you were a bitch and I had to see you every time I visit Zeke."

Oh right. Better smile.

"Well, yeah. Thanks for not thinking I'm a bitch." And I snap my attention back to look for Mr Smooshy, and all of his friends are gone!

This calls for action! Jumping off my perch, "Sorry Tom, I'll be back in a bit." And I dash down the stairs toward the entrance, looking for Richard. My heart sinks when I see the three of them turning the corner down the next street. Shit! My pride just won't let me run after a guy, no matter how nice he seems,

Sighing heavily, I go back inside. I guess I'd better get used to Tom then, as we're the two extra wheels on this ride. But right now I'm really annoyed with him for distracting me at such a crucial moment. Just my crappy luck.

Chapter 40

It's been an excruciating three days waiting for Saturday night. Thanks to my endless nagging we're going to The Swinging Door again. I'm oddly attached to the Richard debacle. He seemed super nice and is obviously blind to his own good looks. He's so shy it took him two years just to talk to me. If only he'd tried it earlier, Gary and that whole disaster might not have happened again. I could have been living happily ever after without any of the mess that my heart's still trying to mop up.

However, I got my way for nothing. There's no Richard here to be found, and no one else interests me. He's left a lingering impression and I can't stop thinking about him. His build reminds me of mmmmMarty. Except Richard's face is trusting. There's nothing sophisticated about him. He has a vulnerable appeal. He looked utterly ravishing in the black jeans he was wearing the other night. Long legs that remind me of a sexy cowboy fresh from the rodeo. If that doesn't paint a vivid picture, then drool on this. After all that dancing, his shirt was unbuttoned, and he has super wide shoulders without the bulk that Zeke and Tom have. His skin was creamy and glistening all the way down those three open buttons, he has full red lips, and a pointy chin, like the elf from Lord of the Rings, with hair that's about two inches long on top but short short, yummy yummy short, in the nape. Which means easy access for kissing.

See? Now I have the stud brigade for comparison. Tom's hair is dead straight and down to his shoulders. He oozes vanity and egotistical urgh. And to top it all off he dresses to showcase the muscles he's so proud of. But Richard covers his up. I prefer that. I prefer the unknown factor. It makes you curious to imagine what he'd look like without that shirt, just wearing those tall jeans announced with a rather bold silver buckle on the black belt hugging him, but without any bling or flash. He's understated hot. And if it took him two years to talk to me, he sure won't be a hunter like Gary was.

Speaking of which, guess who I'm going shopping with tomorrow? Yes, I am bored, how can you tell? Stop distracting me.

Back to the point of my horror; I've been roped into going shopping with Mr Vain, Tom. Sigh. Wish me luck.

* * *

You see! I knew it. There had to be a reason Tom wanted me to go shopping with him. He wants a female opinion on his choice of clothing. In other words, "Do I look hot in this?"

What's really funny is that this morning, I walked into the kitchen to make coffee, still wearing my pyjamas, where I encountered Zeke already there making himself a cup of tea. We've lived together for a week now, but I leave for work before him, so we hardly ever cross paths. And yesterday morning he was at Selene's after staying the night. So my shock was that I waltzed into the kitchen, to find him standing there in shorts and a baggy t-shirt. Ohmigod! I couldn't stop myself from calling him chicken legs. You cannot imagine when you see a man in jeans and shirts, what his legs look like. Zeke seems so bulky, but it's all arms, chest and shoulders. Mr Lats has no calves! He looks just like a chicken! And I don't think he'll ever forgive me for popping his ego with that blurted out remark. Although one afternoon after work, I walked in, and he was sitting at the kitchen counter with a gun laid out in pieces in front of him. That freaked me out. He seemed quite blasé about the fact that he was cleaning his gun. So he's not just built to squeeze your skull in with one hand, but he's packing as back up too. Best I don't tease him too much about having KFC legs.

"And this?"

Returning my attention to Tom, "Yeah, looks good."

Ass; he's such a prick. He's now trying to shock me by taking the jeans he just tried on, off, right in front of me. God he loves himself. He's parading for all the boys and girls to have a peek. Except, oh lordy! Darling, that will never do. Although in his defence, his legs are a lot hotter than Zeke's.

"Um, Tom."

He pauses, an evil grin displayed between designer stubble. He thinks I'm about to drool. Reality check.

"Yes?"

"You are never going to get laid in underwear that gross."

216

"What's wrong with my underwear?"

EVERYTHING! Y-fronts went out of fashion with the cold war!

"Any girl seeing that won't ever call you again. Haven't you heard of Calvin Klein?"

"Yeah, obviously."

"Yeah, so? Mark Wahlberg ring a bell? If you spend that much time earning a six-pack and pecs, you don't want to blow your lick-appeal with those. Hot underwear leaves a lasting impression, trust me."

He gives me a strange look. Instantly self-conscious he disappears back into the change rooms. He's all business when he reappears, hooking my elbow with his arm and shunting me to the men's underwear where he nudges his head at rows of briefs, "Go on then."

"Go on what?"

"Pick out underwear for me."

Lordy, I've never had to buy men's underwear before, and somehow this wasn't how I pictured it was going to be when I did. But I peruse the racks and pick out what I think would look good. Gary is the model I think of. When he dropped his jeans I just wanted to shag the bastard. Grumpy with that thought, I shove a pile of the black, pure white, burgundy and dark navy short looking undies at him. "Here."

He inspects them with concentration, replacing them with the right size, and off we go to the check out point. Thank God. Ten minutes later he's treating me to coffee in a little café right underneath the escalators in the mall.

Relaxing I watch him as I sip my mochaccino. Look at him! He's bloody scandalous! He rubber necks more than half the women in here, and then leans back to stare up their skirts as they take the escalator. He shoots me a sardonic grin, "Now she's hot."

"You are an education and a half."

He smiles again, laughing indulgently. He kicks my foot with his under the table, "Thanks."

"For what?"

"All your help."

I nod. Whatever. I guess Tom could always be my back-up date for weddings. I'm not even remotely attracted to him, which means I can get plastered and maintain my dignity in the process.

Forty-three minutes later, I'm delighted to be stretched out on the couch at home, while Zeke makes me coffee and Selene chooses a CD, when Tom whistles for me from the passage leading to the bedrooms. "Stefanie, come here a sec."

Half-heartedly I push myself off the couch, padding barefoot to the passage where Tom is standing in *only* new underwear. Jesus Tom!

"Whaddayathink?"

He does the model thing for me, turning around to show off his new man-undies. Damn, okay, now even I have to admit he looks good in those. Not that I'd ever tell him. I give him an approving nod, "Much better."

For half a second the bravado drops and he looks at me with all his insecurity exposed, piercing green eyes worried, "But are they sexy?"

I can't stop the smile, "Yes Tom, very sexy."

His smile is lip splitting, the arrogance pops back into his visage and he turns, wiggles his ass and disappears back into Zeke's bedroom. I return to the lounge with Selene giving me a suspicious stare, "What's going on?"

"Nothing." I grin and flop back into my chair.

And before I can prove my innocence, Tom reappears pulling his shirt over his head, flops down next to me, splays an arm around my shoulders and gives me a crushing hug to his side, "This is my girl."

Great, just great. I'm going to be in shit with Selene 'cos now she thinks I just scored. Fucking fabulous.

Zeke joins us with coffee, deliberately squashing his impossible bulk between me and Tom, announcing, "Not on my watch."

Tom punches his leg. Ouch. God that must have hurt. "She rocks, I should have had a girl friend years ago."

Zeke hands me his coffee to choke Tom round the neck, and I'm so concerned about spilling I scoot off the couch with a mug in each hand.

"Fuck off, Tom," accompanies lots of wrestling.

218

Tom starts laughing, his ponytail stuck under Zeke's thick forearm. "Chill out moron. I meant for shopping."

Selene gives me an odd stare again, "You went shopping?"

I nod, "Yes. It was an education."

Tom winks at me, enjoying arousing suspicion, giving me his 'I'm so irresistible' smile, "It sure was."

Let's start a rumour shall we? He has no idea what it's like being in shit with a girlfriend. Thanks asshole.

The thing is, you can't help but like him. Yes he's arrogant, and yes he's vain, but he's also normal. Watching Zeke and Tom interacting is liberating. This is probably the best way to expose myself to the rest of the world's normal. Oh and speaking of chicken legs, that's probably what Selene finds delicious in Zeke. Since I've known her, she's always fallen for the anorexic, just out of rehab types. I never thought I'd see her with someone who's six-foot-two and built like a man. She dates broom handles. I now know that Zeke is six foot tall exactly.

The four of us have become the new clique. We get takeout, rent movies, and go out together. It's been four weeks of no stress normal. Gary hasn't phoned me, no drama, none of the ex-friends have bombarded my life with hate mail, and I'm finally in that place where I know men and women can be just friends, no funny business.

Going out as Tom's sidekick is like hanging out with a jock brother. It's nice to know he's there, and it's purely platonic. Oh, and can I just mention, Tom is a terrible slut! I thought I had an idea of cold-hearted flirting. That guy is incorrigible, and he never gets a number because he doesn't intend on seeing her ever again. Like I said, he's an education. Although, I have to say, he did mention the underwear works.

Chapter 41

Here we are, again. But it's just the four of us this time. The Swinging Door is my new haunt. You know, Gary never danced with me. Ever! I'm still astounded that Zeke dances with Selene, which usually leaves me dancing next to Tom, while we both check out the talent. Crikey it's hot in here. I'm going outside for a smoke.

The Swinging Door has an open rooftop where you can cool off in the night air. Finding a quiet step to sit on, I relax and enjoy a solitary smoke. Now I'm reminded of why I don't do this often. This is the lover's nook. Fuckenhell, why don't you guys go home and get a room? Ugh. I guess I'll disappear inside again.

Actually this song rocks. Standing on my smoke to snuff it out, I launch through the open doors, strutting my jeaned ass back to my peeps on the dance floor. The dance floor is down three steps, no matter which side you approach it from, which gives someone as short as me a perfect view of the claustrophobic mass of bodies writhing together, hair flaying, sexing it up with lyrics and hip sways. When a man turns around, halfway through the throng from me. My heart boings when he gives me the happiest smile I've ever seen. RICHARD!

I know I'm smiling back like an idiot. Yay! He's walking straight to me and his friends are smiling like their buddy just won the lottery. What sweet friends. Gary's crowd really suck septic piles don't they?

"Good evening Lady Marmalade." Gosh he's all hot and sweaty, and from this vantage I can see inside his button down shirt. YUM!

"Good evening, Richard." I came so close to calling him Dick. Why does my perverse sense of humour always have to fuck with me when it seriously matters?

"Where's your bodyguard?"

I point over to Tom, where he's dancing with the lovebirds. He catches the gesture and smiles at me, waving. He then gives Richard a nod of acknowledgement, which he returns.

Richard steps up. Hello, he's two steps below me and he's still taller than me!

"I'm buying you a drink."

Oooh, Mr Assertive is in the house tonight ladies and gentlemen. But I'm more than happy to comply, letting him hook an arm around my waist and lead me right back the way I just came. Up the black pit of darkness to the upper level. The bar is conveniently right next to the doors leading outside.

"What will it be?"

"Coke please."

"Just Coke?"

"Yes." I give him the challenge stare. I want to stay sober so that I don't make an ass of myself around you. Do you have a problem with that?

"Okay." I watch him lean over the bar without any effort and order drinks. When I order drinks I have to stand on the foot bar to lean over the counter to yell my order to the bartender to be heard over the music. Not fair! Oooh, nice view from here. I've got a swarm of fireflies dancing in my stomach. They're lighting up and giving me a warm glow. Oh dear. I haven't thought about sex once in five weeks. Look what you've done, you naughty man.

And off we go outside, where it's quiet enough to have an intimate conversation. He sits next to me, his leg touching the length of mine. Happy sigh.

"So who is that guy?"

"Tom."

He gives me a solemn stare. I just want to kiss him, his reaction at seeing me was so heart warming. He's so lovely to look at. How do men manage to be manly and look like they need someone to take care of them, all at the same time? "Tom is the best friend to the guy dating my best friend."

"That couple you're always with?"

"Yes."

"Aaaah." He pauses and takes a sip of his drink. Perfect profile, and he smells nice too. He puts his glass down next to him on the step, then captures my hand in both of his, giving it a squeeze and staring into my eyes again, "It's nice to see you again Marmalade."

"My name's Stefanie."

"Not Shirley?"

"No."

"I can't believe a word you say, can I?"

"Yes you can."

"Oh really?"

He looks utterly bemused, a wry twist of humour pouting his lips. Oh look, a dimple in his chin. Please nudge me if I start drooling. "I went through a bad break-up. When you last saw me, I just wanted to be left alone. I called myself Shirley because I Shirley wanted to do everything I wasn't allowed to do with my ex."

He's frowning now. "I remember him. That blonde guy you used to come here with?"

I nod. A lump of emotion has just formed in my throat and I can't breathe. Long ago Gary was normal with me.

"So who are you seeing now? Is he a husband or a boyfriend?"

"Not seeing anyone," I reassure him. Come on! Cut me some slack here.

"So Tom isn't your secret boyfriend who's going to beat my head in for talking to you?"

I can't suppress the laugh at the thought of demented Tom being my boyfriend, "Oh no. Definitely not."

He gives me that pensive frown again, latching beautiful brown eyes onto my blue ones. There's just something about him that oozes gentle. "What? Don't you like studs like Tom?"

I shake my head, "Nope. I like my men normal. Lean and clean."

Haha! He just checked his fingernails. Do I make everyone paranoid?

Breaking the silence I ask, "Why do you call me Marmalade?"

"It's just a name I refer to you as. I never knew your name, I had to call you something."

"So when are you going to shut up and kiss me?"

Well that certainly flabbergasted him. He drew himself to sit upright. He's seriously tall. Now I have to look up, the intimacy of him leaning his head in to be next to mine, vanishing fast. He keeps holding my hand, working my fingers as if they're worry beads imparting good luck.

"Maybe I want to get to know you before I suck your face off."

"Crap. You've wanted to talk to me for two years. That means you want to kiss me."

"Yeah? So how do I know you want to kiss me?"

"Because I haven't stopped thinking about you for five weeks. I thought I'd scared you away for good."

Now that's the smile I'm talking about. I'm melting faster than an icicle in a sauna. And the bugger still has to think about it. Standing up so that we're closer to each other's head level, I push between his legs and kiss him myself, holding onto his legs for support. Oh lordy. His lips just depress. They're so soft and warm. I don't think my knees are going to keep holding me up. He just sucked my bottom lip into his mouth. This is better than hot chocolate on a drizzly day. Well thank you. He just seated me on his leg, wrapping those yummy arms around me.

"There you are!"

Fuck off Tom! I ignore him by wrapping both hands around Richard's face for seclusion, and continue kissing him.

"Stefanie! Come on, we're going for burgers."

Inside sigh. Slowly I disengage my lips from Mr Smooshy, and smile, staring into his mesmerising eyes while my hair still gives us privacy. "Would you and your friends like to join us for burgers?"

He leans in, nips my neck between his teeth before speaking softly into my ear, "I'm happy to go wherever you're going."

Straight to hell darling, but at least we'll enjoy the ride. I finally turn my head to grin at Tom, who's giving me the 'guess who's getting laid soon' smirk, "We're coming."

He laughs, shaking his head, "Too much information."

For the first time Richard loosens up around Tom, when we all burst out laughing.

Tonight has been the best night in living memory. Zeke has left us alone by staying over at Selene's tonight. We've had coffee, we've kissed so much I look like I've had silicone injections in both lips, and we're now snuggled up under a blanket, on a rock, watching the sun come up. This is a memory I'm going to cherish for a long time. It's unadulterated romance. The birds are serenading us, and I've found myself a keeper. Smooshy is my word for someone who seems tough on the outside, but is a soft marshmallow on the inside. He's definitely Mr Smooshy.

Chapter 42

I know you're curious, so was I. Richard isn't a player. He really is completely clueless he's a catch. It took another four weeks of dinners, movies, clubbing and hiking, before I finally got a fix of lust-dust. We'd been to the movies and he invited me home for coffee.

So here I am, in Richard's modest home on the outskirts of Durbanville, when he kicks into routine mode. We've had coffee, and he disappears, coming back with obviously brushed teeth. I follow him like a lost toddler, into his navy bedroom. Oh God! Holy crap! He just yanked his shirt off. Do you know this is the first time I've seen him without his shirt on?

"Fancy cuddling?"

Suuuuuuuurrrre thing! This is strange foreplay, but I don't think I need any. This boy is chiselled perfection. And no, I am not exaggerating. He seriously is unbelievably breath stealing. The playgirl mansion is missing a bunny. He has this V coming out of his jeans, straight to hip bones. Two veins run right from his jeans up to his navel, which is so deeply depressed because of the ravine in the middle of his six-pack. Perfect blocks step the way to smooth tight pecs with the Grand Canyon hiding between them. His shoulders are a mass of muscles and tendons, with more veins standing out in stark relief down both sides of cut arms into ripply forearms, ending with long elegant fingers. All wrapped up tightly in smooth creamy skin. All it's missing is my tongue. Is this how Gary felt about me? If the world knew what you hid under your clothes, and it looked like the demi-god before me, you wouldn't want any of them knowing, would you?

Maybe, for just half a second, I can fool myself into believing Gary was this insecure. Holy guacamole, Richard is phenomenal man bling! His arms. How does he manage to look so insignificant in build when he's wearing clothes? There are deep shadows between his triceps and biceps, and they're utterly lickable. And the way his muscles bunch when he bends his arms. He's angelically beautiful. This is how we procreate. Good luck saying no to this guy.

"Anyone home? You haven't answered me."

Dragging my eyes back up his torso to his face, I catch his worried expression. Forcing myself to swallow, I hope my voice doesn't come out as a squeak. "Affirmative." I joke, "Work out much?"

He's in a serious mood. "No, not much."

Liar!

"Oh really? You just look like you fell off your cloud, and you say not much?"

Aw! How cute is he? He's going a deep magenta in the bottom half of his cheeks, getting all shy and trying to peek at me behind eyelashes.

"If you call rock climbing working out, then yes, whenever I can."

Yes I've cuddled him, and yes he felt lean and toned, but nothing prepared me for this. I feel unworthy. How can he feel threatened by the goon squad when he looks like this? I don't understand men. If anyone has a reason to be vain and prone to flashing muscles, it should be Richard.

Silently I'm thanking my angels for giving me a man who could vaporise a volcano, but is so shy and unaware of it, that he'd never use it as bait. My eyes are melting. He just removed his jeans. What is his definition of cuddling exactly? And thank you very much, but would you please observe specimen A and notice the fabulous CK underwear. Holy cow. He really does rock climb. I have never seen a man with legs that defined and perfectly in proportion. He should be in a museum. They need to put him in Madame Taussards as the most perfect male specimen in living history.

"You're making me feel self-conscious."

How do you think I feel? I'm wearing nothing more than a dress, sandals and knickers. When I take my clothes off, it's going to be – right – here it is. That will teach me to wear a strappy sun-dress that's tight enough to get away with not wearing a bra.

"Sorry." I drop my eyes, not knowing what the hell's really going on.

Then he flicks back the duvet, climbs in with his CK's on, and opens the duvet like a cave door, "Come on then."

Closing my eyes, I take a deep breath for the grand opening moment. Here goes nothing. I step out of my shoes, simultaneously pulling off my dress, and climb between his arms, laying down, hoping that was fast enough for me not to feel examined. I was hoping for romantic. A candlelit evening with seduction on the cards, working up to this moment. I wonder when he last had a girlfriend? Maybe he's just seriously out of practice.

I've been really good. I've been used to being led around by my collar for so long, that I've pretty much lost the art of making the first move. Richard is so unlike everyone else I know. He hasn't been after sex. He really meant it when he said he wanted to get to know me first. Thus, despite finding him adorable and infinitely attractive, I've waited for this moment to arrive, on his terms. Yep, and all we're doing is talking, and talking, and talking. It's very hard to think straight with a virtually naked god lying pressed up against me, and hellooooo, he's turned on, I can feel it, but he's still not making a move.

When I eventually notice the time is three o'clock in the morning, I take the plunge.

"What are we doing?"

"Talking."

You don't say.

"Were you planning on having sex with me tonight or are we just cuddling?"

Silence.

I wait. Staring at a moonlit face next to me from the gap left in the curtain.

"Do you want to?"

DO I WANT TO? Understatement of the century. "Yes."

He really isn't confident, is he? Oh what the hell, here goes nothing, again. Rolling, I pull off my knickers, before excavating his body out of his. And like a porn star in her big moment, I take the lead by sitting on top of him, staring down at the crevices created by the shadows over white-washed moonbeam skin. He's so warm and smooth. Tracing his chest with my fingertips, I could have been transported to faery, the king of the Sidhe so ethereal and out of my league, laying at my mercy. Holy cow, I can't believe I got this lucky.

... Pause...

...Play ...

Did I mention, "Holy cow, I can't believe I got this lucky?" How many times can I say that before you want to behead me? It's not possible, but I've found perfection. He's sweet, thoughtful, a gentleman, and a sex god! I've known him for exactly nine weeks and I want to marry him! I'd be brain dead to let this one get away.

He's so humble, completely contradicting the package he's in and his talent. He's a closet artist. His art is phenomenal. He also has a hidden passion, he's an adrenalin junkie. He sky-dives, rock climbs up sheer cliffs, skateboards down steep roads, and does the whole mountain biking thing with his two man-friends.

He cooks, he's got great dress sense; honestly, I can't wrap my head around this either. He's so opposite to everything I've known. On the bright side, if I hadn't met a jerk like Gary, I wouldn't appreciate Richard the way I do. He holds my hand in public, he kisses me in public too, opens doors, pulls out chairs, walks arm in arm, and he dances with me! I've bagged the only living Woman Whisperer. Who, by the way, tells me all the time how he can't believe how lucky *he* is, and that I'm the most gorgeous woman he's ever laid eyes on. Feel free to slap me if I'm wearing my silly-stupid grin again.

He's letting me watch him climb a cliff today. Just my delicious luck, (I now live on the wheel of fortune. Location, location, location!). Richard also owns a motorbike. I miss the motorbike experience I had with Gary, so I'm super-chuffed that Mr Smooshy has one too. His reason though is practical, unlike Gary's which was purely poser inspired. Richard says it reaches the obscure locations a lot easier than a car, which is essential when rock climbing. I now have my own helmet and biker's jacket. I'm living in bliss. My life is so awesome, I'm finally happy to be alive. I have a decent pay-cheque, I live with a guy who could snap Gary in half if he ever showed up, and I'm dating the best secret on planet Earth.

Four hours later, after watching him climb up the mountain, I'm now watching him abseil down it. And I now understand how he's so lean and carved. He manages to pull his entire body up with three fingers and two toes. Those muscles were straining; all of them! At times he lifts his body sideways the way a gymnast can, flexing his back and stomach, gripping with fingertips, while he locates a new foot hold, over there next to his shoulder! If you have never witnessed such a sight, you can't imagine how intoxicating it is. The next best kept secret in Cape Town, rock climbers, er, rock.

He's also balanced mentally. He likes quiet time. He's not brash, and he doesn't need outside validation encouraging him the way my ex did. He loves rock climbing because it's solitary, just him and nature. And I'm a living victim of heart-punch since that first succulent kiss. You know that overpowering sensation when your heart feels like it's going to burst with love, and your chest aches? Every breath feels tight and my chest cavity feels too small, as if my heart has turned into a rapidly multiplying amoeba and is now pressing against my sternum, making it warp. The pressure is building, and I swear at any moment I'm going to have a heart attack. My breath is constantly shallow, hormones leaping like fleas, and every heartbeat throbs – yes THROBS!

Gahdoof, gahdoof, gahdoof – it's so powerful it steals my breath. Feeling dizzy as if it's cutting off the oxygen to my brain – the veins in my neck are pumping gallons a second. I can feel them taut and uncomfortable and stretching out my skin – whoosh, the blood hurtles through with more throbbing. And yet despite being in the process of death by heart-throb – my body feels light – my feet aren't touching the ground – I'm half human and half spectre – gliding over the earth with my chest hurting like someone bashed it with a Samurai punch.

It's so bruised my lungs can't even function normally and I'm forced to keep my lips parted just to draw enough breath to stay alive in this insane existence of encompassing love. And when I'm not with him, my fingers itch to email – to dial – to text – to drive – to hold. I am overcome with a euphoric heartache, which I'm calling heart-punch. And that hottie, glistening from exercise, did this to me.

I think it's official, I am finally drowning in love. Not lust, (okay, maybe both,) but this doesn't come anywhere near close to anything I thought was love before. This is quantum compared to a one dimensional ball of dung.

Hmmmm! See that? The first thing he does is smile his sensitive man smile at me, happy eyes caressing me, and he kisses me hello before saying a word. And that magic hand is trailing down my spine, which if this continues to be a daily occurrence is going to make me knocked kneed, it's the only way I can remain standing.

Then he kisses my neck, giving me a squeeze before saying, "Let's go home, shower, and then I'll take you out for a late lunch."

Thank you God!

Oh! I also finally discovered why he called me Marmalade. Because it was his dream to spread me. Men!

Chapter 43

Whizzing up the road to Zeke's, I feel lazy and happy, holding on to Mr Smooshy on the back of his bike. I wonder if Zeke's home? Crap! We just went past Selene's, and Zeke was filling the doorway leering at Gary! Gary looks mightily pissed off and he stops shouting just long enough to watch us go past. Casually I turn my head away, grateful that my hair's tied up and he can't see my face behind the visor. My heart just bottomed out of me, my insides are quivering with trepidation.

I manage to say goodbye to Richard, have a decent kiss, and make plans for later tonight. I watch him turn the bike, racing off back down the road. Ducking inside, I snatch off the jacket with shaking hands, lock the house, and sneak as fast as humanly possible to Selene's, down the back way. There's a narrow gap between the houses opposite her place, where I should be able to hide, to see what the hell is going on.

Running, I rush to the alley, whisper down it, and hide behind a roller-bin.

"Fuck you!"

I missed it all. He's just slammed his car door, nearly blowing the head when he forces it to screech to life, choking the gears into reverse to turn around. Changing his mind, he guns away up the road. I wait, to see if he'll come back down it. He does, and I cling to the wall in the shadow of the bin, with fear throttling the strength out of me. My breath is coming in shaky gasps. From up here, you can see the car driving away. Finally satisfied that I'm safe, I force my wobbly legs to Selene's door.

I am so grateful for Zeke now. He is just the right kind of man for Gary the coward to not want to confront. Zeke is fearless. I've seen him in confrontations and he's not afraid of anyone.

After knocking, Zeke opens the door.

"Hey babes. Everything okay?"

He seems calm and normal, pulling me through the doorway with an arm around my shoulders.

"Yeah ..."

Selene pops a worried head out from the kitchen, looking pale. "Hey Stef."

"Hey. Um, I just saw Gary here. What's going on?"

Zeke answers. "He was looking for you."

I feel like I just got fired. The doom I'm feeling is overwhelming. "Why?"

Selene answers this time. "Don't know. But he was insistent we tell him where you live."

I'm coming over faint. Using a last spurt of strength, I get myself to a kitchen chair and sag into it, "What did you tell him?"

"Nothing. I told him to fuck off." Zeke says.

I feel like crying. Why won't he just leave me alone? I'm happy now. I have someone normal who loves me and who likes my friends. An odd thought pops back into my head. He once threatened me via Neville, just because I was dating. Who told him? Is he going to follow through on that threat now and have me taken out?

Zeke rubs my back just as Selene pushes a Brutal Fruit at me. He tells me, "Don't worry. We won't let him near you."

And I believe him too. Can I just say, I'm loving a life full of strong and sensitive men. I don't want to lose this.

... Pause ...

... Play ...

I'm not going to bore you with all of the details. A lot happens to me. I go sky-diving, abseiling and get promoted. Richard is a go-slow man. He doesn't rush things. I love him, but we're staying independent for as long as we can handle not living together. He knows the history and wants me to maintain my independence. At one point he moved away and I fell apart. It was Marty all over again. But he came back, and proposed! Saying he didn't want to be anywhere where I wasn't. But I'll save that all for the next time we hook up for a good gossip. I want to tell you the rest of the Gary story. Because, after all, we started with him, we should end with him.

Six months after the break-up, that fucking bastard phones me. "Stefanie?"

My hand goes weak, and my legs turn to jelly. "Yes?"

"How are you?"

"Fine."

231

"I never stop thinking about you."

"Go to hell, asshole."

"Aw, come on baby, you can't still be angry?"

I answer with silence. He's lucky I'm at work or I'd be swearing at him like a gangster bitch off to prison.

"Can I buy you a drink? I'd love to see you."

Hmmm. Fascinating. "I don't think so."

"Stef, come on. For old time's sake."

Heavy sigh. Yeah, what the hell. Let him see the new Stef. Eat your arm off Hannibal. "Sure, okay ."

"RAD! Excellent. Friday good for you?"

"Fine."

"Where would you like to meet?"

"Under a Full Moon."

"That place?"

"Yes Gary, *that* place." I add, "Take it or leave it."

"I'll see you there at eight. I'm looking forward to seeing you, babe."

"I'm not."

And I hang up. Shaking.

... Pause ...

... Play ...

On Friday, I walk into the den of iniquity with my heart in my throat. I have a nose ring now too. Selene, mad thing, had her tongue and her nipples pierced, and the best I could do was a nose-ring. Call me a wimp. I'm dressed to go out because Richard is waiting across the road with Tom, Selene and Zeke, and we're going for dinner after I say hello to my ex-master. I scan the lounges with a sharp eye. He sees me, as I spy him. I walk purposefully toward him. He stands up and gives me a hug. "Good to see you, Woman."

God, he smells divine!

My hair is very long now. I can almost sit on it. I know I turned heads when I sauntered toward him in my long peasant skirt, white tank top and raw linen waistcoat. He looks damn fine. But then this is Gary we're talking about. He will always look sinfully fabulous.

He's smiling, his blue eyes riveted to mine, "Baby, I miss you."

I sit down and scan for a waitress. If I'm going to do this, I need a really strong drink.

To make conversation he says, "What happened to your tits?"

I feel like he just dumped me in a Norwegian ice pool. "I beg your pardon?"

He looks disconcerted, "Your boobs. They're gone."

"It wasn't nice seeing you again, Gary."

I stand and turn swiftly on my heel and start stalking away. He comes rushing after me. "Woman!"

This guy doesn't learn, does he? Despite his sexiness in blue jeans, thinsulate caterpillars and a black leather biker's jacket, he can't get away with this shit another day. I have a fucking name.

He catches me on the pavement outside. "Wait! I'm sorry! It was just such a shock. You always had such great tits."

I force a sarcastic smile, "Well you don't have to look at them, so what's the big deal?"

I wasn't even aware that they'd shrunk to be honest. How nice of him to point it out to me.

"Don't go. Come on. You just got here."

"We have nothing to say, Gary. You wanted to see me. Now you've seen me. I'm going out now, with my boyfriend and *friends*."

Yes, imagine that. I have friends. Miss Fucked-Up managed to procure friendship and acceptance.

"Stef, just wait!"

He grabs my arm again, and I seriously flirt with the idea of playing a game of conkers with his nuts.

"If you need anything, ever, no matter what time of day or night, I want you to know, I'd like to be that guy for you."

Oh puke! Oh how sweet. Where the hell were you when I *needed* you?

I'm feeling so insulted and repulsed. "Thanks. I've got to go." I scour him coldly, "Take care."

And I bolt. It must have looked sinful from his side of the street when both Tom and Richard stepped out of the coffee shop to walk with their arms around me back to where Zeke waited with Selene. He can think whatever the hell he wants. His opinion no longer matters.

... Pause ...

... Play ...

233

It doesn't take long for Gary Fuchs to make me loathe him even further. A couple of days later, I get a phone call at work.

"Stefanie speaking, how may I assist you?"

"We need to go for a drive baby."

What? "I beg your pardon?"

"Oh, don't play coy. You and me, in the car, now. Hey, what do you say?"

"Who is this?"

"Stef, it's Neville. I've been fantasising about being alone in my car with you."

Gag. "Why?"

"Aw, don't pretend you don't know."

I don't know. What the hell is he talking about? "Neville, assume I'm ignorant and explain yourself."

"Gary told us what you used to do in the car. *OH BABY*."

The blood just drains out of my head, and I get vertigo.

"This conversation is over."

Shaking, I wobble out of my chair, clutching a box of smokes. Going to get air and nicotine outside. Tears threaten to burn my eyes. He just hurt me again. Now he's bragging? It's been so long that I'd forgotten completely about that.

... Pause ...

... Play ...

Neville phones me daily. He wants to be my friend. After he told me he wants to fuck me. Yes, just like that. I answered my phone, and he said, "I want to fuck you."

Those were Gary's magic words, and Neville saying them turned me on instantly, to my revulsion. But honestly, the guy has been nothing but nice to me. He is constant. He doesn't change, and he was the only one for a long time who didn't reject me when I was living in the Gary shackles. He and I have far too many intellectual interests in common, and history, for me to just cut him off. I like him very much as a person; so I maintain sporadic telephonic contact with him and the odd email. But I told him to go fuck himself, I'm not available. Dickhead.

... Pause ...

... Play ...

It's been almost nine months since I last saw Kristy. When she phones me. We tap dance around each other for a while – how are you? What have you been doing? – but I'm pleased when she suggests meeting for coffee at our old place in Tableview. Bygones and all that. She's her old bubbly margarine self. She and Alan broke up. A la Stefanie. She had a vicious meltdown, just like mine.

"Stef, I'm so sorry. That day, I thought you were mad. But just two months later, I knew exactly how you felt."

I give her a wan smile. "It's okay."

"But my lord, Stef. Do you know why we broke up? I was so disgusted. Gary is *such* an evil bastard."

Really? You don't say.

"All those times they said they were going to play pool, they weren't. Neville told me the truth. I saw it with my own eyes, Stef. My God, I can't tell you how shocked I was. Those bastards were going to that whore-house every Thursday night. Spending thousands a night on prostitutes. Stef, can you believe it? I didn't want to, until I saw Alan and Gary there with my own eyes. It was disgusting!"

She's waving her hands around frantically. Dramatising the explanation. But I feel as though she's just punched me. I'm winded. I can't breathe.

"Those fuckers were caught red-handed. Every Thursday while we sat at home, they went to Slippery Satan and spent the whole night with girl after girl. And they were using so much cocaine that I'm surprised neither of them are dead. Stefanie, it broke me in half."

You mean, like I am, now?

"Thank God for Neville. He's the only decent one amongst that scum!"

I nod, numb. I don't know how he managed it, but he's just ripped my heart out again. This is just too much. How much damage can one man do?

... Pause ...

... Play ...

It took me years to gain real perspective. I now know that only an insecure man wants to control you. I now know that a man accuses you when he has a guilty conscience. Not because you actually did anything. But because he's so paranoid that the world is going to do to him, what he's doing to you.

I know that it doesn't matter how long you are with someone, you may never fully know them. Look long and hard at that man in your bed tonight. Do you really know him? I thought I knew Gary. Well Kristy blew that illusion out of the window with military brilliance.

I know now, that I was a prime target for an abusive male. Growing up in a home where my father disciplined his wife so severely, that later on in life the doctors tell her she's going to need traction to fix her badly distorted spine. My parents could not teach us how to love, for they had none. I could not learn how to cherish, because I never witnessed it. I did not understand self-respect, until I lost everything.

I've come a long way, thanks to loving friends like Selene, and from knowing people calm and balanced, like Richard, Zeke and Tom. I've learned how other people function, from my friends. Love isn't explosive and angry, and no one can dictate to you. You have the power to say no. And just because he's not as bad as your parents, doesn't mean he's good to you.

Pay attention, I'm sharing wisdom here.

If Gary taught me anything, it's that love belongs to an equation that does not fail.

Love = Pain

If you love someone, they can hurt you. If you love someone, the loss of that person, through divorce, illness, death or drugs, will destroy something sacred inside you. The parts of you that once were whole, are systematically stripped, by the pain of heartache.

There is only one kind of true love. And I've found it. Or it found me. The day when Gary flippantly made that remark about me being fucked up. In that moment I knew, I love myself far too much to ever let him put me through his shit again.

I finally found a love that lasts. Love for myself. And only by loving myself, am I safe from abuse and control. Because if I love myself, as much as I loved Gary, I will always have the motivation to make me happy. To keep me safe, to fulfil my dreams, my goals and my desires.

Yes. I love me. At last, I love myself enough to make better choices. I love myself enough to be alone if need be. If someone treats me badly, I'm better off without them. Never again can anyone take this away from me. Even death, can't take this away from me.

I know, I'm all gushy and should start sending myself secret admirer notes. Send myself a Valentine's card. But I mean it. I hope you find the love I've found. It's complete. It makes me whole. And I am happy.

I have happy tears right now. I accept myself. I love myself. I'm putting that girl in the mirror with the bright blue eyes FIRST!

I'll let you know what happens but I have a feeling that loving myself like this means I will never be insecure again. Because even though I love Richard, I don't need him to validate my existence. I'm not needy. I think you only find and keep rewarding and nurturing love when you don't *need* to be loved by anyone else. Gary owns people. If someone thinks they can own you, get the fuck away from them as fast as you're able.

Okay, enough chitchat. I have to go. And next time, I promise, I'll give you the dish on the thrilling ride of being engaged to a man-god.

Define man-god. He doesn't need me. I don't need him. Because of that we never stop treasuring each other, because we both think we're the luckiest souls alive.

Must go. Kiss kiss.

Bye.

P.S: Oh wait! I nearly forgot the best bit. Years later, Neville and I were chatting. I was shocked, to be honest, when he told me he'd been talking to Gary about me. Doesn't it ever end? But anyway, to the point: Neville shared what Gary had told him, "I think I fucked her up for life."

Oh puh-lease!

He wishes. He'd love to take the credit for ruining me forever. Although to be fair, I'm surprised he's grown enough as a person to recognise that he damaged me.

So Gary, if anyone ever shares this private conversation with you, I'd like to go on record here. "You are not that powerful. It's time someone popped your ego and gave you a very expensive reality check."

I'm happy asshole. Deal with it!

Acknowledgements

I would like to thank the following bands/musicians for the use of their lyrics and song titles in this novel, and for the added freedom of using their work in promotional materials.

Surrounded By Idiots *(SBI)*
www.surroundedbyidiots.com
Especially Scott Norton and Scott.

Feedback
Especially Nic James and Marc A Klein
www.amazon.com/Pieces/dp/B001FXAQM8/ref=mb_oe_o

Andy Chester
www.recreationrecords.com

Cutting Jade
www.makesomenoise.co.za/members/654/index.php
Especially Nancy

La Paz
www.lapazrocks.com
Especially Chic McSherry

Feedback disbanded. The two members mentioned above have a new band I'm working with, titled Almost Alice. Thank you also to David H who posed for my covers.

My big thanks goes to my husband who gives me endless freedom to write and who supports my work.

Made in the USA
Charleston, SC
30 April 2011